Praise for *The Dilemma*

A *USA Today* Bestseller
One of *Bustle*'s Most Anticipated Horror Novels and Thrillers
of 2020
One of POPSUGAR's New Thrillers and Mysteries to Look
for in 2020
One of *BuzzFeed*'s 17 New Thrillers You Need to Add to Your
Summer Reading List
A *New York Post* Best Book of the Week

"[An] evocative drama. Welcome to B. A. Paris's dilemma. It's the kind of book you can read cover to cover in one sitting, eager to see how the characters' impossible choices play out."
—*Star Tribune*

"The phenomenal B. A. Paris has done it again! I devoured *The Dilemma* in one sitting—it grabbed me from the very first page and wouldn't let go until I'd finished. Secrets, guilt, shame, and heartbreak—this story has it all in spades."
—Sandie Jones, *New York Times* bestselling
author of *The Other Woman*

"An all-encompassing, tightly plotted novel of psychological suspense."
—*Kirkus Reviews*

"A powerful, beautifully crafted story that ratchets up the tension with every page and packs a huge emotional punch."
—T. M. Logan, author of *Lies*

"A beautifully written story of love and loss which will stay with me."
—Louise Jensen, author of *The Sister*

"B. A. Paris is a mistress at tapping into fears you didn't even know you had. This is a poignant, thoughtful family tale with a difference." —Jane Corry, author of *My Husband's Wife*

Praise for *Bring Me Back*

Named one of *Good Morning America*'s Best Books to Bring to the Beach This Summer on GoodMorningAmerica.com
A *Bustle* Best Books of the Week Pick
A *CrimeReads* Summer's Most Anticipated Pick

"We're in a new Golden Age of suspense writing now because of amazing books like *Bring Me Back,* and I for one am loving it." —Lee Child

"[Paris] builds a nice plot and brings some originality to the old 'good sister, bad sister' character dynamic." —*The New York Times Book Review*

"A twisty and seductive new psychological thriller you won't want to miss." —*Bustle*

"B. A. Paris is back with another twisted psychological thriller." —*Daily Beast*

"B. A. Paris . . . is a consistent whiz at stitching any number of random events and devious characters into a winner of a plot." —*Toronto Star*

"Paris once again proves her suspense chops with this can't-put-down psychological thriller." —*Library Journal* (starred review)

"Paris adroitly ramps up tension . . . Compelling." —*Booklist*

"[An] outstanding Hitchcockian thriller . . . Paris plays fair with the reader as she builds to a satisfying resolution. Fans of intelligent psychological suspense will be richly rewarded."

—*Publishers Weekly* (starred and boxed review)

"A daring, stay-up-all-night love story. This should be next on your reading list if you love to read thrilling love stories."

—*The Washington BookReview*

Praise for *The Breakdown*

A Barnes & Noble Best Book of 2017: Mysteries and Thrillers

"A story with a ratcheting sense of unease—a tale of friendship and love, sanity and the terrible unravelling of it."   —*USA Today*

"This novel will keep you on the edge of your seat from page one."

—BookTrib (Top 10 July Reads)

"B. A. Paris has done it again! *The Breakdown* is a page-turning thriller that will leave you questioning the family you love, the friends you trust, and even your own mind."

—Wendy Walker, author of the *USA Today* bestselling novel *All Is Not Forgotten*

"In the same vein as the author's acclaimed debut, *Behind Closed Doors,* this riveting psychological thriller pulls readers into an engrossing narrative in which every character is suspect. With its well-formed protagonists, snappy, authentic dialogue, and clever and twisty plot, this is one not to miss."

—*Library Journal* (starred review)

"This psychological thriller is even harder to put down than Paris's 2016 bestseller debut, *Behind Closed Doors*; schedule reading time accordingly. . . . A skillfully plotted thriller. With two in a row, Paris moves directly to the thriller A-list."

—*Booklist* (starred review)

"British author Paris follows her bestselling debut, 2016's *Behind Closed Doors,* with another first-rate psychological thriller. . . . Tension quickly builds to a crescendo as Cass's fears . . . become palpable."

—*Publishers Weekly* (starred review)

Praise for *Behind Closed Doors*

August Amazon Best Books of the Month: Mystery,
Thriller & Suspense
August 2016 Indie Next Pick
August 2016 LibraryReads Selection
Real Simple's Best Book of the Month for August
iBooks Best Books of August
23 Weeks on the *Publishers Weekly* Bestseller List in 2017

"In B. A. Paris's hair-raising debut, a woman falls in love with a psychopath, only realizing his true nature when she's hidden from the world and suffering unthinkable horrors at the hands of a seemingly perfect man. *Behind Closed Doors* is both unsettling and addictive, and I raced through the pages to find out Grace's fate. A chilling thriller that will keep you reading long into the night."

—Mary Kubica, *New York Times* and *USA Today* bestselling author of *The Good Girl*

"Newlyweds Grace and Jack Angel seem to lead a perfect life in British author Paris's gripping debut, but appearances can be deceiving. . . . Grace's terror is contagious, and Millie's impending peril creates a ticking clock that propels this claustrophobic cat-and-mouse tale toward its grisly, gratifying conclusion."

—*Publishers Weekly*

"Making her smash debut, Paris [keeps] the suspense level high. In the same vein as *Gone Girl* or *Girl on the Train,* this is a can't-put-down psychological thriller."

—*Library Journal* (starred review)

"A clever heroine." —*Kirkus Reviews*

"Debut novelist Paris adroitly toggles between the recent past and the present in building the suspense of Grace's increasingly unbearable situation, as time becomes critical and her possible solutions narrow. This is one readers won't be able to put down."

—*Booklist* (starred review)

"A frighteningly cool portrait of a serious sadist, *Behind Closed Doors* is a gripping, claustrophobia-inducing thriller. . . . Read at the risk of running from every handsome British lawyer who crosses your path." —*Romantic Times*

"B. A. Paris's debut, *Behind Closed Doors,* is a chilling confirmation of the adage that no one ever really knows what transpires in other people's private lives. . . . Paris has created one of the most heinous villains in recent memory, upon whom even the most pacifist of readers might wish torturous revenge. They'll likely remain behind their own closed doors as they race through this thriller to see how, or if, the nightmare ends."

—*Shelf Awareness*

"A gripping domestic thriller . . . the sense of believability and terror that engulfs *Behind Closed Doors* doesn't waver."

—Associated Press, picked up by *The Washington Post*

"If you're hunting for a thriller to give you chills in August, look no further than this book, which is already a big hit in the UK."

—*Real Simple*

"*Behind Closed Doors* takes a classic tale to a whole new level. . . . This was one of the best and [most] terrifying psychological thrillers I have ever read . . . each chapter brings you further in, to the point where you feel how Grace must feel. The desperation, the feeling that no one will believe you and yet still wanting to fight because someone you care deeply about will get hurt."
—*San Francisco Book Review*

"Paris grabs the reader from the beginning with a powerful and electrifying tale. *Behind Closed Doors,* a novel sure to make one's skin crawl, also reveals no one truly knows what does go on behind closed doors." —*New York Journal of Books*

"B. A. Paris takes the cliché about not knowing what goes on beyond closed doors to a nightmarish place. . . . Each chapter escalates the tensions and stakes faced by Grace in the nightmare that is her new 'perfect' marriage to Jack." —*Huff Post*

"This debut is guaranteed to haunt you—especially if you're about to tie the knot. Paris's thriller asks the question: 'The perfect marriage or the perfect lie?' Jack and Grace, the couple at the center of this totally enthralling novel, are so clearly not what they seem you'll have no choice but to read and read and read until their darkest secrets are revealed. Warning: brace yourself."
—*Bustle* (10 New Thrillers to Read This Summer)

"This dark and twisted thriller will keep you on your toes and have you wondering exactly what goes on behind your neighbor's door." —*BuzzFeed* (6 Thriller/Mystery Reads That Will Have You Sleeping With the Lights On)

"Really freaking creepy. And really good. Until the end, which was an honest gasp and imaginary pearl clutching moment. Yes, that good. Reader, if you want to read the thriller that enthralled

even this jaded soul, pick up *Behind Closed Doors* by B. A. Paris. . . .
Then draw the blinds and turn off your phone because you will
not want any interruptions." —*Literary Hub* (18 Books
You Should Read This August)

"This book proves that looks are most definitely deceiving. . . .
Disturbing, to say the least, readers will definitely be shaken as
the story commences and they become immediately absorbed.
The writing was incredible, and the pace is quick, offering up
too many chills to count. . . . *Behind Closed Doors* screams: 'Stay
single!'" —*Suspense Magazine*

"The book dishes out endless tension [and] much creepiness."
—*Toronto Star*

"Oh wow. What a story. What pacing. Already a runaway bestseller in the UK with movie rights sold, B. A. Paris's debut psychological thriller is sure to top many 'must-read summer lists.'
And it should. *Behind Closed Doors* is completely unsettling and
addictive, a true page-turner."
—Leslie A. Lindsay, leslielindsay.com

THE DILEMMA

B. A. PARIS

ST. MARTIN'S GRIFFIN

NEW YORK

Published in the United States by St. Martin's Griffin, an imprint of St. Martin's Publishing Group

THE DILEMMA. Copyright © 2020 by Bernadette MacDougall. All rights reserved. Printed in the United States of America. For information, address St. Martin's Publishing Group, 120 Broadway, New York, NY 10271.

www.stmartins.com

Designed by Steven Seighman

The Library of Congress has cataloged the hardcover edition as follows:

Names: Paris, B. A., author.
Title: The dilemma / B.A. Paris.
Description: First U.S. edition. | New York : St. Martin's Press, 2020
Identifiers: LCCN 2019054419 | ISBN 9781250151360 (hardcover) |
    ISBN 9781250272201 (international, sold outside the U.S., subject to rights
    availability) | ISBN 9781250151384 (ebook)
Subjects: GSAFD: Suspense fiction.
Classification: LCC PR9105.9.P34 D55 2020 | DDC 823/.92—dc23
LC record available at https://lccn.loc.gov/2019054419

ISBN 978-1-250-15137-7 (trade paperback)

Our books may be purchased in bulk for promotional, educational, or business use. Please contact your local bookseller or the Macmillan Corporate and Premium Sales Department at 1-800-221-7945, extension 5442, or by email at MacmillanSpecialMarkets@macmillan.com.

Originally published in the United Kingdom by HQ, an imprint of HarperCollins Publishers Ltd

First St. Martin's Griffin Edition: 2021

10   9   8   7   6   5   4   3   2   1

For M, my inspiration for this novel.
I might not have known you, but I'll never forget you.

SUNDAY, JUNE 9

3:30 A.M.

Livia

It's the cooling bathwater that wakes me. Disorientated, I sit up quickly, splashing suds up the sides, wondering how long I've been asleep. I release the plug and the drain gurgles, a too-loud sound in a silent house.

A shiver pricks my skin as I towel myself dry. A memory tugs at my brain. It was a sound that woke me, the roar of a motorbike in the street outside. I pause, the towel stretched over my back. It couldn't have been Adam, could it? He wouldn't have gone off on his bike, not at this time of night.

Wrapping the towel around me, I hurry to the bedroom and look out of the window. The guilty beating of my heart slows when I see, behind the tent, a yellow glow coming from his shed. He's there, he hasn't gone to settle scores. Part of me wants to go down and check that he's all right, but something, a sixth sense perhaps, tells me not to, that he'll come to me when he's ready. For a moment I feel afraid, as if I'm staring into an abyss. But it's just the dark and the deserted garden that're making me feel that way.

Turning from the window, I lie down on the bed. I'll give him another ten minutes and if he's not back by then, I'll go and find him.

Adam

I race along deserted streets, scattering a scavenging cat, cutting a corner too tight, shattering the night's deathly silence with the roar of my bike. Ahead of me, the slip road to the M4 looms. I open the throttle and take it fast, screaming onto the motorway, slicing in front of a crawling car. My bike shifts under me as I push faster.

The drag of the wind on my face is intoxicating and I have to fight an overwhelming urge to let go of the handlebars and free-fall to my death. Is it terrible that Livia and Josh aren't enough to make me want to live? Guilt adds itself to the torment of the last fourteen hours and a roar of white-hot anger adds to the noise of the bike as I race down the motorway, bent on destruction.

Then, in the mirror, through the water streaming from my eyes, I see a car hammering down the motorway behind me, its blue light flashing, and my roar of grief becomes one of frustration. I take the bike to one hundred mph, knowing that if it comes to it I can push it faster, because nothing is going to stop me now. But the police car quickly closes the distance between us, moving swiftly into the outside lane, and as it levels with me, my peripheral vision catches an officer gesticulating wildly from the passenger seat.

I add more speed, but the car sweeps past and moves into my lane, blocking my bike. I'm about to open the throttle and over-take him, taking my bike to its maximum, but something stops me and he slowly reduces his speed, bringing me in. I'm not sure why I let him. Maybe it's because I don't want Livia to have even more pieces to pick up. Or maybe it was Marnie's voice pleading, "Don't, Dad, don't!" I swear I could feel her arms tightening around my waist for a moment, her head pressing against the back of my neck.

My limbs are trembling as I bring the bike to a stop behind the police car and cut the engine. Two officers get out, one male, one female. The male strides toward me.

"Have you got a death wish or something?" he yells, slamming his cap onto his head.

The second officer—the driver—approaches. "Sir, step away from the bike," she barks. "Sir, did you hear me? Step away from the bike."

I try to unfurl my hands from the handlebars, unstick my legs from the bike. But I seem to be welded to it.

"Sir, if you don't comply, I'm going to have to arrest you."

"We're going to have to arrest him anyway," the first officer says. He takes a step toward me and the sight of handcuffs dangling from his belt shocks me into speech.

I flip up my helmet. "Wait!"

There must be something in my voice, or maybe they read something in my face, because both police officers pause.

"Go on."

"It's about Marnie."

"Marnie?"

"Yes."

"Who's Marnie?"

"My daughter." I swallow painfully. "Marnie's my daughter."

They exchange a glance. "Where is your daughter, sir?"

THE DAY BEFORE

SATURDAY, JUNE 8

8 A.M.–9 A.M.

Adam

Leaving Livia sleeping, I move from the bed and stretch quietly in the warm air coming through the open window. I stifle a yawn and check the sky; not a single sullen rain cloud in sight. Liv will be pleased. The weather is just about the only thing she hasn't been able to control for her party tonight. She's been on top of everything else for months, wanting it to be perfect. But the relentless rain of the last few weekends was beginning to get her down.

I watch the steady rise and fall of her chest as she sleeps, the tiny flicker of her eyelids. She looks so peaceful that I decide not to wake her until I've made coffee. I find the clothes I was wearing last night and pull on my jeans, flattening my hair as I tug the T-shirt over my head.

The stairs creak as I go down to the kitchen and Murphy, our red merle Australian shepherd, raises his head from where he sleeps in his basket by the wood-burning stove. I crouch next to him for a minute, asking him how he is and if he had a good sleep, and tell him that mine was disturbed by a nightmare. He gives my hand a sympathetic lick, then puts his head back down, ready to sleep the rest of the day away. He's fifteen now and not as energetic as he used to be, which is just as well because neither am I. He loves his daily walk, but the days of our long runs together are a thing of the past.

Mimi, Marnie's marmalade cat, who acts as if she's a purebred and is anything but, uncurls herself and comes to brush against my leg, reminding me that she exists too. I fill their bowls, then the kettle. As I switch it on, the splutter of water connecting to heat disturbs the silence. I look out of the window at the huge white tent, crouched on the lawn like a malevolent beast, ready to leap onto the terrace and swallow the house. I remember now, the nightmare that woke me. I dreamed the tent had blown away. I pull it from my memory—that's it, I'd been standing on the lawn with Josh and Marnie when the wind began to pick up, and the gentle rustling of the trees became a sinister hissing, then a deafening roar that ripped the leaves from the branches and tossed them into the air, dragging the string of lights with them into the vortex.

"The tent!" Josh had cried as the wind turned its fury on the tent. And before I could stop her, Marnie was running toward it and had grabbed at one of the flaps.

"Marnie, let go!" I'd yelled. But the wind caught my words and whipped them away so that she couldn't hear, and the tent had carried her high into the sky until we could no longer see her.

Liv will laugh when I tell her—it turns out she's not the only one feeling the pressure of the party. I move restlessly from the window and give my body another stretch, my fingertips brushing the ceiling of our old cottage as I raise my arms above my head. I'm not quite sure when Josh overtook me in height, but he's been able to lay his palms flat on the ceiling for a while now.

His rucksack is where he left it, dumped at the end of the table along with two plastic bags. I move them onto the floor and run a critical eye over the table. It was one of my earliest pieces, a simple structure of varnished pine that I'd tried to make different by re-inforcing the legs with a bridgelike structure, a nod to the dream I once had of becoming a civil engineer. At first, Livia hadn't liked the lack of space underneath. Now, she loves to sit on the cushioned bench seat, her feet resting on one of the beams, her body curved back against the wall.

The kettle clicks off. I fill the French press and leaving it to brew, unlock the door to the garden. The noise disturbs a male blackbird sitting in a nearby bush. There's a panicked flapping of wings, and as I watch him soar into the sky, I'm reminded that Marnie is on her way home.

Smiling at the thought of seeing her again, because nine months is a long time, I walk across the terrace and climb the five craggy steps, enjoying the feel of rough stone against the soles of my feet, followed by dewy grass as I cross the lawn. The morning air smells of a damp mulch I can't quite place, something to do with Livia's roses. There's a huge bed of them, on the right-hand side of the garden, in front of the wooden fence, and as I walk by, I catch the incredible scent of Sweet Juliet. Or maybe it's Lady Emma Hamilton. I can never remember which, even though Livia tells me often enough.

I walk around the tent, checking that it's properly anchored, in case my nightmare was a premonition of some sort, and see that they've taken it so far back it's practically touching my shed, leaving only the smallest of spaces for me to squeeze through. I know why they've done it; they've had to leave room for the tables and chairs that will be set up in front of the tent. But if it's possible to resent a tent, I'm doing it now.

I sit on the low stone wall that borders the other side of the lawn, opposite the fence, and try to imagine what the garden will look like tonight with a hundred people milling around, lights tangled in the branches of the apple and cherry trees, and balloons just about everywhere. I always knew Livia wanted a big party for her fortieth, but I hadn't realized quite how big until a few months ago, when she began to talk about caterers and tents and champagne. It had sounded so over the top that I'd laughed.

"I'm serious, Adam!" she said indignantly. "I want it to be really special."

"I know, and it will be. It's just that it sounds a bit expensive."

"Please don't ruin it before I've had a chance to work things out," she implored. "Anyway, the money isn't important."

"Liv, the money *is* important," I said, wishing I didn't have to mention it. "Josh is going away this summer and Marnie's in Hong Kong, we have to be careful for a while. You know that."

She looked at me, and I knew that look. Guilt.

"What?" I asked.

"I've been saving," she admitted. "For the party. I've been putting money by for years, not huge amounts, just a little each month. I'm sorry, I should have told you."

"It's fine," I said, wondering if the reason she hadn't told me was because of the time I spent her savings on a motorbike. It still makes me cringe even though it happened years ago, before Marnie was born.

The thought of Marnie jogs my memory. I make my way back to the house and, stepping over Mimi, who always manages to get under my feet, find my mobile where I left it charging last night, tucked next to the bread bin. As I was hoping, there's a message from her.

"Dad, you're not going to believe it—my flight's been delayed, so I'm not going to make my connection in Cairo. Which means I'll get to Amsterdam too late for my connection to London. It sucks but don't worry, I'll get there somehow. Maybe they'll put me on a direct flight and I'll be there earlier than we thought! I'll text when I arrive at Heathrow. Love you xxx."

Damn. I love Marnie's optimism, but I doubt they'll put her on a direct flight to London. They'll probably make her wait in Cairo for the next available flight to Amsterdam. Not for the first time, I wonder why I agreed to her taking such a roundabout way to get here.

When Livia began planning her party, the one thing she never imagined was that Marnie might not be there. We've always known the date of the party, so the first thing Marnie did when she knew she was going to be studying in Hong Kong this year was check when she had exams. But then the dates changed.

"I now have exams on the third, fourth, and fifth of June and then again on the thirteenth and fourteenth," she said, her face flushed with frustration when she FaceTimed us back in January. "I can't believe I'm going to miss the party."

"What if I move it to the fifteenth?" Liv asked.

"I still wouldn't be able to get there in time, not with the time difference."

"Or the twenty-second?"

"No, because then Josh wouldn't be there. That's the date he's leaving for New York, remember? He chose it to fit in with your party. He's already got his ticket, so he won't be able to change it. I'm really sorry, Mum, I wish there was something I could do. But there isn't."

We spent hours trying to find a way around it, but in the end, we had to accept that Marnie wouldn't be at the party. It was a huge blow for Liv. She wanted to cancel the party and use the money to buy flights to Hong Kong and celebrate her birthday there. But Marnie wouldn't let her.

"I don't want you to give up on your dream party, Mum. Anyway, Josh wouldn't be able to come because he'll have his finals. I'd have to study, so I wouldn't be able to spend much time with you. And you know Dad is too busy to take more than a week off. And to come for less than ten days wouldn't be worth it, not after paying so much for the tickets."

Then, three weeks ago, she'd texted me.

"Dad, what are you buying Mum for her birthday?"

"A ring," I texted back. *"With diamonds. But don't tell her, it's a surprise."*

"Would you like to give her another surprise?"

"Such as?"

"Can I FaceTime you? Is Mum around?"

"No, she's out, looking for a dress for the party."

"Oh, good, I hope she finds one. Talking of her party . . ."

Then my phone had rung and that's when she told me about the cheap flight she'd found, Hong Kong to Cairo, Cairo to Amsterdam, Amsterdam to London.

"I've worked it out and if I leave after my exam on the Thursday, I'll arrive in London on Saturday evening and could be at the house around nine. What do you think, Dad? It could be a surprise for Mum."

She was sitting on a white desk chair in the student room she shared with Nadia, her roommate from Romania, and behind her I could see the duvet cover she'd taken from home, most of it puddled on the floor. She was wearing one of my old T-shirts and her mahogany red-brown hair was piled on top of her head, secured there, I guessed, by the usual pencil. It always amazed me, the way she did that.

"I think she'd love it," I said, scooping Mimi onto my knee so that they could see each other. "When would you have to go back?"

Marnie bent her head toward the screen, cooing and kissing Mimi. "Not until the following Wednesday, so it means I'd get nearly four days with you. I don't have to go via Amsterdam on the way back, which means I get back to Hong Kong in time for my exam on Thursday."

"That's a lot of traveling for only a few days here," I said, frowning.

"Businesspeople do it all the time," she protested. Now and then her eyes would look down to where I guessed her mobile was, checking for messages as she spoke to me. It was late evening for her, and it felt odd, suddenly, the realization that she had a whole life in Hong Kong that Liv and I only knew snippets about.

"Did you look at direct flights?" I asked.

"Yes, but they're hundreds of pounds more. This one, via Cairo and Amsterdam, is six hundred and fifty. I can pay half out of my savings and if you could lend me the other half, I'll pay you back as soon as I can."

"I don't want you paying anything toward your ticket. It'll be part of my present to your mum."

She gave me one of her huge smiles and pulled at a gold necklace I hadn't seen before.

"Thanks, Dad, you're the best! So, shall I book the ticket before the price goes up?"

I had to battle with myself, I really did. I wanted to tell her to book a direct flight to avoid the hassle of two changes. But only the other day I'd made Josh book his flight to New York via Amsterdam, not only because it was cheaper than flying direct but also because I felt he should rough it a bit and not have it too easy. There was no way I could justify spending hundreds of pounds more on Marnie when I hadn't spent 150 more on Josh. And also, was it really worth her coming home for the party, when she'd have to leave again four days later? I looked at her pretty face, illuminated by the desk lamp that stood next to her computer, and any reservations I might have had melted away. First of all, she looked so much like her mother, and second, I knew how ecstatic Liv would be if Marnie turned up unexpectedly.

"On one condition," I said, aware of Mimi's unblinking green eyes staring up at me. "You don't tell anyone—not Josh, not Cleo, not any of your other friends, and especially not Aunt Izzy—that you're coming home. I want it to be a surprise for everyone."

"I won't say a word, I promise. Thanks, Dad, did I tell you you're the best?"

There are quite a few surprises lined up for Livia today, but Marnie's turning up at the party is going to be the best surprise of all.

Livia

A creak on the stairs wakes me. I stretch out my arm and find the space next to me empty.

"Adam?" I call softly, in case he's in the bathroom. There's no reply, and drawn by the warmth from where he lay, I roll onto his side of the bed and lie on my side, my head on his pillow. My hand slides automatically to my stomach, checking for tautness, glad that watching what I ate for the last week has paid off. Who am I kidding? I've been watching what I eat for the last six months. And exercising. And using way-too-expensive eye cream. All for the party tonight.

I lie for a moment, listening for the sound of rain drumming on the windows, like it did last Saturday, and the three Saturdays before that. But there's only the sound of birds trilling and chirruping in the apple tree and I feel myself relaxing. It's here. The day I've been waiting for, for so long, is finally here. And unbelievably, it isn't raining.

I press harder on my stomach, squashing the thin layer of fat into the line of muscle. There are so many different emotions swirling inside me. I try to pull excitement and happiness from the mix, but guilt overpowers everything else—guilt about the amount of money this party is costing, guilt about it being only for me when, if I'd waited a couple more years, it could have been for us, for our twenty-fifth wedding anniversary. I did suggest it to Adam—at least, I think I did. In fact, I'm sure I did, because I remember being secretly relieved when he refused to consider it.

I flip restlessly onto my back and stare at the ceiling. Is it really so bad that I want this party to be just for me? I seem to have developed a love–hate relationship with it recently. I might have always wanted it, planned for it, saved for it, but I'll be glad when it's over. It's taken up too much space in my head, not only for the last six months but for the last twenty years. What I hate most is that my need for this party came from my parents. If I'd been able to have the wedding they promised me, I wouldn't have become obsessed with having my own special day.

I don't want to think about them today of all days, but I can't help it. I haven't seen them for over twenty years. They were always distant parents; I don't remember ever having a meaningful conversation with my father, and the closest I got to my mother was when she bought bridal magazines, and while we looked at the dresses and cakes and flower arrangements, she would tell me about the lavish wedding she and my father would give me. But when I became pregnant, not long after my seventeenth birthday, they refused to have anything more to do with me. And the lavish wedding became a hurried fifteen-minute ceremony in the local registry office, with only Adam's family and our best friends, Jess and Nelson, as guests.

At the time I told myself it didn't matter that I wasn't having a big wedding. But it did, and I hated myself for caring so much. A few years later, one of the parents at Josh's nursery invited us to her thirtieth birthday party and it had been amazing. Adam and I were only in our early twenties then and had very little money, so this party was from a different world. I was completely in awe and I promised myself that one day, I'd have a huge celebration for one of my birthdays.

When I was pregnant with Marnie and barely able to sleep because of the never-ending sickness, I'd lean against the counter in our tiny kitchenette, working out on the back of a bill how much I'd need to save each month to have a party like Chrissie's. I'd already decided it would be for my fortieth, because it fell on a Saturday. Back then, I couldn't imagine ever being forty. But here I am.

I turn my head toward the window, my attention caught by the wind blowing the last of the blossoms from the tree. Forty. How can I be forty? My thirtieth birthday passed in the rush of looking after two young children, so it barely registered that I'd reached a milestone. This time, it's hitting me harder, maybe because I'm at such a different stage in my life compared to most of my friends. They still have children at home, whereas Josh and Marnie, at twenty-two and nineteen years old, have already begun their own lives. It means I often feel older than I am. Thank God for Jess; with Cleo the same age as Marnie, we were able to go through their teenage years together.

I hear the scrape of the back door opening, then the pad of Adam's feet as he walks across the terrace. I know him so well that I can imagine the face he'll make when he sees the tent so close to his shed. He's been brilliant about this party, which makes me feel even worse about the secret I've been keeping from him for six long weeks. The guilt comes back and I turn and bury my face in his pillow, trying to stifle it. But it won't go away.

Needing something to distract myself, I reach for my phone. Even though the screen says it's only 8:17, birthday messages have already arrived. Marnie's came in first; her WhatsApp is timed at a few seconds after midnight, and I imagine her sitting on her bed in Hong Kong, watching the clock while she waited to press Send, her message already written and ready to go.

"To the best Mum in the world, happy, happy birthday! Enjoy every minute of your special day. Can't wait to see you in a few weeks. Love you millions. Marnie xxx. PS I'm taking myself off for the weekend to revise in peace. I probably won't have a network so don't worry if you don't hear from me, I'll call Sunday evening."

There are emojis of champagne bottles, birthday cakes and

hearts, and I feel the familiar tug of love. But although I miss Marnie, I'm glad she won't be here tonight. I feel terrible because I should be sorry that she's missing my party, and I was at first. Now, I don't even want her home at the end of the month.

She was meant to be away until the end of August, traveling around Asia with friends once her exams were over. Then she changed her mind and in three weeks' time, she'll be here, back in Windsor. I pretend to everyone that I'm delighted she's coming back earlier than expected, but all I feel is dismay. Once she's back, everything will change and we'll no longer be able to live the lovely life we've been living.

I hear Adam's feet on the stairs, and with each step he takes, the weight of what I haven't told him increases. But I can't tell him, not today. He peers around the doorway and breaks into "Happy Birthday." It's so unlike him that I start laughing and some of the pressure is released.

"Shh, you'll wake Josh!" I whisper.

"Don't worry, he's dead to the world." He comes into the room, carrying two mugs of coffee, Mimi following behind. He bends to kiss me and Mimi jumps onto the bed and nudges me jealously. She adores Adam and will push between us when we're sitting on the sofa, watching a film together.

"Happy birthday, sweetheart," he says.

"Thank you." I raise my hand to his cheek and for a moment I forget everything else because all I feel is happiness. I love him so much.

"Don't worry, I'll shave," he jokes, turning his face to kiss my palm.

"I know you will." He hates shaving, he hates wearing anything apart from jeans and a T-shirt, but he's been telling me for weeks that he's going to make an effort tonight. "Coffee in bed—how lovely!"

I take the mug from him and move my feet aside so that he can sit down. The mattress shifts under his weight, almost spilling my drink.

"So, how are you feeling?" he asks.

"Spoiled," I say. "How's the tent?"

"Close to my shed." He raises a dark eyebrow. "Still there," he amends. "This will make you laugh—I dreamed that it blew away, taking Marnie with it."

"Good job she isn't here, then," I say. And immediately feel guilty.

He puts his coffee on the floor and takes a card from his back pocket.

"For you," he says, taking my mug and putting it down next to his.

"Thank you."

He climbs over me to his side of the bed and, propping himself up on his elbow, watches while I open my card. My name is drawn in beautiful 3-D letters on the envelope and shaded in different blues, a classic Adam touch. I slide out the card; it has a silver "40" on the front, and when I open it, I see that he's written: *"I hope today will be everything you want it to be, and more. You deserve it so much. Love you, Adam. PS Together, we're the best."*

I laugh at the last line, because it's something we always say, but then tears well in my eyes. If only he knew. I should have told him six weeks ago, when I first found out about Marnie, but there were so many reasons not to, some of them good and some of them not so good. But later, once my party is over, I'll have no excuse not to tell him. I've rehearsed the words a thousand times in my head— *Adam, there's something I need to tell you*—but I never get any further because I haven't yet worked out the best way to carry on, whether a slow and agonizing step-by-step account will be less painful than a brutal blurting out. Either way, he'll be devastated.

"Hey," he says, looking at me in concern.

I blink the tears away quickly. "I'm fine. Just feeling a bit overwhelmed, that's all."

He reaches out and tucks a stray hair behind my ear. "That's understandable. You've been waiting for today for so long." There's a pause. "You never know, your parents might turn up," he adds carefully.

I shake my head, grateful that he thinks my longed-for reconciliation with my parents is the reason for my momentary wobble. It's not the main reason, but they're definitely part of it. They moved to Norfolk six months after Josh was born because, my father told me, I'd made them ashamed in front of their church and their friends and they could no longer hold up their heads in the community. When I asked if I could visit, he told me to come on my own. I didn't go; it was bad enough that they wouldn't accept Adam, but their rejection of Josh was too much.

I wrote to them again when Marnie was born, to tell them they had a second grandchild, a granddaughter. To my surprise, my father replied that they would like to see her. I wrote to ask when the four of us could visit and was told that the invitation extended only to me and Marnie—he was willing, my father said, to see Marnie because she had been born in wedlock. Again, I didn't go.

Ever since, I've tried to maintain contact with them, sending them cards for their birthdays and Christmas, despite never getting any from them, and inviting them to every family celebration. But they never acknowledge the invitations, let alone turn up. And I don't suppose tonight will be any different.

"They won't come," I say miserably. "Anyway, it doesn't matter anymore. I'm forty years old. It's time I let go."

Adam turns his head toward the window. "Have you seen the weather?" he asks, knowing that I need a change of subject.

"I know, I can't believe it." I lie back on the pillows, another worry gnawing away at me. "I think I might have gone over the top with my dress."

"In what way?"

"It's long, down to the floor. And cream."

"What's wrong with that?"

"I'm worried it might look too much like a wedding dress."

"Does it have lots of frills and stuff?"

"No."

"And do you intend wearing a veil?"

I burst out laughing. "No!"

"Then," he says, raising his arm and tucking me into the space underneath, "it's just a cream dress that happens to be long."

I look up at him. "How do you always manage to make me feel better about myself?"

"Just making up for all those years when I didn't," he says lightly.

I find his hand and link my fingers through his. "Don't. You married me, didn't you? You didn't walk away."

"No—but I did spend a lot of the first two years in Bristol with Nelson, instead of with you and Josh."

"Until Marnie arrived, and gave you a reason to stay home."

He lets go of my hand, and recognizing the closed look on his face, I want to take the words back. He's spent the last twenty years trying to make up for those early days, both to me and to Josh. But it still affects him.

"I got a lovely text from her," I say, because talking about Marnie always lightens his mood. "She said she might not be able to phone today. She wants to be able to revise for her exams without being distracted, so she's taken herself off for the weekend, to somewhere without Wi-Fi."

"How did we make such a sensible child?" he jokes, his good humor back.

"I have no idea."

I give him a weak smile and, thinking I'm nervous about my party, he gives me a kiss.

"Relax. Everything's going to be fine. What time is Kirin picking you up?"

"Not until eleven."

"Then you can rest a bit longer." He gets up from the bed. "Have your coffee while I shower, and when you come down, I'll make you breakfast."

9 A.M.–10 A.M.

Adam

I push at the canvas of the tent with my shoulder and it gives slightly before bouncing back. I push at it again, harder this time, and manage to get the door of my shed open just enough to get inside.

I love my shed, with its earthy smell of the sawdust that powders the floor. Several large blocks of wood—oak, pine, and walnut—sit at different levels under the front wall, where the window looks onto the garden. A twenty-foot workbench runs the length of the back wall, dotted at various intervals with clamps and power tools. Two open shelves hold the smaller tools I use. In the far corner, there's a TV and DVD player and two old armchairs. Nelson and I come here sometimes to watch sports or a black-and-white film. He brings beers for the fridge and admits that he's hiding from Kirin and the kids.

It's the other end of the shed that I'm here for. I've been keeping a box there since Marnie came up with her idea to surprise Livia. It's a meter-long wooden crate that held a large piece of black walnut, and I need to move it into the garden and hide it under the table as soon as Liv leaves.

I drag the box to the doorway. And that's when I realize the tent is too close to the door for it to pass through.

"Damn!"

I look at taking the box apart and putting it back together in the garden, but each of the sides is nailed down tightly. I sit down in one of the armchairs, wondering where the hell I'm going to find another box big enough for Marnie to hide inside. The smell of wood and varnish calms my mind and I prop my feet up on the workbench and let my mind wander. I never intended being a carpenter. Ever since my dad took me to see the Clifton Suspension Bridge when I was seven years old, all I wanted was to build bridges, so when I was offered a place at Edinburgh to study civil engineering, I couldn't wait to go. Josh's arrival changed everything—at least, that was how I saw it at the time.

I'm not making excuses for how I behaved back then, but it was hard seeing Nelson and my other friends having a great time at university when I had to do an apprenticeship I wasn't interested in. I don't know how Mr. Wentworth, the only person who would take me on, or Liv, put up with me. I'd disappear to see Nelson in Bristol, leaving her alone with Josh, sometimes not coming back for days. I'd crash in his room and sneak into his lectures with him, then stay up drinking, living the student life I so badly wanted. It's why I can understand Liv craving this party. When you've been robbed of something you wanted more than anything, it never really goes away.

My ledger is lying open on the table and I pull myself up from the armchair and flip through the pages. I automatically log my orders on my computer, but I also keep a written record, something Mr. Wentworth insisted we did. I've kept all of his ledgers. He loved the idea that one day someone would read about the different pieces he made—the wood he used, the approximate number of hours it took, the amount he charged. He died five years ago, and although I hadn't worked with him for more than ten years, I still miss him.

Most of the wood in my shed has already been commissioned— the biggest piece, a beautiful block of burnished oak, will eventually be a table for a rich banker in Knightsbridge—but the black walnut, my favorite, is reserved for Marnie. I'm going to make a sculpture for her twentieth birthday, in July.

I had zero expectations before she was born. Josh's arrival three years earlier had been so bewildering that I still hadn't adapted to being a dad. But the minute I laid eyes on Marnie, I was besotted. If Josh's arrival brought out the worst in me, Marnie's brought out the best. She taught me how to be a father, simply by being.

When she got older, we became close in a way I wasn't sure I'd ever be with Josh. After school, she'd come and find me in the shed and sit in one of the armchairs, chatting about her day as I worked. I got my first motorbike when she was twelve, and she loved it as much as I did. Livia had always insisted that the children walk the twenty minutes to school, but as Marnie got older, she began to take her time getting ready in the mornings, then ask me to take her on my bike, insisting she'd be late otherwise.

"And there's nothing cooler than arriving on a Triumph Bonneville T120," she'd whisper, once Livia was out of earshot.

Livia disapproved of me indulging her. I'd have done the same for Josh, if he'd asked, but he preferred to get a detention for being late rather than ask me for a lift. Later, when Marnie began going to parties, I'd take and fetch her on my bike. She never worried about her hair getting crushed under a helmet, or her dress crushed by the leathers I insisted on her wearing. I was proud that she shared my love of bikes. Stupidly, I never thought that one day she'd want one of her own.

"I've decided," she announced to me and Liv only a month ago, during one of our FaceTime chats. She was sitting on her bed, her phone balanced between her knees. On the wall behind her, along with a KEEP CALM AND CARRY ON poster, she'd stuck photos of me, Livia, and Josh, and her friends from home. There was also a group shot of her and Cleo, with me and Rob—Cleo's dad—standing behind them. We'd taken them to a pizza place in Windsor not long after they'd finished their exams, I remembered.

"I'm not going traveling when I finish here in June," Marnie continued. "I'm going to come straight home instead."

"What? Why the rush?" Liv said before I could reply. She sounded sharper with Marnie than she'd been for years and I knew she was worried that Marnie was feeling homesick again.

"Because I want to be able to do the Long Walk on my birthday."

Neither of us knew what to say. The Long Walk in Windsor Great Park was something we'd done with Marnie on her birthday for the last ten years, but only because she'd been around. To give up her chance to go traveling just to come home and do a walk she could do anytime, given that we lived nearby, was worrying. And then, unable to keep up the pretense, she burst out laughing.

"I'm joking!" she said. "I'm coming home to study for my motorbike license."

"Right," I said, relieved. "But there's no rush, is there?"

"Yes, because I want to get a motorbike."

"You won't be able to afford one for years," Liv pointed out. "Isn't it better to go traveling? You might never get the chance to visit Vietnam and Cambodia again."

"Mum," Marnie said patiently. "I will—by motorbike!"

Nothing we said would change her mind. I wasn't as concerned as Liv. I missed Marnie and liked the idea of her being home sooner than we thought. I also liked her determination to do what she wanted. Like last year, when we tried to persuade her not to get a motorbike tattooed across her back, from shoulder to shoulder.

"So, do you want to see it?" she asked on a weekend home from university. "My tattoo?"

"You didn't," I said, slightly appalled that she'd gone ahead.

"I did. But don't worry, you're going to like it."

"I'm not sure I will," I warned.

"I'd like to see it," Livia said, even though I knew she hated the thought of Marnie with a huge tattoo.

Laughing, Marnie peeled off her sweater and held out her arm. "I chickened out," she said. "I thought this was more appropriate."

Livia nodded approvingly. "Definitely."

"What do you think, Dad?"

I looked at the words tattooed the length of her forearm in beautiful italic script: *An angel walking to the Devil's beat.*

"Interesting," I said, breathing a sigh of relief that it was relatively small.

The tattoo had given me the idea for her sculpture. I'm going to carve an angel, not a traditional one, but an angel wearing leathers and riding a motorbike. I'd like to make a start on it now, but I should really go and see Liv before she leaves, offer to help Josh with the balloons and decorations he's brought. And find another box, maybe in the attic. The plan is that Marnie will text me a couple of minutes before she arrives at the house; I'll take the box out from under the table and push it to the middle of the terrace. She'll slip in through the side gate and climb inside, hopefully without anyone seeing. Once I've placed the lid back on top, I'll call everyone onto the terrace to see Liv opening her present.

It was clever of Marnie to tell Livia she was going away for the weekend and would be out of reach. That way, Livia won't be disappointed not to have a call from her today. I can't wait to see her face when Marnie turns up. It's going to be the best present we could possibly give her.

Livia

I carry my new red sandals in my hand so that I don't wake Josh by clacking down the stairs. I pause outside his door, the wood floor warm under my feet. There's no sound of him moving around. I'm not surprised. He arrived late last night and had been revising on the train. He told me to wake him early this morning, but I prefer to let him sleep.

Holding on to the banister rail, I double-step over the stairs that creak, and when I get to the bottom, I sit to put my sandals on. There's a pile of cards lying on the mat. I pick them up and carry them through to the kitchen, scanning the envelopes as I go, horribly disappointed that there isn't one from my parents. Despite what I said to Adam earlier, I really need them to turn up tonight, because if they can't do it today, on my fortieth birthday, then they never will. And I'll have to let them go, if only for my sanity, because twenty-two years is long enough to not forgive your child.

The feeling of excitement I've managed to hold on to since Adam sang "Happy Birthday" to me starts to disappear. I actually feel a bit sick, which often happens when I think of my parents. There's no sign of breakfast, or Adam, so I'm guessing he's outside. I felt bad yesterday when I saw how far back they had to take the tent, but if I'm honest, a small part of me is pleased that Nelson probably won't fit through the gap. He and Adam have a habit of sneaking off to the shed for a beer, and I really want Adam around tonight.

I give Murphy his morning cuddle. The kitchen smells faintly of the steak we had for dinner last night so I open the window. Warm air rushes in. I can't believe how beautiful it's turning out to be. I could have saved myself hundreds of pounds and not bothered with the tent. On the other hand, it's good to have somewhere covered for the caterers to put the food. They're coming at five, so there are hours before things really start happening.

I sit down at the table, find the bar where I like to rest my feet, and begin opening my cards. There's a ring at the doorbell, and when I answer it, I find a man on the doorstep holding a beautiful bouquet of yellow roses.

"Mrs. Harman?"

"That's me."

He holds out the flowers. "These are for you."

"Gosh, they're lovely!"

"Cut an inch off the stems before you put them in water," he advises. "But leave the bouquet tied."

"I will. Thank you—" He's off down the path before I can even finish.

I bury my nose in the bouquet, breathing in the heady scent of the roses, wondering who sent them. For one tiny moment I wonder if they might be from my parents. But they're more likely to be from Adam's.

I take them through to the kitchen, lay them on the table, and tug at the card that's attached to the bouquet.

"Have the best day ever, Mum. I'm sorry I can't be with you, but I'll be thinking of you. Love you millions. Your Marnie. PS This is the bouquet you never had."

Tears spring to my eyes. I don't remember telling Marnie I'd planned to carry a bouquet of yellow roses on my wedding day, but I must have. And remembering our last conversation, just over a week ago now, I feel terrible.

Adam had gone for a drink with Nelson and, knowing he wouldn't be back until late, I'd seized my chance to phone her. I waited until ten o'clock to call; it was only six in the morning in Hong Kong, but I didn't care that she might still be asleep.

"Mum?" she said, alarm chasing sleep from her voice. "Is everything all right?"

"Yes, yes, everything's fine," I reassured her quickly. "I thought I'd give you a ring, that's all."

I heard her rummaging for something, her watch maybe. "It's only six o'clock."

"Yes, I know, but I felt like a chat. And I thought you might already be up. Sorry."

"It's fine. Why aren't you on video?"

"Oh—I don't know. I guess I pressed the wrong option. Anyway, how are you?"

"Busy. I have so much revision to do. I'll probably sleep for a month when I get home."

"That's what I wanted to talk to you about, actually."

"Oh?"

"It's just that I don't understand why you're giving up the chance of going traveling," I said, plunging straight in, worried that Adam would arrive and hear me trying to persuade our daughter to only come home at the end of August, as she originally planned to do.

"Because I want to get my motorbike license. I already explained that!"

"But you can do that anytime," I said, knowing that the reason she wanted to come home had nothing to do with wanting to pass her test. "It's not as if you can afford a bike now, anyway."

"Is this coming from Dad?"

"No, it's coming from me."

"I thought you'd be pleased that I was coming home earlier," she said, her voice catching.

"I think it's a shame not to take the chance to see more of Asia.

And I don't understand the rush to get something that isn't going to be of any use to you for ages."

"Well, I've already got my ticket, so it's too late now."

"You could always change it."

There was a pause. "Don't you want me home, Mum?"

"Of course I do!" I said quickly.

"Anyway, it's not only about getting my license. There's other stuff I need to do."

"Like what?" It had been an effort to keep my voice even.

"Just stuff. Sorry, Mum, but if you phoned to tell me not to come back at the end of June, you've had a wasted call. I just want to be home."

The edge to her voice told me it was time to back off. Anyway, I couldn't have the conversation I needed to have with her, not like this.

"I know. And it'll be lovely to see you." I paused, wanting to make things right between us again. "I thought you might think that you had to come home and spend the summer with us—you know, as you haven't seen us for a year."

"I don't feel obliged to come home, I want to come home." She gave a little laugh. "I guess I'm more of a homebody than I thought."

We struggled on for a bit, me asking about her day ahead, Marnie asking me how the run-up to the party was going. But neither of our hearts was in it. Mine was too full of a sense of impending doom and maybe hers was heavy with the knowledge that her mother didn't want her home yet, despite my denials.

"I've got a birthday card for you," she said suddenly. "I'll post it today. It might not get there in time for your birthday, but I'll post it anyway."

"It'll be lovely to have it whenever it arrives," I told her. And then we hung up.

Maybe that's why she decided to send flowers, in case her card didn't arrive in time, which it hasn't. Just as I'm worrying how much the roses must have cost her, I hear the strum of a guitar and see Josh standing at the bottom of the stairs, his dark hair not yet unflattened by water or gel. As he bursts into a rap version of "Happy Birthday," I realize that I owe it to him and Adam, and to everyone else who has helped get my party off the ground, to stop feeling guilty about just about everything, and enjoy the day.

"Thank you!" I call, giving Josh a burst of applause. There's a hollow knock of wood on wood as he puts his guitar down on the stairs.

"So, how does it feel to be forty?" he asks, coming into the kitchen and lifting me off my feet.

"Wonderful!" I say, laughing. "Although the novelty will probably have worn off by tomorrow."

He puts me down, steps back and studies me. "Nice dress."

I smooth down the skirt of my white sundress. "Thanks. I bought it specially for lunch with Kirin today."

He bends down to stroke Murphy. "How are you, boy?" he murmurs. "At least you're pleased to see me, not like Mimi. She's hasn't even come to say hello. Where is she anyway?"

"Asleep on our bed."

"And Dad?"

"In his office."

He straightens up. "His office? Come on, Mum, you can call it a shed, Dad does."

I shrug and go to fill the kettle. The tension between Adam and Josh breaks my heart, but it's Josh's snipes at Adam that hurt the most—his hairstyle, the cliché of him reaching middle age, the fact that he works in a shed. Adam always tries. Maybe that's the issue. He tries too hard.

Josh nods toward the table. "Who sent the flowers?"

"Marnie. Aren't they beautiful?"

"I spoke to her yesterday," he says, opening the fridge and taking out a carton of juice. "She's so upset she won't be here tonight."

"I know, I am too." I carry the roses over to the sink and, ignoring the words of wisdom from the man who delivered them, I cut a tiny bit off each of the stems because an inch seems too much. "I don't suppose you could get me a vase from the dining room, could you?"

"Sure."

"So," I say when he comes back. "How are your exams going?"

"Not bad so far."

"Are you sure you don't need to revise today?"

He lifts his arms above his head and stretches, his hands touching the ceiling. It's funny how habits are passed down instinctively from generation to generation, because it's something Adam always does. His T-shirt rides up, showing his bare stomach. Too thin, I decide, wondering if he's eating properly.

"No, it's all under control," he says, hiding a yawn. "I did some revision on the train last night and I'll do a couple more hours on the way back tomorrow. Today, I'm free to do whatever needs doing."

I give him a grateful smile. "Have you managed to sort out the music—you know, with everybody's choices?"

"Yes, Max helped me make a playlist."

Max. Josh's childhood friend, whose mum died when he was five years old, who's been part of our family ever since, a second son to me and Adam, a brother to Josh and Marnie. Max, who for the last six months I've been avoiding.

"I bet there were some weird and wonderful requests."

"You could say that. It was always going to be an odd mix with such a big age range," he says, poking my arm gently to let me know he's joking. He takes the vase from me. "Where do you want this?"

"On the side for now, so that I can enjoy them. Tea or coffee?"

"Tea. I'll make it."

I sit down at the table. Josh is right, there are a lot of generations coming tonight, from Rob and Jess's daughter, Cleo, who's nineteen, to Adam's parents, who are in their seventies. I want there to be something for everyone, so I asked each person to let Josh know their favorite song, which he'll play during the course of the evening. Part of the fun tonight will be trying to match the guest to the music.

"How's Amy?"

Josh leans back against the countertop. "She's good."

"She still can't make it tonight?"

He gives his chest a scratch. "No. But I can understand that, in her parents' eyes, her grandfather's eightieth is more important than your fortieth."

"True."

He brings over a mug of tea. "Do you want something to eat?"

"Thanks. I'll wait until your dad comes in. He said he'd make breakfast."

"You don't mind if I start without you?" Josh goes to the cupboard, finds the cereal, pours himself a bowl, adds milk, grabs a spoon from the drawer, then leans back against the fridge and starts eating. He always seems to be leaning against something, as if his body can't quite hold itself up. The slightly brooding look on his face as he thinks about Amy not being able to come tonight doesn't make him any less handsome. He looks so much like Adam did at that age.

I stifle a sigh. It isn't just the fact that Amy's not able to come tonight that's bothering him.

"When are you going to speak to Dad?" I ask.

"Soon."

"You need to tell him," I say, horribly aware of the underlying hypocrisy of my words.

He wipes his mouth with the back of his hand. "I know."

"He'll understand."

Josh shakes his head. "No," he says somberly. "I don't think he will."

10 A.M.—11 A.M.

Adam

I'm on my way back to the house from my shed when, through the window, I see Liv chatting to Josh in the kitchen. They're not standing close to each other—Livia is sitting at the table, Josh is leaning against the fridge—but I feel like an outsider looking in. Maybe this is how Josh feels when he sees me and Marnie together, I realize. I always thought he chose not to join in because he didn't want to give me the pleasure of thinking he'd forgiven me. But maybe he feels like I do now, that his presence would be an intrusion.

As I watch, uncomfortable at this odd voyeurism but not able to stop myself, Livia throws her head back, laughing at something Josh said, and I smile in response. I love to see Livia happy, especially as I know how much it affected her when her parents told her she never would be, the day she told them we were getting married. I'll never be able to understand their rejection of her. It breaks my heart each time they don't turn up to something she's invited them to, because although she tells herself that they won't come, the expectation is always there. I've often wanted to jump on my motorbike and go and hunt them down in Norfolk, tell them what they're missing out on, not just in relation to Liv but also in relation to Josh and Marnie, the grandchildren they've never wanted to meet. I want to tell them how amazing Liv is, how happy we are, how much I love her. But I've always been worried that it would make things worse.

I realized recently that there is no worse, not for Livia, which is why I decided to write to her parents and ask them if they could find it in their hearts to come to her party tonight. I said that I understood how disappointed they must have been when Livia became pregnant, but over twenty years have gone by and that it's time to forgive. I used Josh and Marnie as leverage, rather than Livia, telling them that we'd always regretted them not knowing their grandparents. I sent a photograph of the two of them sitting on the wall in the garden, taken just before Marnie left for Hong Kong, and wrote long paragraphs about them, about their lives and what they've been doing—I even told them that Marnie was flying back from Hong Kong especially for the party as a surprise for Livia, hoping it might persuade them to come. I fully expected Livia's father to write straight back, telling me never to contact them again. The fact that he didn't gives me hope that they might actually turn up tonight.

My phone buzzes in my pocket, breaking the moment. I check the window to see if Liv and Josh have caught me staring, but they're still deep in conversation. I take out my phone, wondering if it's an update from Marnie. But it's Nelson.

"Sure you don't need any help today? Please . . . the kids are driving me nuts!"

Last weekend, when we went to see them, Nelson was trying to talk to me about his work while his four-year-old twin boys swarmed over him, and his little daughter decorated his beard with clips and ribbons. I love Nelson, but there's something supremely satisfying about the tables having turned.

"You and I both know you're on babysitting duty today. Kirin would kill me. Sorry!" I text back.

I carry on to the house, already preparing myself for the sense of—I suppose "loss"—that I feel whenever I'm with Josh. On the face of it, we get on fine. But there's something missing, a closeness that I'm not sure we'll ever have, not now.

I'd always been aware of the distance between us, but the first time it was really brought home was the day he left for university, in Bristol, where I'd hidden from him eighteen years before—trust me, the irony isn't lost on me. Nelson and Kirin were at our house and when it was time for Josh to say good-bye, he shook my hand, then went over to Nelson, who enveloped him in a hug. What shocked me was the way Josh hugged him back, as if it was the most natural thing in the world. It almost felt as if Nelson were his father, not me.

I know I concentrated too much on Marnie during those early years, and I've tried to make it up to Josh since, but it's difficult. It's why I'm stupidly proud of having found the New York internship for him. When you're a carpenter, there aren't many strings you can pull for your children. Not that I really pulled strings, I just happened to be chatting to an American friend of Oliver, one of my clients, who'd come to my workshop to see if I could make a bespoke piece of furniture for his home on Martha's Vineyard. He'd seen a piece I'd made for Oliver, and wanted something similar, but three times bigger. We were talking about our lives and our children and I happened to mention that for the last year of his master's, Josh needed to find an internship, preferably in digital marketing.

"Has he thought about coming to the United States?" he inquired, and explained that he was the CEO of Digimax, a large digital marketing company based in New York, which offered internships to master's students. To cut a long story short, Josh sent off his CV, had a couple of phone interviews with someone from the New York office and ended up being offered a place. He's really excited about going and it's great to see him making the most of opportunities that I never had.

Livia

Adam comes in from the garden, trailing sawdust across the kitchen floor. I'm so used to it that it doesn't irritate me anymore.

"Hi, Josh," he says. "Sleep well?"

"Yeah, fine, I always do when I come home. You?"

"Not really. I dreamed that the tent blew away, taking Marnie with it." He turns to me. "Lovely roses—who sent them?"

"Marnie," I say, offering him my plate of buttery toast, because I was too hungry to wait. He takes a slice with an apologetic smile, remembering too late his promise to make breakfast.

"Weren't you meant to be making Mum breakfast?"

Josh's tone isn't exactly accusatory, but the message is there. Adam doesn't say anything; he never does.

"I got some lovely cards too," I say, pointing to the pile on the table. He goes over and riffles through them with one hand, eating toast with the other.

"You should at least put them on display," he says. "Enjoy them for a while."

"Dad's right." Josh takes the cards from Adam and stands them along the countertop. "Presents tonight, Mum, is that OK?"

"Of course."

The mention of presents makes Adam restless. He said yesterday that he needed to go into Windsor this morning, and I'm guessing he hasn't bought me anything yet. I did point out a beautiful leather handbag a couple of weeks ago, but it was quite expensive, so I'm hoping my hint didn't register. I'll feel bad if he pays that much for a bag.

I watch him as he leans against the counter, drinking a second mug of coffee as he tries to talk to Josh about where best to put the tables—their job for the morning—and how he wants to hang the lights. Noticing how tired he looks, I feel a sudden rush of love. He's worked so hard over the last four years—well, for most of his life, really—and I know he's looking forward to things being easier once Josh graduates. With only one set of university fees and accommodation to pay, some of the pressure will be off.

When we were first married, we used to promise ourselves that as soon as we could, we'd continue with the education we'd missed. Adam would study civil engineering, and I'd train as a lawyer. It wasn't a lack of time, or money, or ambition, that prevented Adam from going ahead, just a realization that he loved being a carpenter and sculptor. There's something wonderfully organic about working with wood, he says, which brings with it its own sense of peace and well-being.

Over the years, he's built up an amazing business. It can be difficult financially, as we don't always know when the money will come in and it can take weeks to make one piece. But he's made quite a name for himself as a bespoke craftsman and is able to charge a good price. Orders come in from all over the world. Already this year, he's made beautiful carved desks for clients in Norway, Japan, and the United States. Each one is unique, and some of the requests he receives are real challenges, like the client who wanted him to make a chest of drawers six feet tall by four feet wide, where each drawer had to have a series of smaller secret drawers inside. Or the client who wanted him to make a wooden carriage for one of his children, which could be pulled by their pony. That commission paid for most of Marnie's living costs in Hong Kong.

I began studying for my degree in law via the Open University when Marnie was ten. It took me six years to qualify and another two before I could practice, which came at exactly the right time, because it was the year that Marnie left for university. I love my job and it means we don't have to worry so much about money anymore. Adam has never wanted Josh and Marnie to take out loans to pay for their university fees, which means our outgoings each month are huge. It also means he works long hours, six days a week, but even so, our lives are financially so far removed from when we first got married that sometimes I have to pinch myself.

"What time is Kirin coming, Mum?" Josh asks, breaking off from his conversation, about a box, I think, with Adam.

I check the time. "Any minute now."

"Nelson texted me, wanting to come over," Adam says, a smile in his voice. "I think he was trying to get out of looking after the kids."

"Now why doesn't that surprise me? He knows that Kirin is taking me for lunch today." I shoot him an amused glance. "You could always go and give him a hand. I'm sure Josh can manage on his own."

Adam's face is a picture. "No thanks," he says. "I've done my years of early child care, it's his turn now."

"You see, Dad," Josh says, "there are some really positive things about having your children while you're young."

"Apart from having to put your whole life on hold, you mean?"

I know it's meant to be a joke, but my body freezes as a shadow passes over Josh's face, and I know from the look on Adam's that he wishes he could take the words back.

"You better go and get your stuff together, Mum," Josh says, moving to the other side of the kitchen, physically distancing himself from his dad.

"OK," I say, giving them both a quick kiss. "See you later."

"Have fun!" Adam calls. But the words jar in the atmosphere and I can't bring myself to reply.

I run upstairs to get my phone, stopping in the bathroom to

brush my teeth and put on some lipstick. I'm glad to be getting out of the house for a while and it will be good to see Kirin—a proper distraction from everything else that's going on. I'd thought about booking myself into a spa for the day, but it felt a bit too much, and secretly, I've always hated the idea of people fussing over me. Anyway, I'm perfectly capable of doing my own nails and hair. And it's not as if it's my wedding day.

I'm glad I managed to find a present to give Adam tonight, a thank-you for always backing me up over this party, for never telling me to let it go. It was difficult to come up with something; his passions are black-and-white films, his motorbike, and bridges, and there wasn't much I could do with that. Then, a couple of weeks ago, while I was in Windsor during my lunch break, I saw a display in the travel agent's window offering cheap flights to Bordeaux and Montpellier. One of the photos featured the Millau Viaduct, which I remembered from a documentary Adam and I had seen about feats of engineering. He'd been fascinated, saying that he would have loved to have been involved in the project to build the viaduct, and that he'd like to see it close-up one day. Realizing I'd found the perfect present for him, I went in and, on impulse, booked two flights to Montpellier and four nights in a beautiful auberge in the center of Millau, with amazing views of the viaduct.

We're going this week, leaving on Tuesday and coming back Saturday. Adam doesn't know, as I've kept it a surprise. I know he'll be worried about taking so much time off when his orders are piling up, but he deserves a break. I'm planning to give him the envelope containing the plane tickets, and a photo of the Millau Viaduct, at the party tonight, when I make a little speech thanking everyone for coming. He deserves more thanks than anyone. He's had to live with the specter of my party for years, and if he knew how much I've bent truths and hidden stuff from him so that it will be exactly as I want it to be, he'd be shocked.

I drop my lipstick into my bag and go outside to wait for Kirin. Persuading Adam to buy this house over the larger modern one he preferred is just one example of how I've maneuvered things to suit me. The only thing that makes it bearable is that he came to love it as much as I do and has never regretted buying it.

We first saw it about a year after Marnie was born. We'd been renting a cramped two-bedroomed flat and we knew that once she was out of her cot, which was wedged into our bedroom between the wardrobe and the wall, there'd be nowhere to put a bed for her. Fitting bunk beds into Josh's tiny room was out of the question. When we worked out that mortgage payments would be about the same as we'd be paying in rent for a bigger flat, Adam's parents offered to lend us the money for a deposit on a house. It was the lifeline we needed, especially when they added that they didn't want us to start paying them back until we were in a better financial situation.

We visited a lot of houses and ended up with a short list of two, a new build and this one. The new build, on an estate outside Windsor, was bigger. It had an extra bedroom and a bigger kitchen, and was immaculate. In contrast, this house, a cottage over a hundred years old, needed a lot of work before we could even move in. I fell in love with it at once, because of its beautiful garden, which was already teeming with flowers and shrubs. It would be the perfect setting for a wedding, I thought wistfully, looking at the clematis-covered pergola tucked away in a corner. And then I thought of the party I hoped to have for my fortieth birthday, which seemed so far away I knew I was being ridiculous. But I couldn't let it go.

"It'll be a lovely garden for Marnie to take her first steps in," I told Adam, aiming for his Achilles' heel, because I could see he was leaning toward the easier option of the new build. "Just think of the fun she'll have playing hide-and-seek here. She won't be able to do that in that oblong piece of garden that hasn't even been grassed yet."

That swung it for him, as I knew it would. It wouldn't have had the same impact if I'd mentioned Josh having more room to kick his soccer ball around. I felt bad, because he'd had his eye on the extra bedroom in the new build as a possible study. But, very quickly, the garden won him over, as it had me.

We painted everything white, restored the old oak floors and, a couple of years later, Adam built himself a large shed to work in at the end of the garden, which made me feel better about him missing out on a study. And once the lights are strung in the trees tonight, the garden will look exactly how I knew it could, all those years ago.

11 A.M.–12 P.M.

Adam

I lower the box that something was delivered in—I can't remember what—to Josh, standing in the hall below.

"So, what's this for?" he asks.

I come down the ladder and fold it back into the loft. I can't tell him the real reason, so I've got an answer ready.

"You know I'm buying Mum a ring?" He nods. "Well, she'll guess what it is from the size of the box. So I'm going to put the ring box into this box to delay the surprise a bit."

"Then why don't you get a whole range of boxes that fit one inside the other? There are loads up there from toasters and things, and I've got a shoe box we could use for the one before last." His enthusiasm grows. "Or we could slide the ring box in an empty toilet roll and place that in the shoe box. She'll never guess then!"

"No, only one box, I think."

"But if you want the surprise to last?"

"No, I'm just going to put the ring box inside this one." I pick up the box and upend it so that it'll fit down the stairs. "Can you give me a hand covering it with wrapping paper?"

"But won't the ring box slide around inside? Unless we stuff it with newspaper."

"It'll be fine." He follows me down to the kitchen and I dump the box on the floor. "Let's cover it. There's paper somewhere."

"But isn't it better to do that once you've put the ring box inside?" he says. "Then we can seal it up properly."

"I don't want to seal it."

"Why not?"

"Because it'll take her too long to open it."

He scratches his head. "I thought you wanted to delay the surprise?"

I'm beginning to wish I hadn't asked for his help.

"I do, but not for that long."

"I don't understand."

"You will tonight. For now, just let me do it my way."

"Yeah, because you never got to do anything your way." He says it in such a matter-of-fact way that I know he really believes that everything I've done in my life has been out of duty, not choice.

I give him a quick smile. "I wouldn't change a thing."

His silence tells me that he doesn't believe me. I reach on top of one of the cupboards, find the rolls of paper that Liv keeps there, and we get on with the task of covering the box.

"How's Amy?" I ask, breaking the silence that has grown between us.

"She's fine. Really sorry to be missing the party. When are you getting Mum's ring?"

"I'll go and collect it once we've put the tables up."

It's unbelievable how long it takes the two of us to cover the box. Liv would have done it in half the time with no help from anyone.

"I hope the tables are going to be easier than that was," Josh says. He looks around. "Where do you want to put it?"

"I'm going to hide it under the table on the terrace. But I'll have to wait until the caterers bring the tablecloths, because I don't want your mum to see it."

"She'll be back before they arrive." He thinks for a moment. "I've got a couple of those party packs with balloons and banners and stuff, and there's a paper tablecloth in each one. If we stick them together, we can use them to cover the table."

"Sounds good," I say, smiling at him.

He finds the paper cloths, and when we tape them together, they're exactly the right size to cover the table all the way to the ground. We slide the box underneath.

"Perfect," I say, relieved to have gotten that out of the way. The loss of the wooden crate doesn't seem so bad now. "Right, now for the tables."

We take the trestle tables, twelve in all, from where they're stacked along the wall and put four in the tent and eight on the lawn.

"Do we do the chairs now, or later?" Josh asks.

"May as well do them now."

Ten chairs to each table later, we're done. I check the time; it's 11:40, too early for a beer.

I look at Josh. "Beer?"

"I think we've earned it. Stay there, I'll get them."

Even though I'm nearer to the kitchen than he is, I know it's no use insisting. If Josh can help it, he won't let me do anything for him. He doesn't even like the fact that I've paid his university fees, and has told me he intends paying every penny back once he's working. It's why him accepting the internship means so much to me. I honestly thought he would refuse it, given that I was at the beginning of it all.

He comes back with two bottles and Murphy. We sit on the wall to drink them, Murphy at our feet. And all of a sudden, there's this strange tension between us and I find myself struggling for something to say.

"You'll be off to New York soon. I'm going to miss you," I add, surprising myself, because it's the first time I've ever said anything remotely emotional to him. I brace myself for his rejection, but to my surprise, some of the tension seems to evaporate.

"Really?"

"Yes, of course I will."

He nods slowly, taking time to absorb what I've said. "You know back there when you said you wouldn't change anything? Is that true?"

The air around us stills, as if everything and everyone, from the birds in the trees to the neighbors mowing their lawns, have realized the significance of Josh's question and are holding their collective breath, hoping I'll take this once-in-a-lifetime chance—because we've never come near it before, and might never again—to put things straight between us. What has brought this on, I wonder, what has made Josh reach out to me, if that's what this is? Is it because he's leaving for the States soon and might not see us for a year?

Murphy raises his head and gives me a *Don't mess this up* look. I think back to the remark Josh made this morning about there being advantages in having had my children young, and the way his eyes had darkened when I'd joked at the idea.

"No," I say. "It's not true. There are things I'd change if I could."

"What sort of things? Not married Mum? Had me put up for adoption?" He stretches his long legs out in front of him, and although there's a slight joke in his tone, I know he means every word.

I look at him properly then. His hair is the same color mine was before the gray bits came, and his face has the same angles, the nose slightly hooked at the end. "No, Josh," I say. "Not any of those things."

"What, then?"

"I'd still have married your mum, but later, once I'd been to university."

"You might have met someone else at university. She might have met someone else."

I take a sip of beer, because it's something I've often thought about. Livia and I had known each other only a few months, and if she hadn't become pregnant, maybe we wouldn't have ended up together. I don't suppose I figured in Livia's long-term plans any more than she figured in mine, simply because neither of us was thinking that far ahead. And yet, after the first rocky few years, we've been happy, very happy.

"Well, your mum is definitely the one for me, so I'm sure we'd have ended up together somehow."

"But you wouldn't have had me."

"Of course we would have."

"No. If you'd married Mum later, you might still have had a son, but he wouldn't have been me. I'm me only because I was conceived and born when I was."

It's one of those times when it's like looking at myself in a mirror. He has the hurt of rejection written all over him, just as I have. We're bleeding each other dry, I realize.

My mind flashes back to the day he was building a Lego fort and I became angry at his constant demands to help him.

"Daddy, I only need help with this last bit," he'd said for the fifth time. "I did the rest all by myself, just like you told me to."

"It's too *old* for him," Marnie kept telling me when I ignored him. "He can't do it."

But Josh had persevered, and instead of praising him, I lost my temper and knocked the fort over.

"Why you do that?" Marnie asked, her grammar deserting her as she looked in horror at the trashed fort.

"I—it was an accident," I lied.

The look she gave me, of pure disgust, reminded me of the one Livia used to give me when I eventually turned up after spending days in Bristol with Nelson.

"No, you did it on purpose, I saw you! You went over and you did this." She made a swiping movement with her arm. "You're horrible and I don't like you anymore!" She turned her back on me and went over to Josh. "Don't cry," she said, reaching up and putting her arms around his waist. "I'll help you build it again."

Going over, I crouched down beside Josh, telling him I was

sorry and offering to rebuild the fort with him. But he wouldn't even acknowledge I was there.

"Leave him alone, Daddy, it's too late!" Marnie had cried.

I'd looked up then and seen Livia standing in the doorway, her eyes bright with tears. Not the tears of frustration that I'd seen in the early stages of our marriage, but tears of desperation. And I wondered how long she'd been standing there, and how much she'd seen.

"This can't go on," she said shakily. "It really can't." And I knew she was right.

I tried, but Josh would barely speak to me. He kept the distance I no longer wanted him to keep, and refused to let me help him with anything. Our conversations over the years went something like this.

"Josh, would you like me to help you with your dinosaur project?"

"No, thank you, Daddy."

"Josh, shall I help you paint your bike?"

"No thanks, Dad."

"Josh, can I give you a hand moving that bed?"

"I'm fine, thanks."

"Josh, do you need some help with your university applications?"

"No, I'm all right."

"Josh, when do you want me to move you to Bristol?"

"It's all right, Dad, Nelson's lending me his van."

Nothing, just a barrier between us that we've never managed to breach. Until now, if only I can find the right thing to say.

I bend down and ruffle Murphy's fur.

"I'm really sorry I trashed your fort that day."

"It was years ago, Dad."

"Maybe. But it's still there between us."

"Only because you let it be. You knocked my fort down. It's not as if you beat me or anything. You need to let it go."

I can't look at him. "But you've always resented me because of it."

"No, I've resented the way you tiptoe around me. That's why I needle you—I'm trying to get a reaction. I just want us to be normal."

"I'm not sure I know what normal is."

"It's this, Dad. Having a beer and a chat and being honest."

Can it really be that simple? I wonder.

"Anyway, I'm glad you trashed my fort," he goes on.

I straighten up. "How do you work that out?"

"Because we wouldn't have had Murphy otherwise. That's why you bought him for me, wasn't it? He was a peace offering."

"Yes."

"Except you didn't tell me at the time. I thought you just bought me a dog, especially as you bought Mimi for Marnie a week later."

"Only because she made a fuss about not having a pet of her own. Why—would it have made a difference if I'd told you Murphy was to make up for trashing your fort?"

"Maybe. I mean, if you accept a peace offering, you're kind of accepting to make peace, aren't you? Communication, Dad, it's all about communication."

We sit in silence for a while, finishing our beers.

"I'm glad you accepted that internship in New York," I say, deciding to communicate how much it means to me.

"Right," he says. "Shall we have another beer?"

"Good idea."

I sit there, waiting for him to go and fetch them.

"Go on, then," he says, nudging me.

"What?"

"Go and get the beers. It's your turn."

Such a small thing. But as I make my way to the kitchen, it feels amazing.

Livia

Kirin turns off the main road into an all-too-familiar street and my heart immediately starts beating faster.

"What are we doing here?" I ask, trying to hide my alarm.

Kirin laughs. "Picking up Jess, of course!"

"She's coming with us?"

"Yes! We wanted it to be a surprise."

I take a minute to digest the news, to control my emotions. I'm glad Jess is coming, of course I am, she's my oldest friend. But it's become complicated.

"Will she be all right?" I ask Kirin. "It won't be too much for her, will it?"

"She'll be fine. But she doesn't want to drive anymore, which is why we're picking her up."

As we pull up in front of Jess's house, I take my bag from the floor and rummage inside, feeling awful that I didn't know she no longer felt up to driving. But how could she tell me when I haven't seen her for weeks?

"I need to send a text," I say apologetically, taking out my phone.

Kirin snaps off her seat belt. "No problem, I'll go and get her."

I keep my head bent over my phone, listening to her footsteps as she walks up the path. There's the peal of the doorbell and for a moment I forget to breathe. Then I hear Jess saying hello, the front door closing behind her, and the two of them coming back down the path, chattering excitedly together. Only then do I get out of the car.

"Jess!" I say as she walks toward me, leaning heavily on her stick. I give her a hug, careful not to knock her off balance.

"Happy birthday!" she says, hugging me back.

"Thank you. It's so lovely to see you!"

"It's been a while," she says softly.

"I know and I'm sorry. It's been a really busy time, with the party and everything. Here, let me help you."

"I'm fine sitting in the back," she protests.

"Don't be silly, you're going in the front." I take her arm, helping her in. She seems frailer than I remember and worry stabs at me.

I've known Jess for years. We were at school together and I was with her the night I met Adam at a friend's party. Adam was with Nelson, and although Nelson was the one with all the jokes, I was immediately drawn toward Adam, not just because he was amazingly handsome in the way most boys his age never are but also because of the way he looked right into my eyes when he spoke to me. His eyes have always mesmerized me; they're the most beautiful gray, and Marnie has been lucky enough to inherit them.

By the end of the evening, we'd arranged to go out as a foursome the following week, and I couldn't wait to see him again—until Jess asked me if I'd mind if she paired up with Adam. He must have been looking into her eyes too, I realized miserably. But seeing him with Jess was better than not seeing him at all, I decided, and Nelson was a lot of fun to be with. And it was only for an evening. We went to a club—something my parents would have forbidden if they'd known—and I found myself alone with Adam. He admitted later that he told Nelson he'd only go on the date if Nelson agreed to babysit Jess for the evening, so that he could be with me.

In one of life's unexpected twists, Jess is now married to Rob, Nelson's younger brother. Their daughter, Cleo, is Marnie's best friend, I'm Cleo's godmother and Jess is Marnie's, so we're a kind of extended happy family. Then, two years ago, Jess was diagnosed with multiple sclerosis.

"Everyone in?" Kirin asks, starting up the engine.

"Everyone in," I confirm, fastening my seat belt. "This is such a lovely surprise. I can't think of a better way to spend my birthday than with my two best friends."

I may not have known Kirin as long as I've known Jess, but ever since Nelson introduced her to me and Adam, she's become a really close friend. There were times when Adam and I wondered if Nelson would ever get married. He finally did, at thirty-four, which isn't old, it just seemed that way because we'd been married for fifteen years by then. It happened quickly too. His and Kirin's was definitely a whirlwind romance, but I'm not surprised. Not only is Kirin incredibly lovely, she's also incredibly beautiful, with long, dark, sleek hair and gorgeous olive skin, a legacy of her Indian heritage.

I think Adam was relieved that Nelson was no longer single. It had been hard for him during those early years, seeing Nelson going off on his Harley-Davidson with his friends from the motorcycle club, while he took Josh and Marnie swimming, or to the park, or on nature walks. Even when Nelson met Kirin, our day-to-day lives remained poles apart because they had the freedom to do whatever they wanted, go wherever they wanted, without having to think about anyone else. Then the twins came along, then Lily, and now Nelson doesn't go anywhere without them in tow, except on Sunday mornings, when he gets to ride his bike down to the coast.

"Rob was asking if Adam intends taking his bike out tomorrow," Jess says, catching uncannily on to my train of thought. "You know, as you won't get to bed until the early hours of the morning."

"I doubt that only getting a couple of hours' sleep will stop Adam from doing what he loves best," I say shortly. And then I

THE DILEMMA | 61

want to kick myself because I've made it sound as if I don't want Adam to go out on his bike, which isn't the case at all.

It's true that motorbikes used to be a sore point between us, but only because of what happened a couple of years into our marriage. When Josh was a few months old, we moved from Adam's parents' house, where we'd been living since our wedding, into our own flat. Money was tight, as everything Adam earned seemed to go on Josh, so I began to take in ironing. People would drop off baskets of crumpled clothes on their way to work and pick them up on their way home, neatly ironed. I took only two baskets a day, but ten a week meant we could just about make ends meet because, in an attempt to get Adam to turn up for work on a regular basis, Mr. Wentworth paid him only for the hours he actually worked. It meant that his salary varied from month to month and sometimes we couldn't pay the rent.

After a couple of months, without telling Adam, I began to put ten pounds out of the hundred I earned each week into a shoe box, which I kept at the bottom of the wardrobe. I missed the holidays my parents had taken me on and I wanted to rent a cottage in Cornwall as a surprise for him and Josh.

One Saturday, about the time I was thinking of booking the holiday—because after two years, I'd finally saved enough—I came back from the supermarket, heavily pregnant with Marnie, and saw a motorbike parked in the road outside our flat. Guessing that Rob was there, because I knew from Jess that he'd recently bought a bike, I touched it and found the engine hot. I was glad he'd only just arrived; any earlier and he'd have woken Josh from his afternoon sleep. But when I went up to the flat, there was only Adam, sitting on the sofa, and I knew straightaway that something was wrong from the look on his face.

"Where's Rob?" I asked, putting the shopping bags down on the floor.

"He's left."

I put both hands on my back, easing the ache from it. "Isn't that his motorbike outside?"

"No." He paused. "It's mine."

"Yours?"

"That's right."

Stunned, I sat down opposite him.

"I don't understand. How can you afford a motorbike?" He didn't say anything and my heart sank. "Please don't tell me you took out a loan. I thought we agreed no loans, that we buy only what we can afford."

He laid his head back against the sofa. "Oh, don't worry, we can afford it."

I looked at him, puzzled by his attitude. Had my parents relented and sent a check or something? When I'd found out I was pregnant again, I'd written to ask if they could restore the allowance they'd paid me since my sixteenth birthday from money my grandmother had left me. My father had refused, telling me my grandmother would be as ashamed of me as they were. I didn't think they'd have changed their minds, and even if they had, the allowance was in my name, so Adam wouldn't have been able to touch it. Maybe his parents?

"Did your parents lend you the money?"

"No," he said, his eyes fixed on the ceiling.

"A bonus from Mr. Wentworth?"

He gave a snort of laughter. "I wish."

"Well, maybe if you turned up for work a bit more often, he'd give you one!" I retorted. "Stop playing games, Adam. Where did you get the money from?"

He lowered his head and looked me straight in the eye. "You know damn well where."

It took me a moment to realize what he meant. Running into the bedroom, I found the shoe box open on the bed, empty except for a handful of one- and two-pound coins. When I'd last counted, there'd been over a thousand pounds. Now there were barely ten.

Sick with fear that he could do such a thing, I picked up the box and went tearing back to him.

"How dare you?" I cried. "How dare you steal my money?"

He was on his feet in an instant.

"How dare you?" he countered angrily, his face close to mine. "How dare you keep money from me when you knew how much I wanted a motorbike."

"Only since Rob bought one! You never mentioned wanting a bike before that!"

"Because I thought I'd never be able to have one, not with a child to bring up! But then Rob enlightened me, told me the reason I couldn't afford one was because you'd been hiding money from me. So when, exactly, were you planning to leave me?"

I stared at him. "What are you talking about? When have I ever said that I wanted to leave you?"

"Why else would you have been hoarding money?"

"Not to leave you! I love you, Adam, although sometimes I don't understand why, not when you behave like you do."

"So what was the money for, then?"

"I was saving to take you and Josh on holiday!"

From his bedroom, Josh began to cry, woken by our raised voices. A flash of fear ran through me.

"When? When did you buy the bike?"

"This morning, while you were out."

"I was only gone two hours."

"It was long enough."

"Was Rob here? Did he stay here while you went to buy it?"

"No, it was one of his friends who was selling it, so he came with me."

I stared at him, hating that he hadn't even grasped what I was getting at. "How did you get it back here?"

"How do you think? I rode it!"

"How?"

"What do you mean, how?"

"I mean how did you ride it when you had Josh with you?" I could see him working it out, see him thinking—Josh? The blood drained from his face.

"You forgot, didn't you?" I moved toward him, so mad that I wanted to scratch his eyes out. "You forgot about Josh. You look after him so rarely that you forgot he existed. You went off to buy yourself a motorbike, leaving your son here, your son who could have woken up and found himself alone in the flat." I looked behind him to the open window. "Josh is nearly three, Adam, three! He can climb!"

"I didn't know," he stuttered. "I didn't think."

"You never think, that's the problem! You think about yourself, but you don't think about me, or Josh, you never have and you never will! So this is what you're going to do. I'm going out and when I come back, I want you gone! Go and live with Nelson—you think more of him than you do of us. Here's the money for your fare!" And I flung the contents of the box in his face.

For days after, I could see the marks on his forehead where the coins had hit him.

Although Adam returned the bike that afternoon and managed to get the money back, he's never forgiven Rob for misleading him. Neither have I, because I know that when Jess told him what I'd told her in confidence—that I was secretly saving—she would also have mentioned why. At the time, I wondered at Rob's motive. Then I remembered how persistent he'd been in asking me out, even though I'd already met Adam, even though each time I refused. Even now the only thing I can think of is revenge. As I sit behind Kirin and Jess, watching the beautiful countryside fly past the window, a shiver goes down my spine.

12 P.M.–1 P.M.

Adam

I take my leather jacket from the cupboard under the stairs and head out to the garage. Even if I'm only going into Windsor, I still feel the same sense of excitement when it comes to going out on my bike. I put my helmet on, my music starts playing, and it's like I'm in my own secret world.

I switch on the ignition and the engine roars to life. I can't believe how good it feels to have had that conversation with Josh. As we sat drinking our second beer, we began to talk like we've never talked before, not about anything very meaningful, but about everyday stuff. He wanted to know about the techniques I use to sculpt, so I told him about the angel I want to make for Marnie, and he's going to watch me when I make a start on it tomorrow.

I feel bad that Livia doesn't have something just for her, like I have my bike and my wood. I hadn't realized that she doesn't really have any hobbies until she brought it up a few weeks ago. She'd been working late at the kitchen table and I'd gone in to offer her a glass of wine and found her crying, her tears dripping onto her keyboard.

"Hey," I said, moving her computer out of the way. "What's happened?"

She rubbed her eyes and leaned into me as I bent to hug her.

"I'm just feeling a bit rubbish about everything—at everything."

I kissed her hair, the familiar smell of coconut and perfume pulling me in.

"That," I said. "Couldn't be further from the truth."

"Tell me honestly," she said, looking up at me. "Do you think that because my parents were screwed up, I've screwed up Josh and Marnie?"

The question was so unexpected, I laughed.

"Liv! That's insane! You're an incredible mum, the absolute best. Without you, our kids wouldn't be half the people they are. You've brought them up brilliantly."

She pulled away and attempted to go back to working on her laptop. But I stopped her hands and closed the computer.

"You're amazing," I told her. "I don't know what's happened to make you feel like this, but you are."

She stared through the window into the dark night.

"It's just—I don't know—I suppose I feel that I've lost myself somewhere along the way. I'm a mum, a wife, a lawyer, a friend, but sometimes I wish I had something extra, something that's only for me, like you do. Like your biking and your sculpting. I haven't had a passion just for me for years, if ever. I don't even have any talents, not like you. You're so creative and I'm—nothing."

It hurt that she couldn't see how brilliant she was. I took her wrists and pulled her gently to her feet. When she wrapped her arms around me, I could feel the undulations of her ribs through her sweater. She'd lost weight recently and I kept forgetting to ask her about it. Was it all for the party? Or was she worried about something, something bigger? But she would tell me if she was; she'd never been able to leave things unsaid between us.

"What about your roses?" I said, glad to have found something that was all hers. "I don't know anyone who can name roses like you do. That's an amazing talent."

She started to smile and then began laughing so hard that new tears formed in her eyes.

"What?" I said. "You can!"

"Adam, that is the most depressing thing I've ever heard! I'm thirty-nine! Naming roses is not a talent. It makes me sound like I'm eighty years old . . ." She went quiet and I pulled her back into a hug.

"We'll find you a really cool hobby for your fortieth," I promised. "Just you wait."

I know the underlying problem is her parents, not the fact that she doesn't have a hobby. It's why I'm determined she'll have an amazing party tonight, with or without them. She deserves so much to be spoiled, to have a special day just for her full of surprises, including the ring I've come to pick up.

The jeweler's is part of the maze of pedestrianized streets, so I leave the bike in the usual car park and start the short walk there. It's still warm, the sun stronger as it gets closer to noon, and the thought of Livia on her surprise trip to the spa feels good. As I weave between Saturday shoppers, I peel off my gloves and, tucking them into my jacket pocket, take out my phone to check the time.

The light is too bright to be able to read the screen, so I cup my hand around it. There's a news notification on the home page.

Breaking News

Pyramid Airways plane has crashed near Cairo International Airport.

My eyes freeze on the words *Pyramid Airways*. Marnie is flying Pyramid Airways. I stop, my heart constricting. I know it can't be her flight; it has to be a different one. But the mention of Cairo Airport feels too close.

I press at the screen to open the main BBC News app.

A plane has crashed on takeoff from Cairo International Airport. Pyramid Airways flight PA206 to Amsterdam crashed 11:55 local time.

My mouth goes dry. Is that the flight Marnie was meant to be on, the one she said she'd miss? Or a later one?

A child shouts out. Something—a bag—hits the side of my leg. I look up, my eyes unfocused, trying to take in what I've just read.

I need to find Marnie's flight number, but for a moment I can't make my hands work. I move into the shade by a shop window and bring up the WhatsApp conversation where she sent me her flight details. My fingers fumble on the screen as I scroll down.

HK—Cairo HK945 DEP 06:10 ARR 10:15
Cairo–Ams PA206 DEP 11:35 ARR 17:40
Ams—Ldn EK749 DEP 19:30 ARR 19:55
Ldn—Home ETA 21:00!!!

Cairo to Amsterdam PA206 DEP 11:35. I repeat it twice: PA206 Departure 11:35, PA206 Departure 11:35. The flight number in the news story is *PA206*. It's Marnie's flight, the one she would have been on if her flight from Hong Kong hadn't been delayed.

The shock sends tremors through my body. It's not only shock; it's also relief. I unzip my jacket, the leather suddenly too heavy. Thank God Marnie missed the flight, thank God her flight was delayed. But I need to make sure, I need to check that she couldn't have arrived in Cairo in time to get the Amsterdam flight.

I find the flight app I installed on my mobile when Marnie first left, then flip back to our WhatsApp conversation to get her flight number from Hong Kong. I put it into the app: *HK945*. The details come up—her plane landed in Cairo at 11:25 local time, so over an hour late—and only ten minutes before the Amsterdam flight left. I'm weak with relief. She couldn't have made it, not with only ten minutes to spare. She'll be at Cairo Airport, stuck between flights. She'll be distraught, of course, but at least she's safe.

But—why hasn't she been in touch? Maybe she tried to call, maybe I missed it. I check my missed calls log; there's nothing. I press the FaceTime call logo and watch the screen, waiting for her face to appear. Nothing. I cut the call and try on audio, in case the signal isn't strong enough for the video link to work. There's still nothing. I try sending a text: *Marnie, something happened to a flight out of Cairo. Text or call me as soon as you can, Love xxx.*

I send it by WhatsApp too, to double my chances, then hold my breath, waiting for a sign that Marnie has seen it—the two blue ticks, the *Typing* . . . at the top of the screen. Nothing. There are no ticks to say it's been delivered. I check the status—undelivered. The network must be down in Cairo because of the crash. It must be chaos at the airport. There probably won't have been an announcement about the crash, but everyone will know something is wrong because all the departures boards will suddenly show *Delayed* or *Canceled* for all subsequent flights out. Poor Marnie, she'll be devastated by what's happened.

I need to think what to do, how I can find out where Marnie is, and if she's all right. There's usually an emergency number that people can call to check whether or not a relative was on a flight. I know Marnie wasn't, but it would be good to have confirmation that she missed it.

I go back to the BBC News story and see an update: *All 243 passengers and crew members are thought to have perished.* The reality of the crash hits again. Livia, I have to tell Livia; she needs to know. The thought of telling her is overwhelming. How can I tell her what's happened without sending her into a panic? She's with Kirin and Jess at the spa—I can't just call her on the phone, not to tell her this.

A group of teenagers walk past, pushing one another and bumping my arm as I refresh the BBC News story. But there's nothing further. I check WhatsApp, but still there are no ticks next to Marnie's message.

I feel a creeping dread. I have no idea what to do.

Livia

The car slows and Kirin takes a left-hand turn down a leafy drive-way lined with rhododendrons before pulling up in front of a beautiful country house.

"What's this?" I ask, peering through the window.

"Our birthday present to you," she says, smiling at me in the rearview mirror. "A spa afternoon, with a facial and massage all booked!"

I unbuckle my seat belt and lean forward, throwing my arms around the two of them.

"Oh my God, you're amazing! Thank you! Thank you!" Something occurs to me. "You are joining me, aren't you? You're not just dropping me off?"

Jess laughs. "Don't worry, we're coming with you."

"I used to do this kind of thing once a month before Nelson and the children came along," Kirin says as we get out of the car. "Our first appointment is at two, so we've got time for lunch first." She links her arms through ours, discreetly helping Jess. "Come on, it's this way."

"I'm so glad to be getting away for a few hours," Jess says as we stroll down a paved pathway where scented clematis cling to an archway of wooden trellises. "Rob's cleaning his bike and there are bits of it in the kitchen sink."

Kirin nods in agreement. "Me too. It's amazing how many things Nelson needed me to go over with him, about when to put Lily down for her nap and what to give the boys for lunch. Anyway, enough about men. How are you feeling, Liv? Does it feel weird that the party is finally here?"

"I think it hasn't really sunk in yet," I tell her.

"It must feel strange," Jess says as we come to the stone steps leading to the entrance. She leans harder on me and shifts her body so that she can climb sideways. "I mean, you've been planning it for so long."

"Twenty years. Isn't that embarrassing? But it's turning out exactly as I imagined. The weather is amazing and there are so many people coming, nearly a hundred. I feel so lucky."

"You deserve it," Kirin says.

We've reached the entrance and I stop. "Do I, though?"

"Yes, of course you do!" Jess says, tugging my arm, forcing me onward. "Why wouldn't you?"

"I don't know—deep down, don't you think there's something morally wrong in spending so much money on one evening, on one person?"

Kirin gives a sigh of exasperation as she walks toward the reception desk. We've had this conversation before and she thinks I'm being ridiculous. "In short—no. I spent a lot more on my wedding," she says, laughing and pushing hard on the gold bell sitting by the sign: RING FOR ASSISTANCE.

"Yes, but that lasted the whole day. And it was your wedding, not just a birthday party."

"Don't worry, I'm going to have a huge party for my fortieth too!"

We're taken to an outdoor terrace, where tables set for lunch are grouped around a huge swimming pool. A few people are lying on sun loungers, all of them on their phones. It sounds clichéd, but the water really is sparkling in the sunlight.

"I should have brought a swimsuit," I say, looking longingly at the pool.

Reaching into her bag, Jess takes out a pretty gift bag and presents it to me with a flourish. "No sooner said than done."

"What's this?" I ask.

"Something to make you feel like a million dollars."

"I already do, with lovely friends like you." I open the bag and take out a beautiful red swimsuit, complete with diamanté straps. It's not something I'd ever consider buying for myself and I love it.

Kirin orders champagne and while we're waiting for it to arrive, we head to the pool house to change.

"It fits perfectly," I say once I've got my swimsuit on. "It's beautiful, thank you! Have we got time for a swim?"

"Of course."

It's only when I'm in the pool that I realize how much strain I've been under during the last few weeks. I lie on my back and close my eyes, letting the tension seep out of me. Everything will be all right, I tell myself. It has to be. I couldn't bear it if it wasn't.

Our drinks arrive, drawing us from the pool.

"Who's that for?" Jess asks, pointing at the glass of orange juice.

Kirin raises her hand. "That would be me—although I will have a sip of champagne," she adds.

Jess looks at her. "You're not—"

She gives a rueful smile. "I am."

"Wow, Kirin, that's wonderful!" I exclaim, giving her a hug.

She sits down suddenly, as if her legs can't hold her up anymore.

"It's twins," she says. "Again."

I do the math quickly and realize she'll have five children under six.

"Oh my God, how lovely!" Jess looks so excited, although I know the news must hurt a little, as she was desperate for more children after Cleo. But after three miscarriages, she and Rob decided to stop trying. It's probably even harder since Nelson and Rob are brothers, but Jess is the most selfless person I know. She doesn't deserve everything that has happened to her these last two years.

"How are you feeling?" I ask Kirin.

"Fine for now. I'm only twelve weeks. I had a scan yesterday and that's when they told me there were two."

"I wish I'd been there to see Nelson's face!"

"He wasn't there."

"Why not?"

"I haven't told him I'm pregnant."

Jess glances at me: *She hasn't told Nelson?*

"But—" She looks anxiously at Kirin. "Hasn't he noticed?"

She shakes her head. "I haven't put on much weight yet and I haven't had any morning sickness. It's always the middle three months that are the worst for me. So, anytime now."

"Why haven't you told him?" I ask. "He'll be fine about it, won't he?"

"We had a conversation about having a fourth child after Lily was born, and he said three was enough. I broached the subject again when I guessed I was pregnant, and he said definitely not."

"Oh, Kirin." I reach over and give her hand a squeeze. "He'll come around to the idea once he knows."

"I know he will. And despite his moaning, he loves being a dad. It's just the fact that there are two." She starts laughing. "I don't think he ever imagined, even in his worst nightmare, that he'd end up with five children under the age of six. He's not going to know what's hit him."

Jess and I start laughing too. "There's something incredibly funny about Nelson being a father of five," Jess says, wiping her eyes. "I think we need a drink." She hands us each a glass of champagne. "Happy birthday! And congratulations," she adds with a smile at Kirin.

"Thank you for this lovely treat," I say, clinking their glasses. "You're the best."

Kirin takes a sip of champagne. "Maybe I'll tell Nelson at the party tonight, once he's had a few drinks."

"That's not a bad idea. With everyone congratulating him and telling him what an amazing family he's going to have, he'll think it's the most wonderful thing in the world."

"It's not just the fact that I'm pregnant, though," she says, swapping her champagne for the glass of juice. "I don't want to carry on working when I have five young children. The cost of child care will be exorbitant, and anyway, I want to be able to spend time with them. Financially, it's going to be difficult." She pauses. "The holidays will have to go, for a start. And other things—the ridiculously expensive wines Nelson loves so much, the bike stuff. It's my salary that pays for all those extras. His really only covers the mortgage and the household bills."

"I'm sure he'll be happy to make a sacrifice for a few years," Jess says.

"But it won't be for a few years, will it? Children get more expensive with age."

"Yes, they do," I say, trying not to imagine how much university fees and accommodation for five children will cost. "But think of what a lovely family you'll have. And chances are that when they're older, some of them will at least live in the same country as you. Paula—you know, my friend at the office who retired last year—has one of her sons living in Australia and the other in Canada. I'd hate it if I ended up with both my children living abroad."

"Well, at least you don't have to worry about Marnie," Jess says. "You must be pleased she's decided to come home instead of going traveling, especially with Josh off to New York in a couple of weeks."

I shift restlessly on my seat. "Yes, I am."

"And don't worry," Kirin adds. "I will tell Nelson. It's just a case of finding the right time."

"Good," I say, wondering if I'll ever find the right time to tell Adam what I should already have told him.

"Tell Adam not to laugh too loud and too long when he hears the news."

"He won't," I promise. "I think he might even be a tiny bit jealous."

Jess looks intrigued. "Really? He's never wanted a third child, has he?"

"Honestly, I thought it was the last thing he wanted. But last September, after Marnie left for Hong Kong and Josh had gone back to university, I think the empty house hit him a bit, because he said we should have had another baby." I take a long drink of my champagne and laugh. "Can you imagine it?"

"It's not too late," Kirin says.

"Oh, I don't mean my age or anything." Kirin is only two years younger than me and I'd hate her to think that's what I meant. "It's just that I'm so far away from all that now."

"Relax!" she says, laughing. "Although it would make Nelson feel so much better if Adam was going to be a father again too."

"No chance," I say firmly. "Sorry!"

A waiter brings menus, and we order lunch. While we're waiting for it to arrive, we have another swim and dry off on the sun loungers. As I apply some of Kirin's sunscreen, my mind goes back to the day Adam made his "We should have had another child" remark.

"Adam, you can't say that now!" I tried to be lighthearted, but underneath I was angry because I would have loved to have had more children.

He looked at me in surprise. "What? You're a great mum, you could totally handle it."

"That's not what I mean. If you wanted another child, it should have been fifteen years ago. That's when I would have liked one."

"You never mentioned it."

"Because I knew what you would say."

He frowned. "I wish you'd at least broached the subject with me. I might have said yes."

"Look, the only reason you think you want a baby is because Marnie has left home. I know this is harsh, but if you remember, you didn't even want a second child."

He flinched and I wished I could take it back. It's something he's never quite forgiven himself for, not wanting Marnie.

1 P.M.–2 P.M.

Adam

I start to walk back toward the car park. It's busier now, people pushing past one another, families walking as groups. Do any of them know about the crash? Nobody seems sad; the world is still turning. Or maybe they know, but because it hasn't happened here, they're detached from it all. The flight was on its way from Cairo to Amsterdam, so most of the people affected by the crash will be from Egypt and the Netherlands. Nobody else will really care, not after the initial shock. It seems wrong, that detachment, selfish. Marnie pushes back into my mind. I should go home, in case she calls there. I don't want Josh answering the house phone and hearing her in hysterics.

How long will she be stranded for, alone at Cairo Airport? I can't imagine how she must be feeling—upset, frightened, completely unprepared for this sort of situation, without any life experience to help her cope. I should be with her; I need to be with her.

I stop walking and look around. There's a travel agent's somewhere near here. They'll be able to help. I can get a flight to Cairo, find Marnie there. I start walking, then jogging, breaking through the crowds of people until I reach the travel agent's.

Inside, I'm the only customer. A young woman—she doesn't seem much older than Marnie—blond, not dark-haired—looks up and smiles.

"Can I help you?"

"Hi, yes, I'd like to book a flight to Cairo, please."

She immediately looks uneasy. She'll have heard about the crash. Of course she will; she'll have been on her phone. I wonder if she's been trained for this sort of situation, where a customer walks in and asks for a ticket to the very place where a plane has come down. I keep my eyes averted, hoping she's not going to mention it.

"When would you like to leave?" she asks.

"Later today, please." My voice sounds strange, even to my ears. She gives me another quick smile.

"Why don't you take a seat while I check?"

I don't want to sit; I feel too claustrophobic.

"It might not be possible today," she says carefully. "There's some disruption with flights into Cairo." She pauses. "I could see if there's a flight to one of the other airports in Egypt."

"No, it has to be Cairo."

She looks behind her toward an open office door, but there's no one there to help.

"There may be something for tomorrow," she says, turning back to her computer. "Would that be a possibility for you?"

I turn it around in my mind. All I want is to get to Marnie, and waiting twenty-four hours seems impossible. And what if Marnie is no longer there by the time I arrive, but has already been put on another flight? I try to think logically. If there aren't any flights into Cairo today, there aren't likely to be any out, so Marnie won't be going anywhere. And I know Marnie; she'll be too frightened to get on a plane now. She's only nineteen; she's too young for this. All she'll want is to speak to me and Liv, and to know that someone is coming to get her.

"Tomorrow, then," I tell the travel agent.

"There's a flight leaving from London Heathrow at ten-thirty," she says. "It may be subject to delays," she adds hesitantly.

"I'll take it."

"When would you like to come back?"

Her question throws me. I have no idea what will happen when I get there. If they put Marnie on a flight to London, I'll need to be on the same flight as her, but I can't know which one they'll put her on. And what if we decide that the best thing is to forget about her coming over and go back to Hong Kong instead?

There are too many scenarios to consider. Sweat begins to pool under my arms, along my hairline. The travel agent is staring at me, her eyes wide. Neither of us blink.

"I'm not sure, so just a one-way ticket for now," I say.

She nods, checks her computer screen, then glances at me.

"Will that be one ticket?"

I'm about to say yes, when I realize that Livia will want to come with me. She'll want to be there too. She'll feel exactly as I do, desperate to see Marnie with her own eyes, to be with her. She won't want to wait at home.

"No, two tickets, please."

She nods. "That will be five hundred and fourteen pounds for the two, flying with Luxor."

"That's fine."

"Name?"

"Sorry?"

"The passengers' names, for the flight."

"Oh—Olivia Harman and Adam Harman."

"Your flight gets into Cairo tomorrow at ten to five in the afternoon, local time."

"Thanks."

I text Marnie.

Marnie, we know what's happened, don't worry, stay where you are, Mum and I are coming to get you. There aren't any flights today, so we're leaving tomorrow morning and will arrive at Cairo Airport at 4:50 p.m. If you have to move, to a hotel or anywhere else, let us know. Call us as soon as you can. We love you.

"Here you are." The travel agent goes over the flights with me, then asks if I want her to print the tickets. I nod, and the printer beside her whirs. She slips the tickets into a blue envelope with the logo of the agency on the front.

"Thank you," I say, pushing it into my jacket.

She smiles, and suddenly I want to tell her about Marnie, about how close she was to being on that flight. But she breaks eye contact and pulls out a card machine.

Without a word, I pay and leave.

Outside, I stop for a moment. My mobile has remained silent in my hand, but I light up the screen, just in case. It's 13:45, nearly two hours since the crash. There's still no message from Marnie. I try calling again, but I can't get through. The message I sent from the travel agent's is undelivered. How long are the networks going to be down for?

The walk back to the bike passes in a blur. I take my helmet from where I left it in the top case and get on my bike, the air cooler now. I should call Liv, but it would be better if I wait until we're together. Then I can show her the flight times and she'll be able to see for herself that Marnie can't possibly have made the connection.

I stop. The party. I'd forgotten about the party. How the hell have I not even thought about the party? Maybe we should cancel it. I pause, thinking it through. Livia will be devastated if we do, and really, there's no reason why it shouldn't go ahead, as long as we hear from Marnie, which we will.

Livia won't be there when I get home, I realize; she'll still be at the spa. For a moment, I think about phoning Kirin to find out exactly where they are so that I can go and tell Livia there. At least I'd have someone to share my anxiety with. But that's selfish. It will ruin her time with her friends and the thought of her feeling like I do—I can't do that to her, I can't.

I check my phone again. No message, nothing. It's now two o'clock.

Livia

Kirin stretches her body and sighs happily.

"This weather is perfect," she murmurs.

"It's amazing, isn't it? Thank you for this, Kirin. I'd never have done it myself."

"It's based in selfishness, because I love coming here." She digs in her bag for her phone and I take a quick look at her stomach. She's right, there isn't even the start of a bump.

I check on Jess, sitting in the shade, a book on her lap. She has her eyes closed and I watch her for a moment. She looks so frail that I have to turn away.

"Oh no," Kirin says, sounding upset.

Jess and I both turn to look at her.

"Is it one of the children?" I ask, wondering if she's had a message from Nelson.

She shakes her head. "There's been a plane crash in Egypt. No survivors." She makes a face. "There were two hundred and fifty people on board, including the crew."

"That's awful," I say, appalled.

"Don't." Jess gives a shiver. "I can't bear it."

My mobile is lying on the table faceup and I turn it over.

"I'm not looking at my phone for the rest of the day," I say. "It doesn't seem right that I'm celebrating when other people are grieving."

"There's always someone grieving somewhere in the world," Kirin says.

"I know. But a plane crash—it's just heartbreaking."

"Are people from your work coming to your party?" Jess asks, and I know she wants to change the subject, because I'm sure I told her they were.

"Yes, all of them, I think."

"Wow," Kirin says.

"I didn't think everyone would come, but they are."

"It's that thing, though, isn't it?" Kirin says. "You start off with friends and family and then you want to invite neighbors and the people you work with and the list keeps getting longer. It was like that for our wedding and we ended up having two hundred guests, a ridiculous amount."

"The best thing about tonight," I say, "is that, unlike at weddings, there's nobody I've invited that I don't want to be there." Except for one person, I think silently, one person who has the potential to spoil the whole evening for me. But only if I let them.

I turn my face to the sun. Before I made them ashamed of me, my parents took me to some lovely hotels, but none as luxurious as this one. Back then, I didn't realize how fortunate I was to have parents who were comfortably off, and I've often wondered what my life would have been like if I hadn't become pregnant, if I'd gone on to do what my parents had planned for me. They'd wanted me to study medicine, something I'd have been happy to go along with, so I'd be a doctor by now, possibly married to another doctor, maybe with more children and a holiday home somewhere abroad. An existence—because, with my parents heavily involved in my life, which they would have been, it would have been only that, an existence. I can't imagine it would have been as happy as the life I live now, not with the imposed ritual of weekly lunches after church, and Christmases spent in their plumped-up-cushioned house, with its rules and regulations, no elbows on the table, no feet on the chairs, no lazing in bed past nine o'clock, no slouching or watching anything other than BBC2. I had a lucky escape, I realize; *we* had a lucky escape. If my parents had accepted Adam and Josh, we'd have been forever in their debt, bound to them by suffocating duty and obligation.

"It's a shame Marnie can't be there tonight," Jess says sympathetically. "Cleo is going to miss her. They've been talking about your party ever since they were little, trying to imagine being nineteen."

"And designing the dresses they'd wear," I say, smiling at the memory. "I used to do it too. I'd think, *On the day of my party Josh will be twenty-two and Marnie will be nineteen,* and I couldn't imagine what they would look like, or how they would be. They were two unknown quantities, but they were always going to be there, present at my party." And I realize that in all my imaginings about my party over the years, it never occurred to me that Marnie wouldn't be with us. Or that I wouldn't want her there.

"Cleo doesn't mind coming?" I ask Jess. "Without Marnie?"

"Don't worry, she wouldn't miss it for the world." She looks over at me. "Talking of Marnie, Cleo wants to throw a surprise party for her, the weekend after she gets back, and invite all their friends. She asked me to ask you if that would be all right."

My throat tightens. "That's lovely of her."

"It would be the first weekend in July. You haven't got anything planned, have you?"

"No," I say, because I've only gotten as far as thinking about the day Marnie arrives. My mind can't go any further than that, not yet. The repercussions of her return are so enormous that I can't see past it.

"We're free too," Kirin says. "Gosh, another party to look forward to, amazing!"

"I don't think we'll be invited," I say, laughing.

"Then you can all come to me and we'll have our own party!"

I smile across at Kirin, but the knowledge that it isn't going to happen fills me with a desperate sadness. And what about all the other things the six of us used to do together? What about the Christmases? I need my Christmases to be filled with people, and love and laughter, because it's at Christmas that I feel my parents' rejection the most, something I've never understood, as I've had more fun with Adam's family than I ever had celebrating Christmas alone with my parents. Yet as soon as I open my eyes on Christmas morning, a great big hole opens up inside me that not even Adam, Josh, Marnie, and every single friend we have can quite fill.

Rejection was something I had to get used to, during those first years with Adam. He abandoned me so many times that it's a miracle we made it through. It's still with me, although I'd never tell him that. He's tried so hard to make up for it that he'd be devastated if he knew how much it still affects me. It creeps up on me in the dark of the night, and resentment gnaws away inside me, at what he made me go through.

The first time he left, I was convinced he'd had an accident or been murdered. I could see his body lying beaten and broken in a ditch, hear the knock at the door, see the policeman, accompanied by a policewoman, standing on the doorstep. He hadn't said where he was going, so I thought he'd gone to the shops. When he didn't come back that evening, I told myself that he must have gone to see Nelson and had decided to stay the night, and I was angry that he hadn't phoned to tell me. I was also sick with worry. Neither of us had mobiles—they were expensive back in 1997, too expensive for us, anyway—so I couldn't contact him to find out where he was.

When he still hadn't turned up the next day, I went to the police. I could see they thought I was making a fuss about nothing. I think they took one look at our situation—little more than children ourselves with a baby in tow—and I'm sure they presumed he was having an affair. They told me to give it a couple more days, but I couldn't believe that Adam would leave me to worry about him, that he wouldn't have tried to contact me if he'd been able to.

Mr. Wentworth was more sympathetic than the police. When I burst into tears in his workshop, he told me not to worry, that he was sure Adam was just letting off steam and would eventually turn up. He did, three days later, and when I realized that not only hadn't he cared enough to let me know he was all right but that he was also unrepentant, saying that I should have known he was with Nelson, something died in me. When he did it again and again, I vowed I'd never forgive him for the worry he made me go through, because each time, there was always the fear that this time, something really had happened to him.

I know it's mean, and I only think like this when I remember those bad times, but sometimes, just sometimes, I'd like him to experience what it feels like to not know where somebody you love is, to be out of your mind with worry. To fear the worst.

2 P.M.—3 P.M.

Adam

I have no memory of how I got home, but I'm here, standing by my bike in the garage, the air around me familiar with the smell of oil, cardboard, dust. It's as if the last two hours never happened. All I can think about is Marnie. She must be alternating between relief that she didn't make her connection and horror at what could have happened. How can she not be thinking about the people on the flight, the ones who made it in time to get to their seats? I know Marnie; she'll be inconsolable with guilt for cursing that she'd missed her flight, guilty that she'll have a story to tell. Guilty that she has lived, when others have died.

My fingers find my phone, unlock the screen and instinctively check WhatsApp. They're still there, my two undelivered messages. *Come on, Marnie, I just need an "I'm OK."* I try to call her again but get the same as before: silence.

I go into the house. Josh is standing in the hall, a doorstop of a sandwich in his hand.

"Can I see it?" he asks eagerly.

Avoiding his eyes, because I don't want him to realize anything is wrong, I take off my jacket and hang it on the hook in the cupboard.

"What?"

"Mum's ring. Can I see it, or is it wrapped?"

It takes me a while to remember. "No, I—it wasn't ready."

"What do you mean, it wasn't ready? Why not?"

"The size," I invent. "They forgot to have it made smaller."

He sits down on the stairs and takes a bite of his sandwich. "You will have it in time for tonight, won't you?"

I move toward the kitchen, needing to be on my own. "Yes, I hope so. They're going to phone me to tell me when I can pick it up."

He follows me in. "Couldn't you have taken it as it was? Mum wouldn't have minded if it was a bit big."

I want to tell him to please stop talking, that I don't give a damn about the ring, that all I want is for Marnie to phone.

"I suppose so. I didn't think," I say instead. "I just wanted it to be the right size so that she can wear it as soon as I give it to her."

"Are they adjusting it now, then?"

"Yes, I think so."

"But did they say it would definitely be ready this afternoon?" he insists, his mouth full. "I can go and get it for you, if you like."

I round on him. "Josh, they're going to phone me. Until they do, I can't do anything!"

He stops in mid-chew. Out of the corner of my eye, I see Murphy look up, disturbed from his sleep by my raised voice.

"Are you OK, Dad?" Josh asks.

I fight to keep calm. "Yes, fine. I'm disappointed, that's all."

"You don't look too good."

"I've got a bit of a migraine."

"That sucks. Have you taken anything?"

"No." The need for space is so strong, my skin physically itches. I head for the stairs. "I'll go and see what there is in the bathroom."

"Why don't you go and lie down or something? There's nothing to do for now, it's all under control. Max is coming over to help with the lights and stuff."

The mention of Max throws me. "Does Mum know Max is coming?"

"Yes, why?"

I shouldn't have said that; my mind is all over the place. Josh hasn't been here enough to notice that Liv is different around Max at the moment. We've known him since he was a child, so he's like family to us. Max is to Josh what Nelson is to me, and until a few months ago, Livia loved having him around. But suddenly, that all changed. She has this closed look on her face whenever he comes to see us on his visits home from university, and she's been using avoidance tactics—an urgent phone call to make, an errand to run. When I mentioned it to her, she told me I was imagining things. But I know Livia. And I know that Max has noticed, even if Josh hasn't, because he's now avoiding her as much as she's avoiding him. I should have pushed Livia harder about it, and I will at some point. But not today.

"No reason," I tell Josh. "Actually, I might go and lie down for a bit." He throws me a look of surprise, because I've never gone to lie down in my life. "Just give me an hour."

I go upstairs, and when I get to the landing, I notice the door to Marnie's bedroom like I've never noticed it before. I've seen it hundreds of times since she left for Hong Kong, on my way up the stairs and on my way down, going into my bedroom, going out of my bedroom, but it's never really registered like it's registering now. The way the white paint is scuffed in the bottom right corner. The worn-down brass of its original doorknob. The three small nail holes left over from when she'd insisted on hanging a little wooden sign with her name on it that she'd found in a Christmas market over ten years ago.

I open the door and go in. There's so much of Marnie here. Her posters are still on the wall—one of them I recognize as an actor from *Game of Thrones*. Her books are on the shelf—Harry Potter, *Lord of the Rings,* the *His Dark Matters* trilogy, but also books by Jane Austen and Nancy Mitford. Her photos are on the marble mantelpiece—a couple of her with me, Livia, and Josh, but the majority with her friends from school and university. Unsurprisingly,

Cleo features in most. In fact, there's a whole section dedicated to photos of the two of them fooling around and making faces.

But there's also so much of Marnie that isn't here. The pile of clothes that I'd have to move onto the bed so that I could sit on the chair whenever I went in to chat with her, the books and magazines strewn over the floor. Her bed is unmade; there's a cover over the mattress to protect it from dust, and her quilt has been neatly folded into a plastic bag. I should at least make her bed for her.

Pushing the silky blue curtains right back, I open the windows to air the room and see Max arriving on his motorbike. Good. There's no danger of Josh coming upstairs and seeing what I'm doing. I fetch sheets from the cupboard and make up Marnie's bed. After a bit of searching I find her pillows on the shelf in her wardrobe.

Her fluffy white robe is hanging on the back of the door and a memory hits me, of her coming into the kitchen wrapped tightly into it. She loves her robe, says it's the most comfortable thing in the world. It must be dusty from hanging here since she left in August. I take it from the hook; there's a faint yellow stain on the collar, so I take it downstairs to the utility room, almost tripping over Mimi as she makes her way down to the kitchen, and put it on a quick thirty-minute cycle.

Back in Marnie's room, I sit on the freshly made bed, wishing there was something else I could do to fill in the time until she calls. I've been trying not to check my phone, hoping to lessen the worry that isn't going to stop building until I hear from her. But it's become like a tic. I take out my phone, look at the screen, curse, put it back in my pocket. I need to stop. When Marnie can call, she will.

Livia

I've never had a facial before. The creams the beautician is using on my face smell so delicious I could eat them. But for some reason, the whole experience is making me tearful. I think it's something to do with the darkness, because the lights are dimmed, and the music playing in the background—gentle breeze and trickling water. Maybe it's regressing me to when I was in my mother's womb. They say that, don't they, that some experiences take us back to before we were born?

The warm blanket covering me is removed and I'm asked to turn over onto my front for the massage. There's a convenient hole cut in the bench for my nose and mouth so that I don't suffocate. When I filled out the form before my treatments, I had to say what sort of massage I wanted, strong, medium or soft, and I went for soft because I've seen those programs where they pummel you to bits. But it's not gentle enough. Her fingers are digging into my neck, kneading away tension that isn't there because, after my facial, I felt totally relaxed for the first time in weeks. Maybe I should tell her, when she asks me if I enjoyed it, that they should have a fourth category, stroking.

I can't help thinking that my mother might have been a better person if she'd been stroked a bit more as a child. I didn't really know my grandmother because she went to live in a home when I was five years old, and we only went to see her once a year, out of duty. I think everything my mother has done has been out of duty. I don't think there's ever been any real joy in her life. In the photos of what should have been her happiest times—her wedding day and my birth—she looks as grim and unsmiling as ever. And I realize that I can't remember her ever smiling, except when she greeted our parish priest on the way out of church.

She certainly never smiled around the house, but then, neither did my father. Were they really that unhappy? She did seem slightly less severe when we looked through bridal magazines together, planning the wedding she and my father would give me when I eventually got married. I still don't understand, for a woman so austere in every way, why it was so important to her. If she hadn't made such a big thing about it, I wouldn't have become so obsessive about having a party.

It's not as if I wasn't happy on my wedding day. I'd already moved in with Adam and his parents, and when I woke up that morning, Jeannie—Adam's mum—brought me breakfast in bed. Adam wasn't there because he'd gone out with his friends the night before and had stayed over with Nelson, who'd been warned to get him to the pub in time for prewedding drinks. Jess had come over to help me get ready—we'd gone shopping together and I'd bought a pretty pale-yellow knee-length dress, paid for by Jeannie. She'd offered to buy me a proper wedding dress, but I knew my parents would be horrified if I dressed like a traditional bride, and anyway, it was only going to be a small wedding.

I knew my parents wouldn't come to the pub, so there were just the nine of us—me and Adam, Jeannie and Mike, Adam's sister, Izzy, and her husband, Ian, Nelson, Rob, and Jess. It had been a happy couple of hours. To Adam's disgust, Ian played soppy song after soppy song from the jukebox playlist.

"Can't we have a bit of Aerosmith or Queen?" he'd groaned. "Bob Dylan, James Brown, even?"

Ian had laughed. "How about this?"

"Unchained Melody" had come on and Adam and Nelson had covered their ears until Ian pushed Adam and me together and insisted we slow-dance while they all sang along. By the time the song finished I was in tears, not just of laughter but also because Adam had stopped fooling around and, as we danced, had held me tight and murmured promises of how he would love me forever. Even though Adam hates it, "Unchained Melody" has become "our" song.

My parents didn't turn up at the registry office, which brought fresh tears to my eyes. But it struck me recently that I'd never really put myself in my mother's position. It must have been a huge shock when she realized I was pregnant, and although our lives and experiences are very different, I know now that sometimes, when you're least expecting it, your children can throw you a massive curveball.

I was at work when the call came through. It was Marnie. She was home from university for the summer holidays, working at Boots to earn some money before leaving for Hong Kong at the end of August.

"Mum, are you busy?"

"Well, yes, I'm expecting clients any minute now."

"Oh."

"Why, what's wrong?"

"I don't feel well."

"Are you at work?"

"No, I didn't go in. I don't suppose you could come home, could you?"

"What, now?" My meeting wouldn't take more than an hour and I hoped that Marnie could wait until it was over.

"Yes. I really don't feel well, Mum."

"Are you vomiting?"

"Yes. No. Mum, could you just come home, please." For the first time, I caught the panic in her voice and all sorts of terrible illnesses flew through my mind, from a violent stomach bug right through to meningitis.

"How bad is it, Marnie?" I asked, already on my feet. "Do you need an ambulance?" I kept my voice as calm as I could, but the word *ambulance* brought worried looks from my colleagues.

"No, I'll be fine until you arrive. Can you leave now?"

I caught Paula's eye and she paused, watching me. "Yes, I'll be home in twenty minutes. Is that OK?"

"Yes." I heard her voice break. "Thanks, Mum."

In fact, I was home in less than ten minutes because Paula insisted on driving me rather than letting me walk, as I usually did.

"Promise to let us know how Marnie is," she said as I got out of the car.

"It's probably that bug we were talking about. Apparently, it's pretty nasty."

I expected to find Marnie lying on the sofa in the sitting room, but her anguished "Mum!" drew me upstairs to the bathroom, where I found her sitting on the floor, bleeding heavily. It took me a moment to realize she was having a miscarriage.

Later, at the hospital, once everything was over, there was so much I wanted to ask her—and so much I was beginning to understand. When she'd first been accepted to study in Hong Kong, she was ecstatic. By the time she came home for the Easter holidays, a couple of months later, she was telling us that she wasn't sure she wanted to go.

"Why not?" I'd asked, amazed that she was thinking of giving up such a wonderful opportunity.

"It's so far away." We were having lunch at the time and she stabbed a potato halfheartedly with her fork. "I wouldn't be able to come home for nine months."

"If you were really homesick, we could see about you coming home for Christmas," Adam said, and I flinched because I knew tickets at that time of the year would cost over a thousand pounds. He looked back at me, a look that said, *Once she's there, she'll be fine.*

For now, she's got cold feet and needs a safety blanket. "But isn't it too late to back out now?" he went on.

"I'm sure there are plenty of students who'd be willing to take my place," she said, pushing at the potato.

"Are you serious, Marnie? Do you really not want to go?"

"I don't know. It's just that I'm enjoying school so much."

Even though her head was bent over her plate, I saw her cheeks flush and wondered if she had a new boyfriend. But Marnie had never been shy about introducing boys she was dating to us, so I really did think it was a case of cold feet—until I was sitting next to her in the hospital.

"How are you feeling?" I asked.

"Tired. Sad." She looked at me and there was so much pain in her eyes that my throat closed. "Relieved," she added guiltily.

"Had you been feeling ill for a while?"

She shook her head. "No. I meant relieved because now I don't have to make a decision. I don't think I'd have been able to keep the baby." Her eyes filled with tears. "I know that's an awful thing for you to have to hear, when you kept Josh. But you had Dad. I wouldn't have had anyone."

"You would have had us, you'll always have us," I told her gently. "We would never have tried to persuade you one way or another, just made sure you knew what your options were." I hesitated. "The father—did he know you were pregnant?"

She nodded, spilling tears from her eyes. "Yes. But he made me understand that I wouldn't be able to keep the baby, that it wasn't the right time for us."

"I'm so sorry, Marnie. How did you feel when he told you that?"

She plucked at the sheet, desperately trying to hold back the tears. "Gutted. I didn't want to have an abortion, but I knew he was right in what he said. I know it worked out for you and Dad, but it wouldn't have worked out for us. Not just now, anyway."

"Is that why you weren't sure about going to Hong Kong? Because you didn't want to leave him?"

"Yes."

"And now?"

"I think it's good that I'm going. Our relationship—it's not healthy."

"Is he at university with you?"

"Please don't ask me about him, Mum. It's over now, anyway. If it hadn't been for this"—she looked down at herself lying in the hospital bed—"you wouldn't have been any wiser. But thank you, thank you for being here with me."

We had to wait until she could be discharged, and while we waited, she slept. And while she slept, I wondered about the father. Her reluctance to tell me anything about him except that their relationship was unhealthy had my brain whirring. The only thing I could think was that she'd become involved with one of her tutors. Marnie was more beautiful than she knew, with her gray eyes, alabaster skin, and hair the color of autumn leaves, with a natural wave I would have given anything for. I felt so upset for her, and mad at him for preying on a young girl. How dare he? It was her first year at university, her first year away from home.

Her other comment, that their relationship wouldn't have worked out—*not just now, anyway*—made me feel I was on the right track. I built a picture of him in my mind, a thirtysomething-year-old, married with children, and wanted to kill him. I was dismayed that Marnie had allowed herself to become involved with someone who wasn't free. I reminded myself that I didn't know if this was the case; maybe the father of her child was a fellow student. But if that was true, she'd have had no reason not to tell me. It was the little she'd told me that made me uneasy.

I was desperate to speak to Adam, but I didn't want to leave Marnie while she was sleeping. I also wanted to check with her that she was all right with Adam knowing about her miscarriage.

"No!" she said forcefully when I asked. "I don't want him to know. Nor Josh. Please don't tell them, Mum. I don't want either of them to know."

I respected her wishes, but it was hard. I hated keeping something so monumental from Adam and it was difficult not being able to confide in him. I kept wondering about the grandchild we might have had if Marnie hadn't had a miscarriage and had decided to keep the baby. I knew it was a useless exercise, thinking about something that would never have been, but at twelve weeks pregnant, Marnie would soon have had to make that decision. And I couldn't be sure that she'd have gone ahead with an abortion. It wasn't something I felt I could ask her, so I mourned in secret for the baby that might have been born if things had been different.

Although I hated that I was judging Marnie, part of me was stunned that she'd embarked on a relationship with someone who presumably had a partner, and maybe children. I blamed myself. I'd never actually warned her not to have an affair with someone who wasn't free, as it didn't occur to me that she'd ever do such a thing. It was something I thought she'd instinctively know was morally wrong. I felt I'd failed as a mother, that it was my fault she'd had to go through the trauma of a miscarriage.

Over the next few days, I spent hours on the internet, trawling through photos of the faculty at her university, wondering if I'd be able to spot the man who had captured my daughter's heart, then treated her so casually. There were barely any who looked under thirty; most seemed in their forties, twice Marnie's age, which supported my feeling that she'd been taken advantage of. I reminded myself that Marnie could be just as much to blame, that she might have chased him. But it didn't make me feel any better.

I remembered looking at Marnie on her seventeenth birthday, the age I'd been when I became pregnant, and thinking, *How could they? How could my parents have disowned me?* I also remember thinking that Marnie could do anything, anything, and I'd forgive her.

Now, I wonder if fate decided I was tempting it, and chose to put me to the test.

3 P.M.—4 P.M.

Adam

My stomach clenches as I pace the floor in Marnie's room. I need—really need—Marnie to phone before Liv gets home. If she doesn't, and I tell Liv about the crash, she won't believe that Marnie is safe even if I show her that Marnie couldn't have made the Cairo flight, not with only ten minutes to spare. Nothing will stop the panic she'll feel from spiraling out of control.

I need someone to talk to, not to tell them anything, but to fill this building void while I wait. Nelson, I'll phone Nelson.

I sit down on the bed, about to call him, when I remember he has the kids. I think about going to find Josh, offer to help him in the garden, do something physical. That would take my mind off things. But he's with Max and they'll be joking and messing around as they get everything ready for tonight.

The person I really want to talk to, I realize, is Dad. I find his number and press Call.

"Hi, Adam, what's up?" The familiar sound of his voice makes my throat tighten. "Adam? Adam, are you there?"

I get to my feet. "Yes, sorry, Dad, Josh was asking me something."

"Do you want to call back?"

I realize too late I shouldn't have called him. He's always had this amazing sixth sense, which picks up when I'm worried about something.

"No, it's fine," I manage to say.

"So, how's Livia feeling?"

I walk to the window and press my forehead against the glass. "Happy, excited. She's out with Kirin and Jess, at a spa."

"Not running around like a headless chicken, then?"

"No, it's unbelievable how organized she is."

"What about you?"

"Me?"

"Yes. How are you?"

I straighten myself up. "Fine."

"Is it Marnie?"

Christ. "Sorry?"

"Marnie. Is that why you're feeling a bit low? Because she's not going to be at the party?"

"I'm not—" I stop. "I wish she was here, that's all."

"We all do. Have you heard from her?"

"Yes, yesterday. She was busy revising. How are you and Mum?"

"Looking forward to seeing everyone tonight." He pauses. "Are you sure everything's all right?"

"Yes, positive. I thought I'd give you a call, that's all."

"Do you want to speak to Mum?"

"No, it's all right, tell her I'll see her later. I'll let you go now."

"Whatever it is that's worrying you, it'll all work out in the end," he says.

It almost bursts out of me; I almost ask him if he's heard about the plane that crashed. But I wouldn't be able to stop myself from telling him about Marnie, and I need to tell Livia before I tell anyone else.

"I should go, Dad," I say, and before he can reply, I cut the call.

I can't stand the silence. I leave Marnie's room and go downstairs. In the utility room, the washing machine has finished its cycle. I take out Marnie's robe and place it in the tumble dryer so that it'll be ready for when she gets back.

Livia

I lay my head against the car seat and close my eyes. We've just dropped Jess off, so I'm back in the front.

"Don't fight it," Kirin says, throwing me an amused grin.

"Sorry," I groan, forcing my mouth closed after giving the biggest yawn of my life. "It was the massage. I feel so relaxed and sleepy now."

"Nothing to do with that extra glass of champagne, then?" she says, laughing. "You may as well rest, it's going to take us a while to get back." She peers through the windscreen. "Where has all this traffic come from?"

"Saturday shoppers," I say. "As long as you get me back in time for the party, it's fine."

"How do you think Jess looked?" I hear the worry in her voice and wish I could tell her that I thought Jess looked great.

"I've seen her looking better," I say sadly. "She was a bit unsteady on her feet, even with her stick."

"I'm really worried about her. Nelson is too." She pauses. "Actually, he's more concerned about Rob. He told him that we thought the MS was beginning to take its toll on Jess, but Rob seems to be in denial. He doesn't think she's gone downhill at all; he insists that she's still very independent. But Jess told me herself that she's having difficulty getting up the stairs and that sometimes her hands go numb. Nelson's worried that Rob isn't going to be able to cope if Jess's symptoms become worse. She'll always have me and Nelson to help her, of course, but once the babies arrive, I'm not sure how much time I'll actually have."

"Which is why it's important to tell Nelson that you're pregnant," I remind her.

"I'm going to, as soon as I get home." The car grinds to a halt again and she reaches for the radio. "I'll put on some music, I'm sure there'll be something to send you to sleep. You may as well have a bit of nap before the party. There's nothing last-minute to do, is there?"

"No, and if there is, Josh and Max are there."

"Relax, then."

But although I want to, the mention of Max means that I can't. I don't know when I first began to suspect that he was the father of Marnie's baby, but it was probably when she called me from Hong Kong last October to tell me that he wanted to go and see her—and that she didn't want him to.

"Why not?" I asked, because she's always loved Max.

"Because he wants to come in December and I'll be too busy working on my assignment to be able to show him around."

"I'm sure he won't mind doing some sightseeing on his own while you're studying," I said, taking her objections at face value.

"That's what he said. So, I'm going to tell him I'm going away with friends. It's not true, but will you back me up, Mum? If Max mentions to you that he wants to come and see me in December, will you tell him that I'm going away?"

"Well," I began doubtfully. "I'm not sure it's a good thing to lie to him. Anyway, wouldn't it cheer you up to see him?"

"I'm fine now."

She did seem more upbeat, which was a relief. It had been horrible waving her off to Hong Kong just six weeks after her miscarriage. I'd offered to go with her, but she hadn't wanted me to. Although she wouldn't talk about it, the breakup with her baby's father had hit her hard. Sometimes, when I passed her room, I'd hear her crying and knock tentatively on her door. She never told me to go away, so I'd go in and sit with my arms around her, not saying anything, just holding her.

"Really? Are you really feeling better?" I asked, mentally crossing my fingers, because there's nothing worse than knowing your child is hurting but being too far away to give her a hug.

"Yes. So, will you back me up? Please, Mum. I don't want Max here."

I couldn't see her face because she'd audio-called, rather than video-called as she usually did, and suddenly everything fell into place. She had audio-called exactly so that I couldn't see her face, so that I wouldn't be able to see the look on it when she spoke about Max, her almost-brother, who was so much part of our family that for Marnie to be in a relationship with him would be—well, unhealthy. Everything fitted, I realized. She was at university in Durham, he was in his fourth year at Newcastle, twenty minutes away, and I remembered how persuasive he'd been when she had to decide between Durham and Edinburgh, where Adam would have liked her to go.

"If you're in Durham, I'll be near you," Max had told her. "I'll be able to look after you."

And she had laughed and replied, "I won't need looking after. But it will be lovely to have you around."

I'd been making a salad while I talked to Marnie on speakerphone, but I left the sink, took my phone over to the table and sat down heavily.

"Marnie," I began, wanting to know if I was right. But maybe she sensed that I'd guessed and so cut me off quickly.

"Just back me up, Mum," she pleaded.

I never did finish making the salad. When Adam got home from his ride to the coast and found me staring into space, he took over.

"You look worried," he said, throwing me a glance. "Is everything all right?"

"Marnie phoned."

"Oh." His face fell. "It's a shame I missed her. How is she?"

"Fine," I said automatically, because I'd just realized something else, which was that Marnie never normally phoned on a Sunday morning because she knew Adam would be out. If she had chosen to phone this morning, it was because she hadn't wanted her dad to hear her asking me to dissuade Max from going to see her.

"What was her news?"

"Nothing much." He waited, wanting more. "Max wants to go and see her in December, but she's going away with friends," I said, aware that I was already lying for her.

"That's a shame, it would have done her good to see Max. I never expected her to be so homesick, not after two months."

Because he didn't know about Marnie's miscarriage, or her broken relationship, Adam had always put Marnie's low spirits down to her missing everyone.

"She was more cheerful this time," I told him, wishing I could confide in him, wishing I could ask him if he thought it was possible that Marnie and Max had been in a relationship. But if I started that conversation, I'd end up telling him about the miscarriage and I didn't want to break Marnie's confidence. I turned it over and over in my mind, remembering how determined she'd been that Josh shouldn't know about the baby. I'd understood why she hadn't wanted Adam to know—she'd have been worried he'd be disappointed in her—but she and Josh were so close, they told each other everything. If she hadn't wanted him to know, it was because she didn't want to tell him who the father of her baby was. And unlike me, Josh would have insisted on knowing.

Other things began to fall into place. While Marnie was still at home, before she went to university, Max tried to come home to see his dad the same weekend that Josh came to see us, so they could catch up with each other. But there were several occasions when he didn't have the excuse of Josh being home, but came over anyway, pretending it was to see me and Adam, telling us that he missed my cooking or that he needed Adam's help with something. It never occurred to me that the person he was really coming to see was Marnie, and I felt mad that I'd been so gullible. Had something already been going on between them back then? Or had it only started when Marnie left for Durham?

Stupidly, I'd felt used. And how could he have made Marnie "understand" that she shouldn't keep the baby when he knew the circumstances of Josh's birth, and must have known that Adam and I would be supportive after going through the same thing ourselves. Had he looked at us, our family, and decided it wasn't what he wanted? It felt like a horrible betrayal of Josh, of me and Adam.

After that, whenever he came over—always asking about Marnie, about what she was up to in Hong Kong—I could barely look at him. I lost count of the number of times I wanted to challenge him, or the number of times I wanted to tell Adam not to offer him a beer, or take him for a drink. I knew that if Adam ever found out that Max had fathered a baby with Marnie, and had more or less told her to get rid of it, he'd probably kill him.

It's why I'm glad I didn't tell him.

4 P.M.–5 P.M.

Adam

I sit on our bed, the house quiet around me. Josh's and Max's voices come to me from the garden, but I can't make out what they're saying. A few moments ago, I heard them talking as they passed under the bedroom window, something about the music for tonight, I think. But it didn't really register.

The house phone lies next to me on the bed, its screen dull and deactivated. Before, when I was in Marnie's room, I suddenly remembered that she might have called the landline, and as I ran downstairs, I allowed myself to believe there'd be a voice mail from her. But there wasn't, just three messages for Liv, friends singing and wishing her a happy birthday.

My mobile lights up in my hand and my eyes fly to the screen. Not a WhatsApp message, but an email alert—an ad for a motorbike accessories sale. And I realize that, stupidly, I hadn't thought to check my emails. There might be one from Marnie.

I open my in-box and scroll through quickly, looking for her email address, her name listed somewhere. There's nothing. I hear a car door slamming and then Liv's voice. An emotion I can't quite place hits me, as if I've been caught doing something wrong. I quickly type an email to Marnie, asking her to call or email back, and telling her that we love her very much.

"Mum, you can't come up here yet, the tent isn't ready!" Josh's voice is too loud; he must be on the terrace. Liv will have come through the side gate.

I get to my feet and move to the window. Josh is leaping around, his arms outstretched, blocking her way.

"Stay there!" he shouts.

"No problem," Liv says, laughing and tugging at the strap of her bag, which has slipped from her shoulder. "Can I at least sit here?"

She's by the table, where Josh and I hid the box this morning for Marnie to hide inside when she arrives. We'll have to delay that now. A wave of anger hits me. Liv doesn't deserve this; neither does Marnie. How did today go so horribly wrong?

Josh's voice pulls me back. "OK, you can stay there. As long as you don't come any farther and definitely don't look in the tent!"

"I won't. It's just that Kirin gave me this." She pulls a bottle of champagne from her bag. "She says I have to have it with Dad now, before the party starts. It's so kind of her—she had it in an ice bag, ready for us to drink."

My heart sinks. A glass of champagne is the last thing I want.

"Max and I won't mind if you leave some for us."

She bends to stroke Murphy, who's emerged at her legs.

"I'm sure that can be arranged," she says, her tone light.

"Did you have a nice day?"

"Yes, it was wonderful! I had a massage and facial." She looks mock-severely at Josh. "You were meant to notice the difference."

"I did think you looked a bit more—radiant?—than usual," he says, making Livia laugh.

She lifts a hand, shading her eyes. "Where's Dad?"

"He's upstairs. He's got a migraine."

"Oh no! He hasn't had one of those for a while. Didn't he go into town, then?"

"Yes, but he was a bit off when he came back, and when I asked him if he was all right, he said he had a migraine." He lowers his voice but not low enough so that I can't hear. "I probably shouldn't say this but I think it might have something to do with your present."

"Gosh, I don't want him stressing if he hasn't gotten me anything. It really doesn't matter. Do you think I should say something, put his mind at rest?"

"No, leave it for now, because it might turn out all right. But if it doesn't, at least you'll have been warned. I have done the right thing telling you, haven't I?" he adds.

Livia nods. "Yes, definitely." She looks resignedly at the champagne. "I don't suppose he'll feel like this if he's got a migraine." She slides her bag from her shoulder and puts it on the table. "I'd better go and check on him."

Her disappointment gives me the push I need. I move toward the bedroom door. I can do this, I can do it for Livia. One glass of champagne, that's all.

I run down the stairs, through the kitchen and onto the terrace.

"Dad!" Josh says. "How're you feeling?"

I find myself faltering because Max has joined Livia and Josh on the terrace. Liv comes toward me.

"Josh says you've got a migraine," she says, giving me a hug.

"Had," I correct. "It's gone. I took some ibuprofen."

She searches my eyes. "Are you sure?"

"Yes. You smell wonderful."

"It's the creams they used at the spa. They smelled so good I wanted to eat them."

Josh makes a face. "Gross."

"Hi, Adam."

"Hi there." I don't look at Max; I look at the bottle in Livia's hand. "What's that?" I ask.

"Champagne. It's from Kirin. I don't suppose you feel like a glass?"

"I'd love some," I lie.

"Great! Josh, Max, would you like some too?"

"No, thank you," Max says politely.

"Are you sure? There's plenty."

I look at Livia, wondering why she's suddenly going out of her way to be nice to Max.

"Let's have it on our own," I suggest.

Josh throws me a look. But then he gets it—or thinks he does, because he raises his hands in a backing-off gesture.

"You're right, we've got stuff to do. We need to take Murphy round to Max's dad before five P.M."

At the sound of his name, Murphy nudges Livia's hand. "He could stay here, in one of the bedrooms," she says. "In Marnie's room. She won't mind."

"No!" Josh and I say at exactly the same time. He laughs and shakes his head.

"He'll still be able to hear the noise, Mum. He'll hate it." His brown eyes meet mine. "Drink the champagne with Mum, Dad, and don't let her go up to the grass. It's out-of-bounds. Come on, Max."

"See you later." Livia gives them a little wave, then turns to me. "Shall I fetch some glasses?"

"No, sit here and don't move." I take a chair and place it alongside the table so that she won't be tempted to put her legs under it. I don't think she'll be able to feel the box, but I'm not taking any chances.

"I'm being spoiled today," she says, sitting down with a smile.

It takes me a while to find champagne glasses. I find two at the back of the cupboard and carry them out to the terrace. I know Josh thought I wanted him gone so that I could explain about the present and so does Liv, because as soon as I've poured the champagne, she asks how my trip into town went. At the same time as the nightmare of the crash comes back, I glance in her bag and see her phone wedged down the side, almost hidden by a clear plastic bag containing a wet swimsuit. A wave of alarm spreads through me. It hadn't occurred to me that she might already have read about the crash. What if she decides to check her messages and starts talking about it?

"It was fine," I say, replying to her question about my trip to town. "So"—I reach for one of the glasses and hand it to her—"you OK with Max?"

"Of course. Why?"

I look at her curiously, but she refuses to meet my eyes, lifting her glass so that the crystal sparkles in the sunlight.

"These were a wedding present," she says.

"That explains why they were still in the box."

"Do you remember who gave them to us?"

"Well, it certainly wasn't your parents."

"No, it was their friends Mary and David. I wonder if they ever told Mum and Dad that they gave us a wedding present and came to see me in the hospital when Josh was born. We had wedding and birth presents from a lot of their friends, from nearly all of them, in fact."

I raise my glass; if she prefers to pretend she didn't have a problem with Max, there's not a lot I can do. "Happy birthday, sweetheart."

She smiles happily. "Thank you. I can't believe I'm forty today, it's crazy! I don't feel any different from how I did at twenty." She laughs at this; we've both come a long way since then.

"Tell me about the spa." I nod toward her bag. "I see you went swimming."

"Yes, Jess gave me a beautiful swimsuit for my birthday and there was a pool there. I'm guessing that you had a lot to do with organizing it?"

"I had to be in on the secret in case you changed your mind and went ahead and booked a spa yourself. If you had, I was meant to tell you that I thought it was too expensive and that you shouldn't be wasting your money on it."

"Except that you'd never say anything like that, so I'd have guessed straightaway."

I take a sip of champagne.

"Aren't you going to sit down?" she asks.

"I will. But first I'm going to rinse your swimsuit."

"I can do it," she protests. "Anyway, I rinsed it at the spa."

"I'll hang it up to dry, then." Before she can tell me that she'll do it later, I reach into her bag and gather her phone into the folds of the plastic bag containing the swimsuit. "I won't be a moment."

In the utility room, I put her phone on silent, bury it at the bottom of the laundry basket, then drape her swimsuit on the drying rack.

"Done," I say, walking back out onto the terrace and sitting down opposite her. "So you had a good time, then? At the spa?"

"I loved the facial, but I wasn't as keen on the massage. I feel very relaxed, though. And we had a lovely lunch, with champagne."

I raise my eyebrows. "This isn't your first glass, then?" I say, trying to joke with her as I usually do about how she quickly feels drunk on small amounts of alcohol.

"No, and Jess and I had to drink Kirin's because she's—" She stumbles over her words. "—she was driving."

"She could have had one glass, surely?"

"She had a little, but she's very strict about drinking and driving. She needs to be; she'd be stuck if she couldn't drive."

I nod. "How's Jess?"

"Not so good. She didn't look great and her balance was a bit off."

"Poor Jess. It's just as well that Rob is working from home now."

When Jess was first diagnosed with MS, we were all in shock and none of us really knew what to expect. Jess lost some of her mobility fairly quickly, and her confidence along with it, and everyone around her reacted in different ways. Rob, initially supportive, changed jobs within his company, which meant he began traveling a lot, leaving Jess alone and vulnerable. We were in the pub together when Nelson challenged him about it.

"Surely if you explained Jess's situation to your boss, he'd give you your old job back?" he said.

"I've already told you—this job is a promotion, which is exactly what Jess and I need, with her future being so uncertain," Rob explained petulantly, unused to his normally protective and adoring big brother disapproving of him. "She's managing to carry on working for now, but how long will that last?"

"But with you not around to help, won't her health deteriorate faster?"

"It's a chance we have to take. I've talked it over with Jess. She's fine with me being away a couple of days a week. And if her health does get worse, then I'll see about asking for a desk job again. Jesus, Nelson, let it go, OK?"

I get on all right with Rob, but I'm not close to him, not since he tried to drive a wedge between me and Livia during the early years of our marriage over the motorbike. It used to drive me mad when we were younger, the way he tagged along whenever Nelson and I met up. Nelson, for some reason, has always felt responsible for him. Rob can be funny, but most of the time he irritates the hell out of me. It's not just the way he plays on his film-star good looks, pulling out his aviator sunglasses at the first ray of sunshine, or the way he turns on the charm; it's more the way he has to be the center of attention. But I was probably the only one who worked out that the reason he accepted his new job without complaint was because he was glad to get away, glad to have a break from the worry of Jess's illness. I could sort of understand, even if I'd never do the same to Livia if she was ever in Jess's position.

Rob finally bowed to family pressure, from Jess's family as well as his own, and went back to his desk job in January this year. The only time he left Jess was at the end of April, when he took Cleo to see Marnie in Hong Kong for her birthday, because Jess didn't want Cleo going on her own.

Jess moved in with us while Rob was away, and although there weren't any problems, there's been a bit of a shift in the relationship between her and Livia, not on Jess's part, but on Livia's. It's really sad, but I think being with Jess on a daily basis for ten days made Livia realize how much Jess can't do for herself, and is having a hard time coming to terms with what's happening to her friend.

Because ever since, she's been keeping her distance, arranging for us to see her friends from the office on weekends instead of Jess and Kirin, like we usually do, almost as if she wants to have an excuse not to socialize with them anymore. When I asked her about it, she didn't deny it.

"Don't you sometimes feel that the six of us live a little too much in each other's pockets? Surely it's good to widen our circle of friends."

I couldn't disagree, because I like her colleagues and we always have a great time with them. But I miss our weekend dinners and impromptu lunches with the others. It's why, a couple of weeks ago, I told Nelson and Rob to bring Kirin and Jess over for a barbecue on the weekend. Livia was fine when I mentioned it, but we ended up canceling on the day because she wasn't feeling well. I'm not saying that she pretended to be ill, because she did look awful. But it felt too much of a coincidence and I hate that Liv can't cope with Jess's illness.

Liv touches my arm. "What are you thinking about?"

I realize I've been miles away. "Sorry. I was thinking how good the garden looks."

She reaches for my hand. "I want to remember this moment forever," she says softly. "You, me, Josh, the party. And Marnie, of course."

Marnie. How could I have forgotten, even for a second? If only I knew for sure that she was safe. Livia has her eyes closed, her face tilted toward the sun. I take my phone from my pocket and give it a quick glance.

Nothing.

Livia

"Isn't this lovely?" I murmur.

Adam doesn't answer, so I turn my head and squint in his direction to check he's all right. His eyes are closed and I realize from the tautness in his face that he lied about his migraine having gone. I'm glad he didn't probe too much about Jess. I know he's wondering what's going on, why I no longer see her as much as I used to. I've told him that we need to widen our circle of friends, but he doesn't know why; he doesn't know that I'm preparing for the future.

My friends have always been more important to me than they are to most people, because I don't have any family. I've always considered Jess and Kirin as the sisters I've never had, and Nelson and Rob as my brothers. But I know how fragile the future is; I know that very soon, everything is going to change. It's why every time I'm with Jess, my heart breaks a little bit more.

She looked so frail today. Maybe I should send her a text, tell her that I'll understand if she prefers to stay at home and rest tonight. The rush of relief I feel, that she might not be up to coming to the party, makes me hate myself. I couldn't do that to Jess; she'd be so hurt if I suggested she didn't come. She knows that I know she wouldn't miss my party for the world, even if she has to be carried here.

Max is another person I could do without tonight. It was

awkward back there. I haven't seen him for a while, so I thought he might have forgotten that since October I've barely been speaking to him. I thought that if I behaved toward him as I used to, everything would go back to normal. But it doesn't work like that. He must be so confused. The thought of all the explaining I'm going to have to do is depressing.

I grope for my glass and take a sip of now-warm champagne. Marnie has a lot to answer for. It was such a relief to hear her sounding happier back in October, when she called to tell me that she didn't want Max to go and see her, and it carried her all the way through Christmas and into January. But when February came, she seemed depressed again. Adam thought it was because she'd just worked out that she wouldn't be able to come home for my party, and he suggested I go to Hong Kong to see her. I spoke to people at work about it and we agreed that the best time for me to go would be at the beginning of April.

But before I could tell Marnie, she FaceTimed me. She was sitting on a bench outside her university building, her sunglasses perched on her head. I could see the glass entrance doors behind her and students coming through them, some carrying books, their bags slung over their shoulders. I loved it when I got these glimpses of her life in Hong Kong, instead of views of her bedroom wall.

"Mum, guess what? Cleo is coming to see me!"

"That's wonderful!" I said, relieved to see her upbeat again. "When?"

"April, for her birthday. Rob is bringing her because Jess doesn't want her coming on her own."

"That's funny, I saw Jess a few days ago and she didn't mention it."

"That's because she and Rob have only just thought of it. It's going to be Cleo's birthday present."

"Wow, that's nice of them."

"I know, I can't wait!"

"Good job I didn't book my ticket, then," I said, smiling at her excitement.

"What do you mean?"

"I was thinking of coming to see you."

"Really? When?"

"I was going to come at the beginning of April. But now that you have Cleo and Rob coming, maybe I should come in May instead."

"Mum, you don't need to come, honestly. I mean, it'll be lovely if you do and I'd love to see you, of course, but once Cleo and Rob leave, it'll only be a couple of months until I come home."

"I'm sorry you haven't enjoyed your year in Hong Kong more," I said.

"I have enjoyed it," she insisted. "It's just that it's a long way from everyone." She hesitated. "It hasn't been easy."

"I know," I said, understanding that she was referring to the breakup. "But it would have been harder if you'd been in England. Distance is a great leveler."

"You're right there," she said. "It is."

When Adam came back from seeing Nelson, I told him I probably wouldn't be going to Hong Kong after all.

"Jess and Rob are buying Cleo a ticket for her birthday and there's no point both of us going in April. Did you know about it? Cleo's birthday present?"

"Yes, Rob mentioned it to Nelson in the pub just now. They thought of it a while back, but Jess was worried about Cleo going on her own, which is why Rob is going with her."

"She'll only have to make the journey by herself," I protested. "She'll have Marnie once she arrives."

Remembering that conversation, I turn my head toward Adam. I'm sure he knows I'm looking at him and is keeping his eyes closed so that he doesn't have to talk to me. The party's going to be a nightmare for him if he's not feeling well. I should have canceled it weeks ago. And when I tell Adam what I need to tell him, he's not going to understand why I didn't. He's going to think that I wanted my party to go ahead no matter what. He won't understand that I wanted to preserve him for as long as possible, before his world falls apart.

Mine fell apart six weeks and three days ago, about a week into Cleo's visit to Hong Kong, when I FaceTimed Marnie for a chat before I went to work. It was eight in the morning, so four o'clock in the afternoon Hong Kong time. Adam had already left to go to his workshop and Jess, who was staying with us, was still in bed. I knew Marnie's timetable pretty well, so I knew she'd be back from lessons, waiting at the hotel for Cleo and Rob to come back from sightseeing. Marnie had practically moved into Cleo's room for the duration of their stay, glad to get away from her cramped student room, if only for a while.

"How's it going?" I asked.

"Brilliantly! It's so lovely having them here. It makes me realize how long I've been away." She was sitting at a wooden desk in front of her computer and behind her on the far wall I could make out beautiful prints of lotus flowers. She was wearing one of the hotel's white bathrobes and from the way her head was bent over her hand as we talked, I guessed she was painting her nails.

"Do you want me to call back when you've finished?" I offered.

"No, it's fine, as long as you don't mind only seeing the top of my head. We're going out to dinner later, to a really nice restaurant. I'm going to have a lovely long bath in a minute."

"You're going to miss the hotel when they leave," I teased. "Where have they gone today?"

"To Stanley Market." She raised her head. "I wish you could see it, Mum, it's amazing. You should have come with Cleo and Rob. You could have gone sightseeing with Rob and given me and Cleo a bit of time together."

"Is he cramping your style?" I asked, amused.

"No, it's fine actually."

"Well, it's certainly done you good to see them," I said. "You look happy."

"Who wouldn't be happy in this beautiful hotel?" she said, laughing.

I peered into the screen. "Has Cleo changed rooms?"

"What do you mean?" Her head was bent over her nails again.

"The prints on the wall," I explained. "They weren't lotus flowers."

"Oh yes—the other room she had was next to the lift and it was so noisy she asked to change."

I was about to point out that they now had the luxury of a huge king-size bed instead of two singles, when the door behind her opened and I saw a man standing in the doorway, rubbing his hair dry with a towel, obviously straight out of the shower. My shock was nothing to do with the fact that he was naked but more to do with the fact that Marnie had brought her boyfriend to Cleo's hotel room. But I supposed Cleo was fine with it, because Marnie must have asked her.

"It's so lovely here, far more comfortable than my own grotty room in the halls of residence," Marnie was saying, oblivious to her boyfriend in full frontal view. At the sound of her voice, he raised his head from the towel and, realizing she was on FaceTime, stepped quickly back into the bathroom and closed the door. But not before I'd seen his face.

My heart almost stopped. Then, aware that I needed to say something, because I didn't want Marnie to look up and see how devastated I was, I forced words from my mouth.

"Well, you may as well make the most of it," I said, hoping my voice sounded the same as it had before.

"That's what I thought. So, how are preparations going for your party, only six weeks to go now!"

"I know, I can't believe it! Liz came over yesterday with samples of food," I told her, talking too fast. "It was delicious. I'm so glad I chose her to do the catering. She's bringing three staff with her to serve the food and clear up after, so I won't have anything to do."

"I wish I could be there," she said with a sigh.

"Me too."

She straightened up and dangled her fingers in front of the screen. The sleeves of her bathrobe fell back, and I could see her tattoo: *An angel walking to the Devil's beat*.

"There," she said. "What do you think?"

"Navy blue isn't really my color," I said, amazed that I managed to force out a laugh. "But they look lovely. Are you wearing your blue dress tonight?"

"How did you guess? Sorry, Mum, I'd better go. Cleo and Rob will be back soon, so I need to go and have that bath."

"Make sure your varnish is dry first," I warned.

She waggled her hands in the air. "I will, don't worry. Speak soon?"

"Yes, I'll call you in a couple of days."

"Bye. Send Dad my love."

"Will do."

I don't know how long I sat there, staring at the blank screen, unable to move my body but unable to still my mind, which was careering all over the place, trying to make sense of what I'd just seen. I tried to tell myself that I'd been mistaken, that it hadn't been Rob standing naked in the doorway, but another man. And when I could no longer lie to myself, I tried to find excuses—Rob was using Cleo's bathroom because there was a problem with his and he hadn't known Marnie was there when he'd come out naked, which was why he'd ducked back in again quickly. I didn't want to believe that Marnie had been lying to me from the beginning of the conversation, when she'd told me that Rob was out with Cleo, and that Cleo had changed rooms. I didn't want to believe that the reason she was painting her nails in Rob's room, waiting to use the bathroom he'd just come out of, was because the two of them were having an affair. There had to be some other explanation.

I felt sick as I went onto Cleo's Facebook page. There were photos of Stanley Market, and other views of Hong Kong, but Rob wasn't in any of them. There were a couple of selfies of Cleo, one with a caption underneath: *Visiting on my own again today,* followed by a sad-faced emoji. Looking back at other posts, it was clear that since she and Rob had arrived in Hong Kong, Cleo had been doing a lot of sightseeing on her own. I tried to close my eyes to the truth staring me in the face, telling myself that Marnie would never have done something so immoral, so damaging, as embarking on an affair with someone who had been part of our family since before she'd been born. It was inconceivable. Not only was Rob twenty years older than Marnie, he was also Jess's husband, Nelson's brother and the father of her best friend.

I remember the nausea that rose up inside me, the panic that swept through me when the floorboards creaked in the bedroom upstairs, a sign that Jess was out of bed and on her way down to the kitchen. Snatching up my bag, I ran into the hall and out of the door, grabbing my car keys as I went. And then I drove, not to the office, but out to the country, where I parked and burst into tears.

5 P.M.–6 P.M.

Adam

"Do you need me to do anything?" I ask Livia, desperate to leave the terrace.

"No, it's fine," she says, getting to her feet at the sound of the caterers arriving. "Why don't you go and get ready? I'll need the bathroom from six o'clock."

As I go into the house, my phone beeps, telling me a message has come in. I stop at the bottom of the stairs, my heart crashing in my chest, my hands shaking as I pull my mobile from my pocket. I close my eyes, offer a silent prayer, then look. It's a message from Izzy.

Hey bro! Hope Liv's having a great day. Ian and I are running a bit late but will see you as soon as we can get there. Can't wait! xx

Crushing disappointment makes me want to hurl my phone at the wall. I can't go on like this, I can't keep waiting for Marnie to get through. As I go upstairs, I open the BBC News app to find the emergency number set up for relatives of those on the flight. If I explain that Marnie missed the flight and is somewhere at the airport, they might be able to get a message to her via the Pyramid Airways desk. A wave of guilt hits when I think of the families who are having to call the number for another reason, but I can't think of any other way of contacting her.

Flooding in Indonesia is the main news, then a fatal stabbing in London. The plane crash is the third item down. There's a photo next to the headline, a tangle of debris and flames. I sit down heavily on the bed and scroll quickly past it, looking for the number. Two words jump out at me—*local reports*. But—if there are videos coming out of Cairo Airport, why hasn't Marnie been able to call me, message me? With a horrible sense of foreboding, I play one of the videos.

A young man is gesticulating. *"I was standing right here,"* a voice translates, *"and I could hear a plane. It was louder than usual and I looked up and I saw it. It was very low in the sky. I knew it should have been higher at that point, because I often watch them. I see them just after they've taken off. But this one, instead of climbing higher, it stopped, right there, in the middle of the sky. And then it fell."*

The blood is pounding so hard in my ears that I struggle to keep up with what he's saying. *I knew it should have been higher at that point, because I often watch them. I see them just after they've taken off.* But the plane that crashed, the one Marnie should have been on, crashed twenty minutes into its flight. I remember calculating it, it crashed at 11:55, twenty minutes after its departure time of 11:35. So why did the man in the video say it had crashed just after takeoff?

My fingers are shaking so much I can hardly hold my phone. I scroll back to the news report and scan the text, searching, searching for the information that will tell me that I'm right and everyone else is wrong, that the plane didn't crash just after takeoff but twenty minutes into its flight. Then I see it, in black and white— *The plane crashed three minutes after takeoff from Cairo International Airport*—and I freeze, because the only way it can have crashed after takeoff, at 11:55, is if it left late.

I can't breathe. For a moment, the room spins. I close my eyes, tell myself to get a grip. I mustn't panic; it's going to be OK. I just need to calculate what time the flight actually left. It seems impossible to do the simple sum. I force myself to focus—it crashed three minutes into its flight and I know it crashed at 11:55, so all I need to do is take three from fifty-five to find its departure time. Fifty-two, the plane would have taken off at 11:52, not 11:35, so seventeen minutes late. Marnie's flight from Hong Kong was meant to arrive in Cairo at 10:15, but the flight app I checked earlier confirmed her flight arrived at 11:25. If the Amsterdam flight only left at 11:52 then—

Nausea rises inside me. I lurch to the bathroom and stand over the sink, my hands gripping the sides, willing myself not to be sick. I stare at my face in the mirror, searching desperately for something to ground me, to stop my panic from spiraling out of control. What if Marnie made the flight? But she couldn't have. I'd know, I'd know if something had happened to her. She's such a part of me, I'd just know. Marnie's safe; she has to be.

Sweat springs from my pores. I feel suffocatingly hot and begin tearing off my clothes, the button of my jeans too stiff for my fingers, tugging and pulling until I'm standing naked, the whole of me shaking. I pull open the shower door and almost fall inside. I reach blindly for the lever and water cascades down, drumming onto my head, filling my mouth, my nose, my throat until instinct forces me to take a breath. And all I can think is, *Marnie's safe; she has to be. Marnie's safe; she has to be.*

I push my way out of the shower, pull a towel around me. A blast of music comes from the garden, dragging me back to reality. I can't carry on fooling myself. Marnie might not be safe. She could have made the flight that crashed. She had twenty-seven minutes to make the connection, not ten.

Unless she had to change terminals. I don't know if there's more than one terminal at the airport in Cairo, but I can find out. I sit on the edge of the curved bath and type "How many terminals at Cairo Airport?" into my search engine. "THREE" comes up, and I almost laugh, because it's as if they've used big letters to reassure me. All I need to know now is that Marnie's flight from Hong Kong arrived at a different terminal from the one that left for Amsterdam.

"Please," I mutter. "Please let it be a different terminal."

I find her first flight, the one from Hong Kong; it arrived at Terminal 3. Then I type in the flight number of the Pyramid Airways flight, holding my breath while I wait to find out. It comes up—Terminal 2.

I close my eyes in relief. Even if the terminals are close enough to each other to walk, she would only have had twenty-seven minutes to get off her plane and make it out of Terminal 3 and into Terminal 2. She'd still have to find the gate.

My fingers move quickly on the screen, searching for more information on Cairo International Airport. I find the official website and read that terminals 2 and 3 are linked by a footbridge. OK, so how long would it take to disembark from one flight, find the footbridge, walk all the way across it to the other terminal, find the gate—and still be there twenty minutes before the departure time? Marnie couldn't have made it.

I should feel reassured. But I can't get away from the fact that if she had missed the flight, she would have contacted me. If news reports are getting through, the phone networks must be working.

I'm so damn scared.

I need to tell Livia. I turn to leave the bathroom, and catch a glimpse of my face in the mirror. I stare at my clammy skin, at the pulse beating in my temple—I can't let Livia see me like this. I don't want her to guess that something is wrong before I've made her sit down, before I've taken her hands in mine and have somehow found the words to tell her that Marnie, our daughter, could have been on a plane that crashed. First, I need to chase the fear from my eyes. And the only way I'm going to be able to do that is by believing there's still hope.

I'm not going to call the emergency number, not until I've spoken to Livia.

Livia

The food looks amazing. I can't stop walking around the kitchen, in awe of it all. My birthday cards have been moved to the sitting room and all the work surfaces are now covered with trays of delicious canapés.

"This is lovely, Liz, thank you. It looks beautiful!"

"And I can guarantee it tastes delicious too," she says, smiling at me, which I already know, because I tasted one when I first booked her.

There's also food in the dining room—two whole salmon, a huge side of cold beef, platters of other cold meats, wonderfully colored salads, the biggest cheese board I've ever seen, and a variety of desserts, which will be taken out to the tent at different stages throughout the evening. And for when people first arrive, the trays of canapés. Liz and her team will be there to serve and clear away, which means I'll be free to enjoy the evening.

I can't help worrying about Adam. Expecting him to make small talk for approximately seven hours, because the party won't finish until two in the morning, might be a bit much if he's got a migraine. It won't all be small talk, but I need to make sure he doesn't get stuck with Paula, as she tends to talk about her health in too much detail. I also need to steer him away from Sara, who has a habit of cornering people and showing them a stream of holiday photos on her phone. But if I know Adam, after a brief chat with everyone he'll spend most of the evening with Nelson and Ian.

The house phone rings and I go to answer it, wondering if it's Marnie, if she changed her mind about being off-radar so that she could wish me a happy birthday in person. But it's Jeannie.

"Hello, love, I just wanted to wish you a happy birthday," she says.

"Thank you—but you and Mike are coming tonight, aren't you?"

"Yes, of course, we wouldn't miss it for the world. You'll be busy, though, and we might not get the chance to speak very much."

"I'll always have time for you and Mike. You've been more of a mum and dad to me than my own parents."

"They're the ones who've missed out. They've missed the joy of seeing their grandchildren grow up into lovely young adults." She pauses. "How's Adam bearing up?"

"He's fine. He had a migraine earlier, but he's just had some champagne—Kirin gave us a bottle for the two of us to have before the party—so he must be feeling better."

"That's good. Well, I'll let you get on. Good-bye, love, see you later."

Jeannie hangs up and I stand for a moment, wondering what I'd have been like if I'd had parents like Jeannie and Mike. A different version of myself? I think of Izzy and her confidence. And Adam with his quiet self-belief.

I take a minute, watching everything going on around me, at the piles of plates and baskets of cutlery being carried out to the tent, at Emily, the young girl from the caterer's, filling small vases with the flowers that I ordered. They arrived when I was out, along with another bouquet, this time from Jess's mum, who can't come tonight. Although I'm glad Marnie isn't here, I hate that she's missing out on all this, because she would have loved it. I look for my phone to take some photos to send her, but it isn't in my bag. I look around; I must have put it down somewhere. I check the terrace, but it isn't on the table, or anywhere in the kitchen.

Going into the hall, I phone my mobile from our house phone. When it starts ringing, I put down the landline and listen carefully, hoping to hear where it's coming from. But I can't locate it, not even when I try again. Maybe I left it at the spa. I remember seeing it facedown on the table when we had lunch, but I don't know what I did with it after that. Hopefully, Jess or Kirin will have picked it up. I'm about to phone and ask them, when I realize that their numbers are in my mobile. I think about asking Adam to phone Nelson and get him to ask Kirin. But I'll be seeing them later, so I can ask them then. And I don't really have time to worry about my phone.

Liz comes to ask me where I want the cutlery, set out on trays in the tent or in a pot in the middle of each table. She asks me about Marnie, and I tell her that I'm secretly hoping she'll Face-Time during the evening. If I can show her the garden, if she can see everything, she'll be able to be part of it.

A sudden thought hits me—that maybe the reason Marnie has gone away for the weekend to a place without Wi-Fi is because she needs an excuse not to FaceTime tonight, because Rob will be here and she's worried she might give something away. Or, more probably, because she can't face looking Jess in the eye and asking her how she is when she's having an affair with her husband. I'm so *angry* with her. How could she? How could she have an affair with Rob? I still can't get my head around it. I've tried to make excuses for her, blame it all on Rob, tell myself that he took advantage of her, that he played on her vulnerability and slowly reeled her in. But at some point, she consciously crossed the line.

There are no words to describe how I feel about Rob. As I sat in my car that day, the day I discovered the truth, I tried to work out when their affair had started. Even though it made me ill to think about it, I was certain he was the father of the baby Marnie lost. I was sure—hoped—that there hadn't been anything between them while she was still at school, which meant it must have started once she was at university. But she was at Durham, nearly three hundred miles and a four-hour drive away from Windsor, so how had they been able to see each other to start an affair? Rob worked five days a week and, to my knowledge, he'd never gone away for the weekend on some pretext, or missed a Sunday bike ride with Adam and Nelson.

Then it dawned on me—those two days a week last year, when he'd worked away from home, he went to the Darlington offices of his company. I knew Darlington was somewhere in the north of England, but I didn't know where exactly. I scrabbled in my bag for my phone and located Darlington on Google Maps. It wasn't as far north as Durham—but was it near enough for him to have gone to see Marnie while he was there? When I discovered that it would have taken him half an hour to get there by car, I felt ill. I wanted to phone his boss and ask him if it really had been as Rob had said, that he hadn't had any choice about the new job—that although the company knew his wife had MS, they'd forced him to work away from home. But I was too scared I'd be told what I suspected was the truth, that Rob had asked—or at least put himself forward—for the job.

There was something else too. Because of the relationship among us all, it would have been normal for Rob to have looked Marnie up when he was in Darlington. We wouldn't have thought anything about him taking her out for a drink or a meal. It's what an uncle would do for his student niece, because that was how we considered Nelson and Rob, as Marnie's uncles—she had even called him Uncle Rob until a few years ago, for God's sake! Yet he had never mentioned to us that it was something he was going to do, and no bells had rung for me because I hadn't realized how close the two places were. But once I realized, his silence damned him. What surprised me was that Adam had never questioned it. If he had gone anywhere near Aberystwyth, where Cleo was studying, he would have automatically looked her up.

It took me a long time to pluck up the courage to go back and face Jess that day. I phoned Paula and asked her to tell the office that I was ill, then told Jess I'd come home early because I wasn't feeling well. She made me a cup of tea and insisted I go to bed, and I lay there, staring at the ceiling, trying to work out how I was going to tell her that her husband was having an affair with my daughter. But my mind wouldn't go there, just as it wouldn't let me tell Adam what I suspected when he came to see how I was. I wanted to think everything through before I destroyed their worlds.

I walk restlessly around the kitchen, realizing that although the food looks lovely, I'm not going to be able to eat any of it, feeling as I do. I know I'll enjoy my party once it's gotten going, as long as I can avoid Rob. To fill in the time, because I don't have my phone, I go to the sitting room and look through my cards again. Most of them are from people I'll be seeing tonight, but there are some from those I didn't invite, and even though there's no reason why I should have invited Kirin's two cousins, or Ian's mum, or the girl from the hairdresser's, I still feel bad that I didn't.

I check the time; it's almost six. I'm dying to see the garden, but I need to wait until Josh tells me I can. He and Max have been hard at it since they came back from dropping off Murphy. Adam should be down soon, so we'll be able to see it together. He had the longest shower he's ever had in his life, judging by the length of time the water was running, trying to wash away his migraine, maybe.

There's the sound of footsteps on the stairs and I go out to the hall. When Adam sees me, he comes to a stop and just stands there, halfway down the stairs. It's as if he's looking at me, thinking, *OK, this is it, the evening Liv has been waiting for forever, so I better get it right*. And I want to tell him that he's got it exactly right, that dressed in his beige chinos and white shirt, he's perfect. He's filled out since I married him, and is in amazing shape, thanks to the fact that he never gets much of a chance to sit down. He's forgotten to shave, but I don't mind.

He comes the rest of the way down the stairs and takes my hands in his.

"Livia." I can see from the way he's looking at me and from the way he's called me Livia that he's feeling a bit emotional and I know he's going to tell me that he loves me.

"Mum! You can come out now!" Josh calls from the garden.

Excitement surges through me. "I love you too," I say, kissing Adam softly. "Thank you for making me the happiest person in the world." I pull him toward the door. "Come on, Josh needs us."

6 P.M.–7 P.M.

Adam

I let Liv lead me into the garden. As we walk out onto the terrace, the evening sun, still high in the sky, sears my eyes. What am I doing, letting her bring me out here? I need to tell her; I need to tell her about Marnie. I'd been ready to; I'd prepared myself mentally. But Josh had interrupted us and before I could say anything else, she told me she loved me too. Why had she said that? Had she really believed I was going to tell her that I loved her? Or had some sixth sense told her I was going to say something that she wouldn't want to hear?

She said I'd made her the happiest person in the world. Now, as we step onto the lawn, that's exactly how she looks. She turns slowly, taking everything in, and I'm glad that Max is filming her, because one day, if the worst has happened and—I can't bear to think about it—Marnie was on the flight, I'll want to look back and remember how happy she was at this moment in time. The words resonate through my brain—*how happy she was*—and my heart breaks. I have to tell her before she gets carried away. There's no way this party can happen.

"Livia," I say again.

"I know," she says, turning to look at me, her eyes shining. "It's beautiful!"

I catch her hand, pull her toward me, fold her into my arms. But she turns so that she's facing the garden, her back warm against my chest.

"It's so much more than I imagined," she says. "Haven't we got the best children in the world? Have you seen what Josh has done? Over there on the fence?"

I hadn't really taken in anything when we'd come up the steps onto the lawn. I was aware of the lights and flowers and balloons, but it massed together in a blur. All my senses are affected, I realize. Livia's voice seems to come from a long way off and I can barely feel the touch of her hand as she pulls me toward the fence. The air must be heavy with the scent of her roses, but I smell nothing, except my fear.

We reach the fence and my whole world shatters. I drop Livia's hand and move clumsily away from her. There are photos of Marnie everywhere—photos of her as a baby, at school, in the garden, on holiday, in Hong Kong, photos I've never seen before—tacked all the way along the fence. And above, a sign saying HAPPY BIRTHDAY, MUM!

Fortunately, Livia mistakes the breath I take.

"I know, isn't it amazing?" she says.

I close my eyes and Marnie's voice rings out, *Happy birthday, Mum!* She sounds so close that if I reached out, I could touch her.

Josh comes over and puts an arm around each of us, drawing me in. For one terrible second, I want to lay my head on his shoulder and weep.

"So," he says. "What do you think?"

"Wonderful." I can't bear to look. I keep my eyes fixed above fence level and try to focus on the chance that Marnie is still alive.

"I think it's the best thing ever!" Livia says, hugging him. "Thank you so much, Josh. You've gone to a lot of trouble."

"It was Marnie's idea; it's her present to you."

"I couldn't have asked for anything better. I remember taking that photo," she says, pointing. "And that one of her in her *Star Wars* outfit. Where did you get them?"

"Marnie gave me most of them, others I got from your albums. I took photos of the photos and had them enlarged."

"I wish I could tell her how much I love it." She turns to me. "Shall I try to call her?"

"No!" Aware that I spoke too fast, I try to speak more reasonably. "It's the middle of the night for her and anyway, didn't she say that she was going to revise where there wasn't any Wi-Fi, so that she wouldn't be disturbed?"

"She'll still have a phone signal," Livia says. "It feels wrong not to call, to say thank you."

"Dad's right," Josh says. "We'll hear from her tomorrow, when she gets back from her weekend away." He drops his arms from our shoulders and I feel suddenly cold. "Right, I'll leave you to it. I've got things to do."

He leaves and there's only me and Livia. Is this the place to tell her, here on the lawn, in front of the photos of Marnie? Or should I take her into the house?

"By the way, your mum phoned," Livia says.

"Did she? When?"

"While you were in the shower."

"What did she want?"

"Just to wish me a happy birthday." She pauses. "I thought it might be Marnie phoning. Isn't it lovely, what she's done?"

"Yes," I say, glad I hadn't heard the phone ring, that I was spared the crushing disappointment of it not being Marnie.

"I could stand here all evening looking at these photos, but I'd better go and get ready." She starts to move away and I catch hold of her hand again.

"Livia, wait—"

But she gives me a kiss and pulls away, her mind already elsewhere.

She gets as far as the steps before she realizes.

"Sorry!" she says, turning around and laughing. "Did you want to tell me something?"

I look at her, her hair burnished by the sun, her face flushed with excitement, and all I can think is that this might be the last time she'll ever be truly happy. In the future, the very distant future—if Marnie isn't all right—there might be moments when she forgets. But for the rest of the time, for every second of every minute of every hour, for every hour of every day for the rest of her life, Livia will feel the desperate pain of grief. As she stands there waiting for my answer, all I can think is that these might be her last few moments of happiness.

So I prolong them a bit. I take my time answering, stretching out the seconds.

"Adam! Can it wait?"

Her words echo in my ears. *Can it wait?* I draw in my breath, overwhelmed by a sudden thought. What if—what if I only tell her once the party is over? I don't have official confirmation that Marnie was on the flight, and there's a fair chance that she wasn't. What if I tell Livia that Marnie might never be coming home, that we might never see her again—and then, a few hours later, she walks through the door? I'll have caused Livia unimaginable pain and anguish for nothing. And if she doesn't walk through the door, if the very worst has happened—

"Adam!" Waiting for my reply, Livia becomes impatient.

I take a steadying breath. If the very worst has happened, then it won't make any difference to Marnie whether I tell Livia now or not. If Livia can have another few hours of happiness, then surely that's the greatest gift I can give her.

"It can wait!" I call. And she blows me a kiss and runs down the steps toward the house.

She deserves so much to be happy.

Livia

I take the towel from my head and shake out my wet hair. As I reach for a comb, I catch sight of myself in the full-length mirror and move to stand in front of it, running a critical eye over my body. I'm in my underwear, so I can see that watching what I ate has gotten rid of the extra pounds that crept up on me over the years. It wasn't that hard. I lost my appetite the moment I found out about Marnie and Rob.

The level of deception that he and Marnie have stooped to is bewildering. A couple of days after I saw Rob naked in the hotel room, when I was still piecing everything together, a couple of days before he and Cleo were due home, I had a conversation with Jess.

"Didn't Cleo mind Rob going to Hong Kong with her?" I asked, remembering that she hadn't wanted Cleo to travel on her own. I hoped she hadn't noticed that I'd almost choked on his name. What I'd discovered weighed so heavily on me that I could hardly bear to be around Jess, and I was glad I could escape to work during the day, that Adam was with us in the evenings, and that she'd soon be going back to her own house.

Jess threw back her head and laughed. "Yes, of course she did! No self-respecting nineteen-year-old wants their dad chaperoning them when they go to see their best friend. But Rob insisted that Cleo wasn't going without him. I tried to persuade him to let her go on her own, but he wouldn't budge, saying it wasn't safe. Cleo was furious and said there was no way that he was going with her and that she'd pay for the ticket herself. But Marnie told her that if it was the only way they were going to be able to see each other, it was best to accept Rob as part of the package."

To know that Marnie was part of the deceit crushed me even more. It made me question everything she'd told me about her time in Hong Kong. I could think about nothing else, and when I remembered how depressed she'd been when she first arrived there, I also remembered how she'd suddenly perked up in December. And then I remembered Rob's big trip away, supposedly to the Singapore office of his company. We were all so impressed that he was going somewhere more exotic than Darlington that nobody thought to wonder why he'd suddenly been sent to the Singapore, not even Nelson, because it wouldn't have occurred to any of us that he could possibly be lying. We were best friends, family. People don't lie to their families.

I was so obsessed, so determined to have all the facts, that I trawled Rob's Facebook page, scrolling down his timeline until I came to the corresponding date. There weren't many posts, certainly not as many as I'd have expected from someone like Rob in somewhere like Singapore, because he loved to brag. And what he had posted was tellingly vague—no views at all, just a couple of selfies, one sitting in a restaurant in front of a platter of seafood with the caption "*loving Asia*" and another of him holding a cocktail and the caption "*unsurprisingly hot in Asia*." But I didn't know for sure.

I run the comb angrily through my hair, tugging the knots hard, the eternal question trapped in my brain—how could Rob do that to Jess? I'll never get an answer I can understand. Jess is the kindest, loveliest person I know. She doesn't deserve to have a cheating, lying husband, especially now, when she's ill. What I can't bear is the thought that it's happened *because* she's ill, that Rob no longer loves her because of her illness. Surely it should have brought them closer, made him want to protect her. I know 100 percent that if I was ill, Adam would be there for me, just as I would be there for him.

Out of nowhere, a sudden fear takes hold of me. I put down the comb slowly, turning it over in my mind. Is that what's wrong with Adam, is that why he's behaving so strangely, because he's ill? Josh said he was stressed when he got back from town. What if he had a doctor's appointment that he didn't tell me about because he didn't want to worry me? What if he received bad news? *Don't let it be that, please don't let it be that Adam is ill,* I pray. But I can't think what else it can be.

Grabbing my dressing gown, I shrug it on and run down the stairs, tying the belt as I go. It must be bad if Adam wanted to tell me before the party. Maybe he wants me to cancel it. But he'd only want me to cancel it if it was something really bad.

I can't see Adam in the garden, even Josh and Max have disappeared, so I head to the work shed. As I squeeze behind the tent, I see Adam through the window, standing at his workbench, his head bent over a piece of dark wood.

"Hey," he says when I burst through the door. "Aren't you meant to be getting ready?" He sees my face and freezes. "Livia, what is it? What's the matter?" The fear on his face mirrors my own. He knows that I know.

I go toward him because he seems unable to move.

"Adam." I take his hands in mine and find them ice-cold. "Adam—please, tell me the truth. Are you ill? Is that what you wanted to tell me? That you're ill?"

The long pause makes my heart race.

"No." He shakes his head, puzzled. "No, I'm not ill. Apart from my migraine. I didn't want to say anything, but it's come back."

I swallow a shaky breath. "You didn't go and see the doctor today?"

"The doctor? No, I would have told you if I'd had an appointment."

"Really?"

"Yes."

I give a half sob, half laugh of relief. "You don't have some terrible illness that you're keeping from me until after the party's over?"

"No, Liv, no." He pulls me into his arms. "I'm sorry you thought that, I'm sorry you were worried."

"Promise?"

"Yes. I'm not ill, I promise."

"Then what was it you wanted to tell me? You tried to tell me several times, so it must be important. I should have listened."

His arms tighten around me. "I just want you to know how much I love you, how I'll always be here to look after you, no matter what."

"I know you will be."

"All I want is for you to be happy."

There's a darkness in his eyes that I don't understand. "I am happy," I say, kissing him softly, wanting to chase it away. "I'm happier than I've ever been."

"Good. Now, if you don't go and get ready, you'll be welcoming your guests in your robe." He looks at the old battered clock standing on his workbench. "It's quarter to seven, so you have exactly forty-five minutes."

"I'm already gone!" I call, running from the shed, my feet no longer heavy with dread, but light with relief. I could bear anything, anything, except Adam being ill. I think of Jess and I know that's why I made that jump, because before she told us about her diagnosis, I'd known there was something on her mind. But she waited until we came back from holiday, knowing we'd worry about her as soon as we knew.

I reach the house and slow my pace. Adam is keeping something from me, I know he is. I don't believe that what he wanted to tell me was that he loves me and will always be here for me, not with the darkness I saw in his eyes. It reminds me of the haunted look I see in my own eyes, and suddenly I'm struck by the possibility that maybe he knows what I know, and has been looking for a way to tell me. But then I realize that it can't be that, because if he had the slightest inkling that Rob was having an affair with his beloved Marnie, there's no way that Rob would still be standing.

7 P.M.–8 P.M.

Adam

I haven't left my shed since Livia came to find me. The first thing I thought, when she came bursting in, was that she knew, that she'd somehow worked out that Marnie was meant to be coming home and had been on the plane that crashed. But she'd thought I was ill, and I wished it could be that—that I could swap everything around so that Marnie was definitely coming home, and that I was ill.

I'd been studying the block of walnut that I'd bought for Marnie's angel sculpture, trying to ground myself by thinking about how I would start, where I would make the first cut. Liv's interruption had me pacing the floor, unable to stay still. I tried to call Marnie again, but the call wouldn't connect. To calm myself, I put my hands on the wood and focused on the thought that, on her birthday in July, Marnie would be here in the shed with me, delighted with her sculpture.

The stifling air in the shed becomes oppressive. I push my way outside. Livia will be down soon. I circle the tent and walk across the lawn, psyching myself up to be as normal as I can possibly be so that I don't spoil anything for her. I wait on the terrace; and then she's here, walking toward me, her movements nervous, the expression on her face almost embarrassed, so beautiful in her long cream dress that she takes my breath away.

"You look beautiful," I say, kissing her.

A faint blush appears on her cheeks. "Do you really think so?"

"Yes, even more beautiful than on our wedding day."

"We were so young. You were only nineteen, the same age as Marnie. Imagine if she told us she was getting married—and that she was pregnant." She stops abruptly.

I try not to flinch at the searing pain the mention of Marnie brings. It's going to happen a lot tonight, I realize. People are going to be talking about her, saying it's a shame that she couldn't be here, asking when she'll be back. How am I going to cope with having to pretend that she'll soon be home when I don't know if she will be? *You'll focus on Livia,* I tell myself, *you'll be strong for her.*

"I was going to curl my hair and leave it loose, but I ran out of time," Livia says. "Is it all right, do you think?"

She's put it up and some strands have fallen around her neck. "It's perfect. You're perfect." I give her another kiss. "Stop worrying."

"I wonder who'll be the first to arrive."

"Normally, I'd say Izzy and Ian, but Izzy messaged to say they're going to be late. So, it'll probably be Kirin and Nelson. Nelson will be itching to get away from the children."

"And I imagine he'll be needing a stiff drink," she says with a smile.

"Well, there's everything here he could possibly want."

"We haven't forgotten anything, have we?"

"No, I don't think so."

"Where's Josh?"

"Upstairs, getting changed."

"And Max?"

"Upstairs, getting changed."

She gives a sudden laugh. "This is the worst bit, waiting for everyone to arrive." She turns toward me. "And do you know when the best bit will be? Not when everyone is here but when it's all over and it's just you and me."

I swallow painfully. There are footsteps on the path. "I think someone's coming."

As if in answer, Nelson's voice comes to us.

"It's seven-thirty, let the party begin!"

And he and Kirin burst through the side gate and onto the terrace.

"Oh my God, Livia, you look amazing!" Kirin squeals. "And you don't look so bad yourself," she says, giving me a kiss and then hugging Livia. "I love your shirt."

I give a quick smile. "New on today."

"Livia, you look stunning." Nelson turns to me and gives me a man hug. "I've missed you."

"You saw me only a week ago."

"And that's seven days too long."

Kirin takes her phone from her bag and I realize I'm not going to be able to stop people from asking about Marnie tonight, but what if they start talking about the plane crash? I move away from them quickly, my heart hammering as I hurry to the kitchen. The caterers are there, taking up too much space. I push past Liz, reach into the cupboard next to the dishwasher, grab a large bowl and go back outside.

"Sorry, Kirin," I say, interrupting her as she talks to Livia. "It's a no-phone policy tonight. In here, please. You too, Nelson."

Liv looks at me in surprise. "Is that really necessary?"

"Absolutely," I say, faking cheerfulness. "We don't want people on their phones when they should be enjoying the party."

"But what about photos?"

"Max is the official photographer, isn't he?"

Kirin frowns. "What if Mum and Dad need me? They're looking after the children."

"They'll phone on the house phone."

"But will we hear it?"

"Hopefully not," Nelson jokes. "Kirin, if they need us, one of them can drive two minutes up the road."

"All right," Kirin says, reluctantly dropping her phone in the bowl.

"You can have mine, with pleasure," Nelson says. "At least I won't hear a million messages coming in."

More people arrive. Neighbors from across the street, colleagues from Livia's law firm, friends we don't see as often as we'd like because they live farther away. Soon the terrace is full of people with bottles of wine and presents for Livia. I'm relieved that everyone is going along with the no-phone policy without too much grumbling, joking about going home with the wrong phone—I hadn't thought of that. But Josh hears and, with a hand on my shoulder, says he'll sort it. He disappears for a couple of minutes while I struggle to make conversation with one of Livia's work friends, and comes back with some stickers and a pen.

I leave him with the bowl and move to the side, listening as he tries to get people, once they've given him their phones, to move up the steps and onto the lawn. At first, no one responds, so he starts shouting that there are drinks in the tent. It works; the terrace empties and Livia goes with them. She's quickly surrounded by a group of people and all I can see is her auburn hair. Then it's just me and Nelson.

"Have a drink with me," he says.

"What would you like—beer, wine, champagne?"

He sits down on the steps. "I don't suppose I could have a whiskey, could I?"

"Sure. Wait there."

I go to the dining room, find a single malt and two glasses and half-fill them.

"Here," I say, handing him one.

"Thanks. Exactly what I need." He pauses. "Kirin's pregnant." He clinks his glass against mine. "Here's to big families."

I wade through the mess of emotions coursing through me, trying to find an appropriate response. "Wow."

"You can say that again." He takes a drink. "It's twins."

I can't keep the shock off my face. "Twins?"

"That's right."

"Christ."

He looks at me, a frown furrowing his brow. "Right now, I'd be expecting you to be rolling on the floor laughing."

He's right; normally I would be. "It's great news, Nelson, really. You are pleased about it, aren't you?"

"I'm sure I will be, once I've gotten used to the idea. Kirin sort of sprang it on me earlier. She couldn't get into the dress she wanted to wear and that's when she told me. It was quite brutal. My fault—I told her she'd better go on a diet if she didn't want to bust the zip, and she told me I'd better get a vasectomy if I didn't want to end up with more than five children. You know Kirin, she gives as good as she gets." He takes another long drink from his glass. "Father of five, who would have thought it? But, you know, after I'd gotten over the initial—pretty awful, I have to say—shock, I began to think it might be quite nice. As long as they're girls. I don't want another pair of little monsters. I don't know where the boys get their energy from. That's the only thing that worries me. I'm already permanently knackered. Sometimes I envy you. We're the same age and yours are off your hands."

"Don't envy me," I say quietly, so quietly that I'm not sure he's heard.

"I suppose I must be OK about it," he goes on, "because while I was having my shower I began to think about names. I thought, if they're girls, it might be nice to continue with the flower theme. I was thinking Poppy and Dahlia. They go well with Lily, don't you think?"

"Dahlia? Poppy's all right—but why Dahlia?"

"They're the only two flowers I know. Apart from Chrysanthemum and Carnation, and I don't think Kirin will like either of those," he says with a grin.

"I don't think she'll like Dahlia much either. What's wrong with Rose?"

He turns to me, a look of amazement on his face. "Adam, you're a genius! Rose!"

"They might not be girls," I remind him.

"They bloody better be," he growls. Then he starts laughing.

"What?" I ask.

"Five years ago, we'd have been talking about motorbikes and who won the Grand Prix. Now we're sitting here talking about babies and flower names for girls."

I find a smile. "You started it."

He gives me a nudge. "People arriving."

"I'll see you later," I say, getting to my feet. "Go and get drunk, you deserve it."

"Adam!" I turn and see Jess smiling at me. "Where's the birthday girl?"

I give her a hug, taking care not to knock her off balance. "On the lawn. Where's Cleo?"

"Here!" I look past Rob, who is standing in front of her, dressed in a tuxedo and bow tie. He's fiddling with his hair and I have to reach around him to give Cleo a hug.

"This is amazing," Cleo says, her blue eyes moving around the garden, taking everything in. "Those lights in the trees—they're beautiful!"

"How are you?" I ask, and I feel even worse because all I can think is that here is another person who's going to be devastated if anything has happened to Marnie.

"I'm good—apart from Charlie, who's being a bit of a child at the moment."

"I'll kick his ass if he upsets my little girl," Rob threatens.

Jess casts her eyes to the sky. "Your little girl is perfectly capable of taking care of herself, aren't you, darling?"

"Absolutely," Cleo says.

I hold out the bowl, now nearly full with mobiles. "Phones in here, drinks this way," I say, showing them the steps, and thankfully, they leave, Rob going up the steps first, leaving Cleo to help Jess.

An arm comes around my shoulder. "So, how are you?"

"Dad. I'm good. Hi, Mum. Wow, you're looking glamorous."

Her eyes search my face. "How's the migraine?"

"Fine. Not great," I amend. I'm beginning to lose track of whether I still have my migraine or not. Although I'm no longer lying, because a huge band of pressure is building up inside my head.

"Is that why you forgot to shave?"

I run a hand over my chin. She's right, I did forget.

"The drinks are on the lawn," I tell them.

"Are you trying to get rid of us?" Dad jokes.

"Only until everybody has arrived. Why don't you go and see Nelson? He's got some news I'm sure he'd love to share with you."

"Sounds intriguing. Catch up with you later, Adam."

More people arrive. I chat with them for a bit, take their phones, the bowl nearly overflowing now, send them up the steps. I can't remember who's arrived and who hasn't. I fish my own phone from my pocket, but nothing has come in since that message from Izzy. I feel the now-familiar wave of panic. *Where are you, Marnie?* I ask silently. *Shouldn't I have heard from you by now?*

I check the time; it's eight o'clock. The party is supposed to go on until three in the morning, when the music has to stop.

I don't know if I can do this.

Livia

Josh stands on a chair, his tanned legs showing under the cutoff jeans he's wearing with a loose white shirt. I watch as he waves his arms at the guests, who are busy chatting, trying to attract their attention. Max steps next to him and taps a fork against his bottle of beer until there are only murmurs.

"Hello!" he shouts, and people cheer back.

I'm standing with my friends from work, smiling at Josh when, out of the corner of my eye, I see *him*. He's standing in front of the tent, wearing a tuxedo with a red bow tie, and my stomach clenches horribly. He looks so confident and sure of himself that for a moment I don't know how I'm going to be able to bear being in the same place as him. Since I found out about him and Marnie, I've managed to avoid him completely, arranging dinners with other friends, pretending to be ill so that Adam would have to cancel the dinner he'd arranged at our house—although it wasn't really a pretense, because the thought of having to sit down and eat with Rob made me physically sick. But I was damned if I was going to cancel the party I'd dreamed about for so long. All I needed was to avoid him, I told myself, which wouldn't be difficult with another ninety-nine people around. But now that it's here, the reality is very different.

The rush of hate I feel is so violent that I have to turn away for a second, and my cheeks flare as I try to control my breathing.

"So for tonight," Josh continues, "we have a musical adventure for you all! At certain times during the evening I'm going to play a song that one of you chose, and it's up to you to guess who chose it."

There are more cheers and laughs and I try to focus on this, everyone's enjoyment, to take my mind off Rob.

"Do you understand?" he cries.

"Yes!" everyone shouts back.

"Then let the party begin!"

"Celebration" starts playing through the speakers, and before anyone can stop me, I move away from the tent and go and stand at the top of the steps, as far from Rob as I can. Max is hovering nearby, filming and taking photos, and I'm glad he insisted on being the photographer, because otherwise we might not have had any. Adam confiscating everyone's phones was so unlike him, I nearly laughed, thinking at first he was joking. We'd never talked about a no-phone policy, so it must have been a spur-of-the-moment decision. Maybe he was worried that people would spend half of the evening checking their messages, but I don't think any of our friends would do that.

I take a few deep breaths. This moment of solitude among so many people has calmed me and I smile as I watch my friends laughing together, already having a good time. I smooth my dress down, rearranging the skirt so that the hem is straight, and flattening the material that has bunched slightly around my waist. I've been worrying about this dress since I bought it, wondering if it was the right thing to wear, wondering if people would think, because of the color, that I was trying to reenact my wedding. But I've only had compliments and no one has said that I look like a bride.

I did have a moment earlier, though, after I'd done my hair and makeup. As I checked my appearance in the mirror, I suddenly thought of the roses Marnie had sent me and ran downstairs to get them. Back upstairs, I took them from the vase, dried the stems with a towel and put them to one side while I slid into my dress. Then, before looking at myself in the mirror, I picked up the bouquet and held it in front of me, like a bride would, walking up the aisle. When I looked up and saw my reflection, tears sprang to my eyes.

I wish there'd been someone to take a photo so that I could have taken it out and looked at it in secret, a reminder of what could have been. But only Adam and Josh were there, and I was too embarrassed to let them see me playing at being a bride. I stared at myself for a long time, imprinting the image on my brain, because I wanted to remember how I might have looked on my wedding day. And then I raised the roses to my face and breathed in their heady smell.

"Thank you, Marnie," I murmured. "Thank you for making it possible for me to see."

The sad thing is, if she had been here, and if what has happened hadn't happened, we'd have shared the moment together, messing around and giggling. Maybe later, once everyone has left, I'll ask Adam to take a photo of me with the roses to send to Marnie. Or if I preserve the roses, I can wait until she comes home at the end of the month, put the dress back on, and re-create the scene for her. But I'm not sure I'll feel like dressing up then.

It was strange, that moment on the terrace with Adam, when we were waiting for everyone to arrive. There was a sort of gap, a moment in time when nothing was happening and there was nothing to do. A moment when Adam and I ran out of words. A moment where it seemed as if the world had stopped turning and we were suspended in time, waiting for it to move on.

I see Kirin waving and go over, lifting my hem as I walk.

"I told him," she says, smiling. She takes a glass of juice from a passing tray and I do the same. I will have alcohol, but later, once everyone has arrived. "I told Nelson I was pregnant."

"How did he take it?"

"Well, after I resuscitated him, he seemed OK. Dazed, but OK." She sweeps her arm around the garden. "This is beautiful, Liv."

"I know, and it's all due to Josh and Max. They've done a fantastic job. I can't wait until it gets dark, it's going to look amazing."

"So, was it worth the wait?" The sound of Jess's voice behind me makes my heart start hammering, terrified that Rob will be standing next to her. I turn slowly, giving myself time, wondering if I'm going to be able to hold it together.

Relief at finding Jess on her own brings tears to my eyes.

"Yes," I say, blinking them back. "It was worth the wait."

Jess takes my tears as tears of happiness, that at last I'm having my "big day," and gives me a hug. "You look beautiful!"

"Not too much like a bride?"

"Not at all."

I peer over her shoulder. "Where's Cleo?" I ask, looking for Rob at the same time.

"Talking to Josh and Max."

"Oh yes, I can see her. I'll catch her later. By the way, did either of you pick up my phone at the spa?"

"I didn't," says Kirin.

"Me neither." Jess looks worried. "Why, have you lost it?"

"I don't know. It's not in my bag, so I thought I must have left it on the table when we were having lunch."

"Do you want me to phone them?" Kirin asks. "Oh—I can't, Adam's confiscated our phones."

"Don't worry, I'll call them tomorrow." I turn to Jess. "Shall I get you a chair?"

She gives me a grateful smile. "I'm fine for now."

"Have you seen the photos of Marnie?" Kirin asks her.

"Not yet."

Out of the corner of my eye, I see Rob approaching.

"Oh look, there's Izzy!" I say, ducking away. "Sorry, I need to go and say hello."

I have a hug and a catch-up with Izzy, who wants to go and make sure the caterers are doing their job. I tell her that everything is under control, but Izzy loves organizing everyone and manages to do it without causing offense.

"Have you heard from Marnie?" she asks, reaching out and taking a canapé from a passing tray.

"Yes, I got a message from her this morning. And she sent me some lovely yellow roses."

"The ones in the kitchen? They're beautiful! I can't wait to see her when she comes back, I miss my favorite niece."

I smile, because Marnie is her only niece. Izzy and Ian can't have children, so Marnie is hugely important to them. Since she was old enough to hold a teacup, Izzy has taken Marnie for afternoon tea in London for every birthday, trying a different hotel each year and rating them afterward according to the quality of the scones, the freshness of the sandwiches, and the variety of cakes.

"You should go and see the photos," I say, pointing to the fence. "There's one of you holding her just after she was born."

"I'm glad I'm in at least one of them!"

I had such mixed emotions when I saw the photos earlier. Delight and pride, of course, but also a slight dismay that there were some I couldn't remember. I couldn't remember if I'd taken them or if they'd been taken by someone else, where they'd been taken, why they'd been taken. The one where she's wearing her school uniform, what occasion was that to mark—a first day back at school, an end-of-term event, or simply because she'd looked cute that morning? And the one on the beach—where, when, why? I was haunted by the memories the photos didn't bring back—and haunted by the innocence of them. And disbelief that Marnie, my beautiful Marnie, could do what she's done.

I'd been proud of the way that, during her calls to us, she would always ask how Jess was doing, and how she was managing her symptoms. But after what Kirin told me earlier today, about Rob being in denial, about the way he insists to Nelson that Jess is still independent, I have a horrible sense of foreboding. What if the real reason Marnie is coming back at the end of the month is not just to see Rob but also because he's planning to leave Jess and she wants to be here to secretly support him through it?

Izzy leaves to look at the photos and, after checking that Rob is nowhere near me, I look down toward the terrace to see if anyone else has arrived. I know it's not logical, not when I haven't seen them for over twenty years, not when they didn't reply to the invitation I sent them, or send me a card, but I can't let go of the faint hope that my parents will turn up. But there's only Adam, his head bent over something that I suspect is his mobile. He looks so forlorn standing there on his own that I'm suddenly overwhelmed by a weird feeling of displacement, that we aren't where we should be, that everything going on around us is wrong. I want to shout at Josh to stop the music, to turn off the lights, to tell everyone that there's been a terrible mistake and could they please go home. But Jeannie and Mike are coming up the steps, their faces lit with smiles, and the feeling passes as quickly as it came.

8 P.M.–9 P.M.

Adam

More people arrive. I stand on the terrace and go through the motions: meet, greet, move them toward the steps and onto the lawn. The caterers stop to offer me things to eat as they walk by with trays of food, but I can't bring myself to take anything. And then, at last, a lull.

"Dad!" I look up and see Josh waving to me. "Can you come here?"

"Has everybody arrived, do you think?" I call, reluctant to leave the terrace until I'm sure. I have to shout over the sound of Aretha Franklin singing "Respect." Jess's choice, I heard someone say.

"Yes, I think so!"

How is it possible that since Nelson and Kirin arrived at seven-thirty, I've been so focused on what people are saying so they won't guess anything is wrong, that there have been stretches of a few seconds, maybe even a few minutes, when Marnie completely disappeared from my mind? It feels wrong that I'm able to smile and chat when— I quickly close my mind. I can't let doubt in, not with Josh waiting to speak to me.

I close the side gate and make my way over.

"Mum's ring. Did you pick it up?"

I stare at him. "No, I—"

"Aw, Dad! You disappeared for ages after Mum got back, so I thought you'd gone to get it."

"I was upstairs, getting ready." I rub at my face. "The jeweler's phoned to tell me they couldn't get it done in time."

"I thought you were going to give it to her anyway?" He looks at me, frowning. "If you didn't go and pick it up, does that mean you don't have a present to give her?"

"I'll explain," I say. "She'll understand."

"Right." I can see he's disappointed. "It's just that I've heard people asking what you'd given her and she said that the party was enough. But I think everyone might be expecting you to give her something later. Do you have a photo of the ring? You could at least give her that."

"No. No, I don't."

"Well, could you maybe find a photo of something similar?"

"Yes, good idea," I say, glad of an excuse to get away. "I'll go and do that now."

"Don't be long!" he calls as I head toward the house. "I don't want to have to explain to everyone why you've gone missing!"

I go up to the bedroom, but instead of looking for a photo on my iPad, I sit down on the bed. Mimi is in her favorite place, watching me with those unblinking green eyes. Ignoring her, I take out my phone and sit staring at it for a moment. I should call the emergency number now. I should have called before. I don't know what the hell I'm doing, not calling.

A burst of laughter comes through the window and, glad of the excuse, I get to my feet and look outside. Nelson is standing in the middle of a group of people and I realize that he, or Kirin, has just announced that she's expecting twins. The music stops and then the song "Congratulations" starts playing. Everyone is applauding, and I'm struck by the terrible irony of the situation; there's been a plane crash, a crash that our daughter might have been part of, and people are singing along to "Congratulations," and applauding.

It hits me then, the enormity of what I've done. I've let the party go on. I've let people drink champagne and laugh and sing. I sink onto the bed and bury my face in my hands. What was I thinking? Mimi, sensing my distress, comes to investigate, but I push her away. She comes closer again, not used to my reaction, and I round on her.

"No, Mimi, leave it!"

She darts off the bed and I sink further. What have I done? I have to stop the party now, this minute, before it goes any further. I shouldn't have let it get this far; I should have canceled it before it had even started. Now, if the worst has happened, I'm going to have to go down and ask everyone to go home—and then tell them why.

I can't, I couldn't. My mind starts spiraling. Maybe I could ask Nelson. If I find out that Marnie was on the flight, maybe Nelson could tell everyone. So would I tell Nelson before I tell Livia? I get to my feet and start pacing the room. No, I need to tell Livia first, then Josh. Mum and Dad too, they should hear it from me, but once I've told Livia, once I've told Josh. Maybe I should include Izzy and Ian with Mum and Dad, because they're family too. Or should I tell them after, once I've told Livia, once I've told Josh, once I've told Mum and Dad? Or maybe leave Nelson to tell them along with everyone else?

And how will I tell them? There are no words. Even the thought is unthinkable.

And then—a ring of the doorbell. I whip around, staring at the bedroom door, my heart already racing. We're not expecting anyone else; all the guests have arrived. The bell sounds again, more timidly this time, as if whoever is on the other side of the door is having second thoughts about having pressed the bell the first time. Just as Marnie might do if she was worried that someone other than me might open the door and spoil the surprise. Just as Marnie might do if she'd gone around to the side gate and hadn't found me there, waiting to help her into the box.

I look down at my phone. It's 8:35, earlier than she was due to arrive—but what if she was put on a direct flight to London, straight from Cairo, like she'd said in her message this morning? I run down the stairs, stupidly near to tears. I could have saved myself so much anguish if I'd thought things through. Of course they'd try to get passengers stranded in Cairo to their final destination as quickly as possible. I fumble with the latch; I can already see myself hugging her, telling her that I thought she was on the plane that crashed.

I fling open the door.

"M—" Her name dies on my lips, and I stare in disbelief, because it isn't Marnie, but someone else. Someone smaller than Marnie, with darker hair, someone I know but whom, in my confusion, I can't place.

The young woman takes a sudden step back. "Hello, Mr. Harman," she says, flustered. "I hope it's all right that I'm here. We changed my grandad's celebration to tomorrow so that I could come to the party tonight. I didn't tell Josh because I wanted to surprise him. Maybe I should have let you or Mrs. Harman know. I—I didn't think. I'm sorry."

Josh's girlfriend, I realize dully. Not Marnie.

"Amy," I say.

I don't want her here. All I want is to slam the door in her face, scream at her to go away.

She looks behind me into the hall, her movement faltering when she sees my face.

"I'm sorry," she says again. "I should have called."

I stand back, not trusting myself to speak. She steps into the hallway and waits, hovering uncertainly.

"Well, go on through," I say roughly. "I'm sure Josh will be pleased to see you." She hurries off and I lean against the wall, adrenaline making my heart thump painfully. It's not her fault, I tell myself. It's not her fault she's not Marnie.

I walk slowly after her, and watch from the door as she tiptoes across the lawn, around groups of people, to where Josh is standing next to Max, his back to her. She reaches up and puts her hands over his eyes and when he swivels around, it's not Amy I see laughing at the look on his face, but Marnie, because she did the same to me, the time she came home unexpectedly from university to surprise me on my birthday. I can still feel the touch of her hands as she sneaked up behind me and covered my eyes.

"You OK, Adam?" Overwhelmed by the memory, it takes me a moment to realize that Nelson is talking to me.

I pull myself back to the present. "Yes, I'm fine. I didn't know she was coming, that's all."

"Amy?"

"Yes." I take a step onto the terrace, moving myself away from him. "Sorry, Nelson, I need to go and socialize."

I walk unsteadily up the steps. People crowd around, telling me what a wonderful party it is and how lovely Livia looks and isn't it a shame that Marnie isn't here. It becomes too much. I look around desperately—I shouldn't be here, none of us should be. And then I hear Livia laugh from somewhere behind me and when I turn, I see her standing in the middle of a group of her friends. She looks so beautiful, so happy, so—I search for the word—free.

And I know that I'm only going to make the call once the party is over.

Livia

There are so many people talking at the same time that I'm finding it hard to concentrate. Luckily the music is loud and I'm able to smile, laugh, and nod without anyone realizing how distracted I am. The effort needed to avoid Rob is beginning to weigh on me. I hate that I'm having to play this stupid game of cat and mouse at the party I've been waiting for, for so long. Tears prick my eyelids and I bow my head, blinking them away quickly.

Someone hands me a drink and, looking up, I see Ian, Izzy's husband.

"Thank you," I say gratefully.

"It must be quite overwhelming," he says, studying my face. We're the same height and his eyes, level with mine, are almost black. With Izzy being so extroverted, it's easy to overlook Ian, who is quieter and gentler. But he's one of my favorite people, even though, most of the time, I have no idea what he's really thinking.

"It's amazing to have everyone here," I tell him.

He nods. "But there are people missing."

My mind flits to Marnie, and away again, because it's too painful to think of her, then turns to my parents. They haven't come, of course they haven't, and I know they won't now.

"I thought my parents might come," I say. "I invited them. Stupid, I know."

"It's not stupid," he replies, and I want to hug him. "I'm sorry they haven't turned up."

"If my fortieth birthday isn't enough of a reason for them to hold out an olive branch, there's not much more I can do," I say with a shrug. "I can't believe they still hold a grudge after all these years."

"Time can either mend bridges or push them further apart," he says.

I look quizzically at him. "What made you so wise?"

"Being with Izzy, probably."

We laugh softly and, with a quick smile, he goes to get himself another drink. I take a sip of the one he gave me, knowing it's time to stop wishing for something that will never happen. It's too late, anyway. What I wanted was for my parents to be part of Josh's and Marnie's lives. But Josh and Marnie have already left home; they have their own lives, which might not have room for grandparents they barely know. My mother is sixty-eight now, my father seventy-two. Ian is right, time hasn't mended anything between us. Their hearts will only harden more with age, not soften.

"Livia!" A hand touches my arm. I turn and see Paula looking fabulous in a long floaty dress. She's carrying silver heels in her hand and her face is flushed from dancing.

"Hello, Paula," I say, giving her a hug. "It's lovely to see you. Are you having a good time?"

"Yes, it's so nice to be able to catch up with everybody from the office. I've missed them."

"So, how are you?" I say, prepared to give her my full attention because I know how lonely she is now that she's retired and has no close family nearby.

While she talks about the book club she's recently become a member of, I keep my eye out for Rob. At one point I see him heading my way, but when he sees I'm with Paula, he turns back quickly. She's joined us a couple of times for lunch on the weekends, so he's met her before and knows how much she loves to talk. He couldn't possibly have anyone talk more than he does, could he?

From the lawn I hear Josh announce that the next song is some-one's choice and that we have to guess whose it is.

"I know this one," Paula says as it begins to play. "It's 'We Are Family.'"

She takes my hand and pulls me to where a group of people are dancing.

"It has to be Kirin," I say. "Look at the way she's grinning." I point at Kirin. "It's Kirin!" I shout.

Josh gives me the thumbs-up and people clap and laugh as Nelson races across the lawn, dodging around people, to scoop Kirin into his arms.

"*We are family,*" he sings. "*I got all my daughters with me!*"

"I wish I had my sons with me," Paula says sadly. "I hate that they're living so far away."

Before I can reply, Jeannie comes over, wanting, I'm guessing, to talk about Nelson and Kirin having another set of twins.

"Five children!" she says, laughing, and I can see Adam so clearly in her face when she smiles. "He's going to have to swap that great big motorbike of his for a people carrier."

"I think he'd rather sell the house than his motorbike," I joke.

"He'll probably have to sell it anyway. Kirin was saying she doesn't know where she'll put another two babies—to which Nelson re-plied that there's a perfectly good shed in the garden!"

Somebody comes onto the terrace and I crane my neck around Jeannie, expecting to see Adam. But it's Amy and my delight at seeing her—because I know how happy Josh will be that she's here—is short-lived when I see the look on her face. Something has obviously upset her and I hope it's not to do with her grand-father.

I'm about to go over to her, when she runs up the steps and tiptoes toward Josh. She puts her hands over his eyes, her frown replaced by a smile, and I laugh at Josh's surprise. But then she says something and they both look toward the kitchen, where Adam is standing in the doorway. He must have let Amy in, I realize.

I excuse myself to Jeannie and Paula, intending to go to him. But Nelson beats me to it, so I make my way over to Josh and Amy instead.

"Hello, Amy," I say, aware that Max has moved away. "It's lovely to see you. I didn't think you'd be able to come."

"Happy birthday!" she says, hugging me. "My mum told my grandfather about your party and he insisted I come. He said that at his age it didn't matter if we didn't celebrate his birthday on the day, so we're having his party tomorrow afternoon instead."

"That's lovely of him. Well, I'm very glad you're here."

"I'm not sure Mr. Harman is," she says, the frown returning to her pretty face.

"What do you mean?"

"Just that he didn't seem very happy to see me."

Josh turns to me. "You didn't tell him, did you, Mum?"

"No, of course not."

"Well, he must have found out somehow. There's no reason for him to have been off with Amy otherwise."

"Why don't you go and speak to him?"

"What, now?"

"No time like the present," I say lightly.

"He's going to be so disappointed," Josh mutters.

"He'll understand."

"I'm not so sure."

"You won't know until you talk to him."

"Go on," Amy says, giving him a little push. "You may as well get it over and done with."

He goes off reluctantly and, feeling eyes on me, I realize that Max wants to speak to Amy and is waiting for me to leave.

"I'd better go and circulate," I say, giving Amy a quick smile. "I'll see you later."

I turn away and see Rob only yards from me. I want to run, but like a rabbit caught in the glare of a car's headlights, I don't seem to be able to move. And then Max, coming over to talk to Amy, walks clumsily into Rob with his rugby-player build and knocks him momentarily off balance.

"You drunk already?" I hear him say good-naturedly to Max, because that's Rob, everyone's best friend. I don't stay around to hear the rest of their conversation, but duck into the empty tent, needing a few minutes on my own.

I press my palms to my face, feeling the heat in my cheeks. I must have been mad to think I was going to be able to avoid Rob this evening. At some point we're going to come face-to-face. He's not going to stop seeking me out, because he won't know why he shouldn't. What I should have done, I realize with hindsight, was email him yesterday and tell him not to come tonight, to pretend he was ill so that Jess could still come, because I know about him and Marnie.

But he'd have told Marnie that I know, and I need to speak to her, to get her side of the story before Rob tells her what to say, before she has time to prepare to lie about how and when it all started, if only to protect Rob. And while she's caught unawares, I want to ask her if she realizes the full extent of what she's done, because I can't believe that she does. I can't believe that she's gone into this relationship with Rob with her eyes wide open. She can't have realized that once their affair becomes common knowledge, Adam will never speak to Rob again, which will affect his friendship with Nelson. She can't have realized that Nelson might never speak to Rob again, which will affect their whole family. She can't know that Jess might never speak to me again, or realize that Kirin's loyalties will be torn because Jess is her sister-in-law. She can't know that Josh will be horrified at what she's done, or realize that for Cleo to know her best friend is having an affair with her father will be devastating. It isn't possible that Marnie has realized any of this, because if she has, I don't think I could ever forgive her.

9 P.M.–10 P.M.

Adam

"Dad?"

I turn my attention away from Izzy. "Yes, Josh?"

"Sorry to interrupt. Aunt Izzy, can I borrow Dad for a minute?"

"Sure. And make him take something for that migraine. He looks terrible."

"Shall we go to your shed?" Josh suggests.

As I turn to follow him, I see Amy talking to Rob and Max, and notice that although Max seems to be listening, he's actually staring over their shoulders at something or someone. I follow his eyes and see that they're fixed on Livia, who is disappearing into the tent. The way he's looking at her makes me pause, throws my mind off balance. What is going on with Livia and Max?

"Are you coming, Dad?"

We push our way into the shed. Josh leans back against the workbench, his arms folded in front of him. I remember now that I'm meant to have found a photo of the ring to give Livia.

"I didn't find one," I say.

"What?"

"A photo."

He takes a really deep breath. "Sorry, Dad, but I'm not going."

"Not going where?" I say. Does he really think that I want him to go and pick up the ring, even though the shop is shut?

"To New York."

"New York?"

"Yes. I don't want to take up my internship."

It's so far removed from what I thought he was going to say that it takes me a moment to catch up.

"Right," I say. "OK."

He pushes away from the bench and begins pacing up and down. "I know you must be disappointed. And I know my reason for not going is a bit pathetic. The thing is, I love Amy and I don't want to be apart from her for a year. It's been hard enough these last six months with me in Bristol and her in Exeter." He gives an embarrassed laugh. "I think she's the one, Dad, I really do. I know I'm only twenty-two—well, nearly twenty-three—and I haven't known her very long, but there's something about Amy—"

"Josh," I say, stopping him. "It's fine. It's not a problem. If you don't want to go to New York, don't go."

He stares, relief washing over his face. "Really?"

"Yes." I swallow painfully. "Life's too short. Just do what makes you happy."

He shakes his head slowly. "You wouldn't believe how worried I've been about telling you."

"Why?"

"Because you found me the internship."

"That doesn't mean you have to take it."

He runs a hand through his hair. "I must seem so ungrateful."

"Not at all." A wave of exhaustion comes over me. "Look, can we talk about this later? I don't know—maybe Bill can switch your internship to London—I presume that's where you want to be, near Amy?"

"Yes. Marnie is with me on this one, by the way. She says it's not worth going abroad if I spend most of my time there being miserable."

Marnie. "Let's talk tomorrow," I say. "We'd better get back out there."

"I need to go and find Amy. She thinks you're annoyed with her, that you think it's her fault I don't want to go to New York."

"Then please tell her I'm not."

He looks at me curiously. "So why were you off with her when she arrived, if you didn't know?"

"It's this migraine, that's all."

"Thanks, Dad." He comes over and gives me an unexpected hug. "You really are the best."

He leaves and I stand there, trying to process what he just told me. It seems so unimportant compared to Marnie. Would I really have been disappointed—bitter, even—if he'd told me any day before today that he wasn't taking up the internship? Probably.

I leave my shed. I'm desperate to know what time it is, but for the first time tonight, I can't face checking my phone. Amy arrived around 8:35, that I know. Then I was stopped by Nelson; then I spoke to another couple of people, got them a drink, made sure Jess was all right, got her and Kirin a drink—all that must have taken thirty minutes. Then Izzy cornered me for at least ten minutes, then Josh for another ten. It must be around half-past nine. In the world I inhabited before, Marnie would have arrived. I'd have gotten her text saying she was at the gate, I'd have met her at the side door and, after a quick, secret hug, I'd have taken the box from under the table and helped her into it. And now, right now, we'd all be down on the terrace.

I walk across the lawn, vaguely aware of Livia disappearing into the house with Max. I keep my eyes fixed ahead so that I don't get ambushed by people wanting to chat, and when I get to the top of the steps, I pause. In my mind, I see everyone gathered on the terrace below, waiting for Livia to open her present. I'm standing next to her and as she bends to open the box, Marnie springs out. Everyone is laughing and exclaiming and Livia, after hugging Marnie until they are both in tears, throws her arms around me and tells me it's the best present ever. I see everything. And then I see nothing.

Except—someone is coming in the side gate, pushing it slowly open. My heart starts racing, just as it did when Amy rang the doorbell. *Don't get your hopes up,* I tell myself. *You'll only be disappointed.* But I'm already running down the steps and across the terrace.

I get to the gate and jerk at it, the wood sticking as I pull it open. And then I stop. Because it's not Marnie. My body slumps against the wooden panels. I bite down hard on the inside of my mouth until I taste blood, and stare at an older woman I've never seen before.

"Hello, Adam," she says, and, recognizing her voice, I realize that I'm looking at Livia's mother.

"Patricia," I say dully.

"I received your letter." She waits for me to say something. "And an invitation for tonight," she says when I don't respond. "I'd like to see Livia, if that's all right."

A wave of panic sweeps through me. Is this something else I've gotten wrong? What if Livia doesn't want to see her mother, not here, not now, not at her party? And what if her mother hasn't come to make peace, but to cause more trouble?

She tries again. "I won't stay long; I have a car waiting for me."

"I don't want any trouble," I say, finding my voice. "It's a special day for Livia."

"Yes, I know."

"No, you don't know," I say roughly. "This party is to make up for the wedding she never had."

Her face flushes. "I wish things could have been different."

"So why are they now?"

She holds my gaze. "Her father died a few months back."

She doesn't say anything more, but it's enough. Livia's father was a domineering bully and, when I think about it now, he was the one who told Livia they didn't want anything more to do with her. Maybe her mother didn't have a choice. I look at her more closely. It's not surprising I didn't recognize her. Her hair was always pulled back in a severe bun; now it hangs to her shoulders in soft waves.

"I'm not sure today's the right time to tell her," I say, wishing more than ever that I hadn't written that letter.

"I'd still like to see her," she says, standing her ground. "Josh and Marnie too, just to say hello. Has Marnie arrived yet?"

Livia

The best thing about so many people being at the party is that nobody has noticed I've been missing for a while. I might have stayed in the tent longer, but Liz and her team started bringing the food in and now people are serving themselves. I duck out of the tent and take a quick look around. Josh is with Amy and Max, and Rob is, thankfully, nowhere to be seen. But safety is in numbers, and spotting a group of my work friends chatting together, I go over. At the same time as I'm encouraging them to go and have something to eat, I'm wondering how Adam took the news that Josh doesn't want to go the States. Fortunately for Josh, his dad's disappointment will soon be trumped by something bigger.

During my time alone in the tent, I was trying to work out whether it would be better to wait until we're in France to tell Adam about Marnie and Rob. I have visions of him jumping on his motorbike and riding off to find Rob, then beating the hell out of him, and although the thought is viciously pleasing, I can't risk him doing that. If we're not in the same country, the fallout will be less immediate, so hopefully less traumatic for everyone. And again, there's that thing—if I tell him as soon as the party is over, he'll think I didn't tell him before because I wanted it to go ahead, no matter what.

I look around and see Cleo sitting on the wall, taking a rest from dancing. I go over and sit down beside her.

"How's my favorite goddaughter?" I ask, putting my arm around her and giving her a hug.

"Happy birthday, Livia," she says, hugging me back. "Are you having a nice day?"

"The best," I tell her.

"I'm sorry I didn't come and say hello when I arrived, but you always seemed to be with someone."

"No one as important as you. Thank you for coming. It's bad enough Marnie's not here." I know I should ask her if she had a nice time in Hong Kong, because it will be strange if I don't, but I hate that the only reason Rob took her there was so that he and Marnie could be together.

"Did you have a good time in Hong Kong?" I ask anyway.

"Yes, it was lovely to see Marnie, although she was at school more than I expected. And Dad ended up having to work, so I spent a lot of time on my own."

How could you, Marnie, I think, *how could you?*

"So, how's life?"

She makes a face. "I think Charlie might be cheating on me. Otherwise, everything's fine."

"Oh, Cleo, I'm sorry. Do you want me to sort him out for you?" I add, trying to lighten the moment.

She smiles. "You sound like Dad."

She couldn't have said anything worse. Rage rises inside me at Rob threatening to sort out his daughter's boyfriend, who might or might not be cheating on her, when he's having an affair with my daughter—his daughter's best friend.

"I love your dress," I say, to hide the fact that I've stood up abruptly. "I'd better go and find Adam, I've barely seen him since the party started. He keeps doing a disappearing act."

"Mum says he's got a migraine."

I nod. "Maybe if I can get him to eat something, he'll feel better. I'll catch you later."

"Enjoy your party!" she calls after me.

"Thank you!"

I move to the center of the lawn and slowly turn myself in a circle, hoping to spot Adam. An arm snakes around my waist.

"Hello, birthday girl. Have you been avoiding me?"

It's here, the moment I've been dreading. My flesh crawls at the touch of his hand. He's always been a flirt—maybe another reason why Adam doesn't particularly like him—and although it bothered me for Jess, I always went along with it. It's how Rob is, how he's always been. But now I'm overwhelmed with disgust at the thought that he has touched me, hugged me, and kissed me in that lingering way of his, when he was also touching, hugging, and kissing my daughter. White-hot anger flares inside me. I wrench my body around, dislodging his arm roughly.

"Hey, what's up?" he asks, looking at me in confusion.

The urge to lunge at him, slap him, scratch him, scream at him is stronger than anything I've ever felt. I take a step toward him, my teeth and fist clenched. But before I can do anything, someone takes hold of my wrist and pulls me back, away from Rob.

"Sorry, Rob." Max's voice comes from behind me. "Livia is needed in the kitchen. Something to do with the desserts melting, apparently."

Rob presses his hands together in a prayer. "Please don't let anything happen to the desserts, Livia. You know how much I love a good dessert!"

It's incredible the way he's able to tell himself that the look on my face couldn't possibly be anything to do with him, because isn't he such a good guy and anyway, nobody could possibly know about him and Marnie because everyone is gullible enough to take both him and what he says at face value.

I'm still seething as Max walks me to the kitchen. There's no sign of Liz.

"She must be in the dining room," Max says, leading me through. She's not there either, but my thoughts are too full of Rob to register that anything is wrong until Max closes the door and leans against it, stopping anyone from coming in.

"What are you doing, Max?" I ask. But I know what he's doing; I just can't believe that he's chosen my party to ask me why I've been off with him for the last few months. "I really need to get back out there."

He doesn't say anything, just looks at me, his blue eyes boring into me, weighing me up.

"Look, I'm sorry if I've been off with you lately," I say impatiently. "I've just been defending Marnie because I know the two of you have fallen out. I know I shouldn't take sides, but Marnie's had a bit of a difficult time lately and I thought—" I stop, because how can I tell him that I thought he and Marnie were in a relationship?

"Go on," he says.

"I thought maybe you wanted a relationship with her and she didn't," I say.

Max frowns. "Gross. Marnie's like a sister to me. Which is why I'm so bloody angry with her!" It bursts out of him. "I know, Livia. I know about her and Rob."

My heart misses a beat. "What do you mean?"

He looks at me in alarm. "Oh God, don't tell me you don't know. I thought, because of the way you've been avoiding Rob all evening, and the way you looked as if you were about to kill him just now, that you knew." He runs a hand through his hair. "Shit."

I lay a hand on his arm. "It's OK, Max, I do know. I just didn't think that anyone else did. How did you find out?"

The relief that washes over him is quickly replaced by anger. "I went to surprise Marnie once in Durham and I saw them together."

"When?"

"About a year ago. Maybe a bit more—March, I think."

Not long after Rob began spending two days a week in Darlington, I realize bitterly.

"Why didn't you say anything to me or Adam?"

"Because when I asked Marnie about it, she said I'd made a mistake. When I told her what I'd seen, she said it was a moment of madness and that it was all over. And I believed her—until last December, when Josh mentioned that Rob's company was sending him to Singapore for a week. I know it's not that close to Hong Kong, but it made me suspicious, because why was he suddenly going to Singapore? I looked up the company and they do have offices there. But it still didn't feel right; I couldn't stop wondering if he was going to see Marnie, so I emailed her and asked if I could visit her around the time of Rob's trip to Singapore. And she did everything to put me off, telling me first that she had to work on her assignment, then that she was going away."

Remembering how Marnie had involved me in that particular lie, I close my eyes. *I don't want him here,* she'd said, which had made me think that Max was the father of the baby she'd lost. Had she known I'd jump to that conclusion, had she said it on purpose so that I'd lie for her?

"I ended up phoning Rob's office, the week he was meant to be in Singapore, asking to speak to him," Max goes on. "They told me he was away on holiday. So I phoned Marnie and asked her straight up if he was with her. She said—I'll give you the polite version— that it was nothing to do with me, and hung up on me. I haven't spoken to her since."

"I'm sorry, Max," I say helplessly.

"I knew I should say something to you, but I couldn't. I mean, Marnie was right, it wasn't really my problem and I didn't have actual proof that he was there." He pauses. "How long have you known?"

"Since he and Cleo went to see Marnie for Cleo's birthday. I FaceTimed her and saw him, in the background, he was—" I stumble over the memory and the word *naked.* "She doesn't know that I know. I need to speak to Adam first."

"Why haven't you? Sorry, but I couldn't believe it when I asked Josh if Rob and Jess were coming tonight and he told me they were. I thought that neither of you must know, especially when I saw that Adam was all right with Rob. And then I saw that you weren't. I'm glad Josh doesn't know; he'd probably kill Rob. Even I want to kill him."

"Adam will too—which is why I'm worried about telling him. It's not only that, though, it's also Marnie. Adam is going to be devastated. She's always been up there on a pedestal for him."

Max shakes his head. "I can't believe she's been so stupid. Sorry," he says, looking guilty.

"Don't apologize. I'm furious with her too."

"You are going to tell Adam, right?"

"Yes, once the party is over. I just wanted us all to have this one last time together." He nods, but I'm not sure he understands.

"I'm scared of what it's going to do to us all," I say, moving toward the door. "I'd better get back out there. And thanks, Max, for stopping me from breaking Rob's face. I will at some point—but my party isn't the time or place to do it."

I walk back outside and see Adam at the side gate, talking to an elderly woman, and I hope she hasn't come to complain about the noise. I pushed a note through the letterbox of every nearby house, warning them that there would be music until 3:00 A.M. Adam looks as if he needs rescuing, so I go over.

"Adam?" I say. "Is everything all right?"

10 P.M.–11 P.M.

Adam

I make my way back to Livia's mother, whom I'd left at the side gate while I went to find Livia.

Remembering that I'd seen her going into the house with Max a few minutes before, I headed inside and heard them talking in the dining room. I was about to open the door when I heard my name, Max saying, *You are going to tell Adam, right?* And instead of interrupting, I stood there, trying to listen to what they were saying, until Livia said she needed to get back to the party.

Now I wish I'd just opened the damned door, because I can't think what Liv might need to tell me. She said something about wanting us all to have this one last time together, but she can't know about Marnie, she can't; she would never do what I've done. The weight of it is so heavy it's a struggle to breathe. I want to be on my own, I want to go upstairs and hide myself away. But Livia's mother is looking at me expectantly.

"She was with someone," I say. "I didn't like to interrupt. But she'll be out in a minute."

"Thank you."

How am I going to be able to warn Livia that her mother is here before she comes out and sees her?

"Adam?" I whip round at the sound of her voice behind me. "Is everything all right?"

I move quickly to block her mother from view, wanting to prepare her.

"There's someone to see you," I say hesitantly.

The color drains from her face because she's guessed, maybe from the strained look on mine, whom I'm referring to.

Neither of us seems able to move, so Livia's mother steps out from behind me.

"Hello, Livia." And as her eyes fall on the daughter she hasn't seen for twenty-two years, they fill with tears.

For a moment Livia just stares. "*Mum?*" She takes a step toward her, as if she can't quite believe what she's seeing and needs to take a closer look. She looks so confused I want to fold her in my arms. "Is that really you?"

Livia's mum raises her hand and touches her hair self-consciously.

"Yes. I thought I'd come and wish you a happy birthday," she says, attempting a smile.

Livia looks behind her. "Is Dad here?"

I turn to the table, where the box is waiting for Marnie, and pull out the two chairs that Livia and I sat on to drink Kirin's champagne.

"Why don't the two of you sit here?" I suggest, and they move slowly toward the table, their eyes still on each other. "Call me if you need me," I tell Livia, giving her a kiss. "I won't be far."

At the top of the steps, I bump straight into Mum, who, without a word, drags me over to where Izzy and Ian are sitting with Jess, Rob, Nelson, and Kirin.

"Sit down," she says, pushing me onto a chair. "I'll get you something to eat."

I fall into the chair. My elbows find the table and I put my head in my hands.

"Everything all right, Adam?" Jess asks.

"Livia's mother just arrived," I say, forcing my head up.

"What?" Kirin almost spills her water.

"Oh gosh, is she OK?" Jess asks worriedly.

Nelson gives me a glass of wine and I take it, my fingers fumbling on the stem.

"I think so. I left her down on the terrace."

"What, with that old battleax?" Rob says. "Was that wise of you?"

I'm so tired I can't find the energy to shut him down. "She seems different. Livia's father is dead, apparently."

"Oh no. Poor Livia!" Kirin looks upset.

"No great loss, if you ask me," Rob says. "He was always a miserable bastard."

He says it as if he knew Livia's father, when I know he never actually met him. I take a sip of wine, then finish the whole glass in one gulp. The alcohol mixes with my exhaustion and begins to numb the fear of never seeing Marnie again. *She can't have been on the plane that crashed,* I tell myself, the alcohol making me bold. *I'd know if something had happened to her, I'd just know.*

Kirin and Izzy are discussing Patricia's arrival, their voices rushed. When Patricia asked me if Marnie had arrived, I told her the flight had been delayed and that she wouldn't be arriving until after midnight. And reminded her not to say anything to Livia.

I've told so many lies tonight. I reach for my glass, then remember it's empty.

"Adam, did you hear me?"

I look across the table at Rob. He's lounging back in his chair, his right foot raised and resting on his left leg, his hands behind his head.

"Sorry?"

"I asked if you ever believed that Aldershot would beat Leeds in the third round of the FA Cup."

I struggle to follow what he's saying. "What?"

"Come on, Rob, of course they never would have!" Nelson says from across the table.

Rob's face momentarily hardens. "I was asking Adam," he says. "Anyway," he adds, his features flipping back into a smile, "Leeds would have beaten Aldershot if the referee hadn't been biased. And then they'd have slaughtered Man United!"

A few people laugh and I feel a weird sense of disorientation. I can't believe that I'm sitting here, listening to people talking about soccer. I need to move. I can't stay here.

I'm pushing my chair back when the words *plane crash* slam into my consciousness. My heart misses a beat and I stare at Rob, because I'm sure it was he who uttered the words. But he's looking at Ian, not me.

"You mean the Pyramid Air flight?" Ian asks. "Yes, I saw it on the news. It's heartbreaking."

"I didn't read any of the news reports, it's too sad," Jess says.

"It crashed on takeoff from Cairo," Rob explains, leaning forward. "It was on its way to Amsterdam. Around two hundred and fifty people on board. No survivors, apparently."

Jess shivers and pulls a shawl over her shoulders. "I hate flying. That's why I didn't want to go to Hong Kong. That, and Rob not wanting me to go."

"Only because I thought the flight would be too much for you," Rob says, putting his hand on her knee.

"I hate flying too," Izzy says. "Every time I hear about a crash, I vow never to get on a plane again. I always do, though."

"Let's change the subject, shall we?" Ian suggests. "It doesn't seem right that we're sitting here drinking and chatting when so many people will be grieving."

"You're right—but life's too short," Rob says. "And it has to go on." He lifts his glass. "Cheers."

There's a sound of breaking glass and I feel a stab of pain. Looking down, I see that the wineglass has shattered in my hand.

"Adam! You're bleeding!" Izzy cries.

As well as bleeding, my hand is also shaking uncontrollably. Grabbing a napkin, I cover it and stand up. "I need to go and get this sorted."

"Do you want me to come with you?"

"No, please don't, it's fine."

"Adam? What's happened?"

I look up and see Livia standing in front of me. *I think Marnie might have been on the plane that crashed, Livia. That's what's happened.*

"He cut himself on a glass," Izzy says. "He's OK, he's going to clean it up."

Livia pulls the napkin from my hand. "Ouch," she says, peering at the gash. "It's deep. It must hurt."

"Are *you* all right, Livia?" Jess asks.

"Yes, I'm fine."

"Adam says your mum is here?"

Livia smiles at her "Was. She just left."

"How did it go?" Kirin asks carefully, as if she's almost afraid to ask.

Livia's breath catches. "Fine, I think."

"So, a bridge mended," Ian says, nodding.

"It's early days." Livia turns to me. "Come on, let me have a proper look at your hand."

I follow her over to the wall. We sit side by side and she takes my hand in hers. If there weren't so many people in the way, we'd be able to see the photos of Marnie.

The gentle touch of her fingers and the sharp physical pain as she probes the wound make everything recede until there's no Marnie, no people, no noise, no party, just me and Livia.

"It should be all right," she says, inspecting the napkin for a clean bit, then pressing it onto the cut and closing my hand over it to keep it in place. "You'll need to disinfect it, though." She reaches up and places her hand on my cheek. "You OK?"

"I forgot to shave, sorry."

"Don't be sorry. I like you exactly as you are."

"What about you, are you all right? With your mother turning up?"

She nods slowly. "She said that you wrote to her."

"I thought I was doing the right thing—but now I don't know."

"You did do the right thing. Thank you." She reaches up and kisses me.

"Your father?"

"I'm glad he's dead," she says fiercely. "I know I shouldn't say that, but I am. If he'd still been alive, Mum wouldn't have been able to come tonight. She told me something of what her life was like with him. I didn't realize how much she was under his control. I was too young to notice, I suppose. I thought she was happy that he was the one who made all the decisions, but it seems she didn't have a choice."

"I'm glad you're pleased she turned up. But you will be careful, won't you?"

"Don't worry, I'm not going to fall into her arms or anything. We need to take it step by step. But she'd like to meet Josh before he leaves tomorrow evening." She turns to me. "She's staying with the Graingers. Do you remember them? It was Irene who brought her over tonight. Mum told me she nearly didn't come, that she lost her courage, but Irene persuaded her to, told her she'd regret it. She was waiting outside in the car, which is why Mum couldn't stay longer. Would you mind if she came over tomorrow afternoon, just for an hour?"

"Of course not," I say. I try to hold an image in my mind, of Livia's mum sitting on the sofa tomorrow afternoon with Josh and Marnie on either side of her. I need so much to believe it will happen.

"So, are you happy?" I go on, needing her to say it, because if she's happy, I can live with the decision I made not to say anything about Marnie.

"Ridiculously happy," she says, smiling up at me, her eyes bright with unshed tears. She lifts her hand and rests it against my cheek. "This is a new beginning for me, Adam. Thank you for making it happen."

Her words cut through me like a knife.

"Are you two lovebirds going to sit there all night?" a voice calls.

"Aren't you meant to be socializing? Adam, your mum's brought your food over. Come back here!"

Livia tenses at Rob's clumsy interruption.

"Come on, we'd better get back to the party."

I nod. "You go and sit with Jess and the others while I sort out my hand."

"No!" She says it so forcefully that I flinch. She gives me a weak smile. "I'd better go and chat with the neighbors."

She starts moving away, but I catch hold of her and draw her toward me.

"Is tonight everything you wanted it to be?"

"It's more than I wanted it to be, if that's possible," she says, wrapping her arms around me and leaning her head against my chest. "Except for Marnie."

A strange weakness comes over me, and if Livia hadn't been holding me, my legs might have given way. Adrenaline kicks back in.

"I know it might not seem like it," she says. "But sometimes things happen for a reason."

Is that what Josh not going to New York is—a reason? A reason for us to be able to carry on without Marnie, because we'll have Josh close by, instead of on another continent?

"Like Mum turning up," Livia goes on. "I know she felt able to come because Dad died, but why did he die now, why not years ago, when she could have gotten to know Josh and Marnie? There must be a reason why she's turned up now, at this moment in time, when it's almost too late to have a relationship with them." She pauses. "She wants to move back to the area, by the way."

Did fate have a hand in her mum turning up tonight? I'm not giving up on Marnie; I could never do that. But there's a small comfort in the thought that if the very worst has happened—if Marnie doesn't make it home—Livia will have her mother nearby.

Livia

"Great party, Livia," Nelson says, smiling at me through his bushy beard. His eyes search my face. "It must have been weird with your mother turning up."

"It was, especially as I didn't recognize her at first. But I'm glad she did. It all came from my father, you know, and she had no choice but to go along with it. It's awful to say, but his death has liberated her. I'm not saying it's going to be easy, but her turning up has been the icing on the cake of this lovely, lovely evening." And then I remember. "Congratulations, by the way. It's wonderful news!"

"It is—but I'm still trying to get my head around it." A slight frown crosses his face. "Livia, is Adam all right?"

"Yes, apart from his migraine. Why?"

"It's just that he didn't tease me about being a dad of five."

"Don't worry, I'm sure he'll get around to it," I say, laughing. Something behind me catches his eye and, turning, I see that he's watching Jess.

"How do you think Jess is?" he asks. "You haven't seen her for a few weeks—did you find a change in her when you went out for lunch today?"

"I found her quite frail," I say. "More unsteady on her feet than before."

He nods slowly. "I think she's gone downhill fast, and so does Kirin, but when I tried to talk to Rob about it, he said that wasn't the case at all. I think he's in denial."

And I think he's a dirty fat cheat, I rant silently.

"He actually said that she's becoming more independent by the day, and that she can manage perfectly on her own. That worried me a bit. Well, a lot actually, although I'm not sure why."

A chill goes down my spine. Please, please don't let me be right about Rob planning to leave Jess for Marnie.

"It seemed a strange thing to say," Nelson goes on. "Maybe his bosses are putting pressure on him to travel again and he's trying to convince himself that Jess will be all right without him."

No, he's preparing us, I realize. He's preparing us so that the day he does leave Jess, he'll say he thought she could manage without him.

"I'm worried about him," Nelson finishes. "Sorry, Livia, I shouldn't have bothered you with this tonight, of all nights."

"It's fine. I'm just glad everybody is here together." *For maybe the last time,* I want to add, and for one crazy moment I want to tell Nelson what Rob has done and what I'm scared he's going to do.

"Except Marnie," he says.

"Yes, except Marnie."

But I can't tell Nelson, not until I've spoken to Adam. For now, it's enough that Max knows, enough that someone is as appalled as I am. It was depressing to have it confirmed that Rob was actually in Hong Kong with Marnie last December, not in Singapore. I'd hoped I'd been wrong about that, I'd hoped that he hadn't lied to Jess, to us, about being on a business trip, to start up his affair with Marnie again. Why couldn't he have left her alone?

Nelson gives my arm a squeeze. "I'll catch you later."

As he moves off, I try to imagine what it would have been like if Marnie hadn't had a miscarriage and had gone on to have Rob's baby. I see now why she didn't want Josh to know about the miscarriage. She would have been worried that he'd tell Max, and that because Max had seen her and Rob together in Durham, he'd have guessed Rob was the father. He might have had reservations about telling me and Adam about their affair, but if he knew there was a baby, he'd have been more likely to tell us.

Again, I feel a flicker of sympathy for my parents—or rather, my father, because maybe Mum would have been all right about me being pregnant if it hadn't been for him. My pregnancy must have seemed the worst possible thing that could happen, the end of his world as he knew it. The difference is that I'm afraid for those I love, while he was only afraid for himself, how it would look to other people.

"Livvy?" I look up and see Mike, his brow crinkled with concern, his tall frame stooped toward me. I love that he came in a jacket and tie tonight, though he's taken both off now. "Are you all right?"

"Never been better," I say, pushing Marnie and Rob to the back of my mind. Jeannie comes over and I put my arms around both of them. "Did you know that Mum turned up?"

"Yes, we heard," Jeannie says. "We're so glad for you, Livvy."

"I still can't believe it. It's the one thing I was really hoping for tonight, that my parents would turn up. If they hadn't, I was prepared to give up on the dream that we'd be reconciled one day. And now my dream has come true, and it's the best feeling ever." I reach up and kiss their cheeks, first Jeannie, then Mike. "I'm so lucky to have you both. I don't know what I'd have done without you over the years. You've been wonderful parents to me."

"We're always here to help, you know that," Mike says.

"I do, and I love you for it. Did Josh tell you that he's decided not to go to New York?"

"Yes, he did. I guess it must have been a bit of a disappointment for Adam. When he phoned this afternoon, I knew he had something on his mind."

"It couldn't have been that, because Josh only told him tonight," I say, puzzled. "Didn't he say why he was calling?"

"No, not really. It felt as if he was all at sea about something."

"I think this party may be the reason," I say ruefully. "He's been more worried about it than I have. He knows how important it is to me, and maybe the pressure got to him. And"—I lower my voice— "I think there's a bit of a problem with my present. Josh gave me the heads-up so that I won't be disappointed. Not that I would be."

Mike nods. "That'll be it. You know Adam, he'll be livid if something has happened, which means that today will be less than perfect. Oh, this is my song choice," he says as "Uptown Girl" starts playing. He holds his arm out to Jeannie. "May I escort you to the dance floor?"

Mike and Jeannie are hugely popular, and as everyone crowds around to watch them dancing together, I take advantage of a few more moments of solitude. I still can't quite believe Mum turned up. It was so strange to see her standing there, because whenever I tried to imagine our reconciliation, I pictured her as I remembered her: her hair drawn back in a bun, her face unsmiling, my father looming over her both physically and—I realize now—mentally. And I hadn't allowed for her having aged. Bizarrely, though, she seems younger, maybe because of the way she has her hair now. She told me she got it cut the day after my father's funeral because as she watched his coffin disappear into the ground, it dawned on her that she was free, that she could do as she liked without having to defer to him for everything. She said that even though she loved my father, she'd felt a great weight lifting from her shoulders.

Mum isn't the only one feeling lighter. It's not just because the need to be reconciled with my parents—a need so raw it hurt— has finally gone. It's because soon, in a few hours, I'll be free of something else that's dominated my life for years, and that's this party. I might not have thought about it every day of those twenty years, but definitely every week. If I saw a beautiful dress in a shop, I'd wonder if it was the kind of dress I might like for my party. If I tasted a delicious dish, I'd think about having it on the menu. If I came across ideas for decorations in a magazine, I'd wonder if I should have something similar. I couldn't get away from my party. It was always there, not necessarily in a bad way, but taking up space in my mind. And now that it's here, now that it's everything I dreamed of, despite Rob, a part of me can't wait until tomorrow evening, when the tent is down, when the last of the food has been eaten, and when everybody has left. And then it'll just be me and Adam.

11 P.M.–12 A.M.

Adam

I can't stay in the bathroom forever. I've been here too long, standing at the sink, watching the blood seep from the gash across my palm, feeling nothing. The throb of the music outside matches the pounding in my head. I'm so close to the edge that I want to go out to the garden and scream at everyone to get the hell out of our house. To stop myself, I imagine the carnage it would cause—everyone staring at me in alarm, then Livia, my dad, Josh, Nelson trying to calm me, asking me what's wrong, worried that I'm having some kind of breakdown.

Would I be able to keep it inside me, the news that Marnie might have been on the plane that crashed? Or would I scream out my pain and anger, tell them that I hate them all, because they're alive and Marnie might be dead? They'd be horrified, devastated. And no one would understand, not even for a second, why I let the party go on.

I hear feet on the stairs. Josh.

"Dad? Where are you?"

I clench my hand, feel the warmth of blood. "Just patching up a cut!"

His voice comes through the door. "I've been looking for you everywhere."

"I'll be right down."

"Two minutes?"

"Yes, two minutes."

"OK. I need you there."

His footsteps thunder down the stairs. I haven't given much thought to Josh in all this, I realize, about how losing Marnie will affect him. But I can't go there now. And there's still hope. I need to believe that there's still hope.

I splash some water on my face and make my way down, trying to avoid looking at Marnie's bedroom door. I'm halfway down when the music cuts out in the middle of the song, leaving behind a sudden silence. There's a low murmuring of people's voices, the occasional loud laugh, a shout. The murmurs get louder, as if something is about to happen—Livia's speech, probably. And then, out of nowhere, I hear, "I'm here, Mum!"

The world comes juddering to a halt. I'm hearing things; it must be in my head. Then Livia gives a cry of delight and everyone is laughing and cheering, and I'm running through the kitchen, across the terrace, up the stone steps, to where everyone is standing on the lawn, straining to see over one another's shoulders to where Livia—I catch a glimpse of her dress through the crowd—is standing. I can hear Marnie talking excitedly about how she arranged this surprise with Josh, and as I push my way through, nobody takes any notice of me, they're too busy laughing. And at last, at last, I get to the front, elbowing Nelson and Rob aside.

"Watch it!" Rob says.

"Let him through, Rob, he wants to see his daughter," Nelson says, and I'm looking for Marnie. I can hear her, but I can only see Livia, and she looks so happy that I know she's looking at Marnie. I follow her eyes until I find where they are focused. And the same terrible weakness I felt earlier comes back and I stumble against Nelson. And Nelson, his eyes still fixed on Josh's computer screen, where Marnie is telling Livia that she can't wait to be home, throws an arm around my shoulders.

"Isn't this brilliant? Look at Livia's face! This has made the party for her. Doesn't Marnie look great!" He turns to me. "Did you know about it?"

But I can only stare at the video of Marnie, caught up in the nightmare of being able to see her but not being able to hold her. Of her being here, yet not being here. And Nelson, recognizing that I can't speak, gives my shoulder a squeeze.

"She'll soon be home," he says. "She'll soon be home."

"And Dad, where are you? Ah, there you are!" Marnie cries, pretending she can see me, and everyone laughs. "I can't wait to see you either. Not long now, only a few weeks. And who knows, maybe we'll be watching this together," she adds, smiling a smile that is just for me. A smile of conspiracy, because I'm the only one who understands the meaning behind her words and everybody is too busy waving good-bye to her as she disappears from the screen to give them any thought.

Livia comes over, her face flushed, her eyes shining with unshed tears. "Wasn't that lovely? Was it you who arranged it?"

"No, it was me," Josh says, coming over to join us, his laptop now closed and tucked under his arm. I can't stop staring at it. "I wanted Marnie to FaceTime tonight, but when she said she might not be able to, as she was going away, I asked her to send a backup video just in case. She said to wait until eleven-thirty and if she hadn't gotten through by then, to play it. She might still FaceTime, though," he adds.

No, she won't, I realize, pain searing through me as I finally accept what I've tried so hard to deny. She'll never FaceTime again. Marnie only agreed to make the video so that Josh wouldn't know she was coming home. She didn't expect it to be played at the party, because she'd already be here. Because everything was going to turn out exactly as we'd planned.

The sounds are too loud, the colors—balloons, dresses, lights—too bright. Everything blurs. I can't move. I can't speak. Next to me, Livia and Josh hug, and the soft material of her dress brushes my hand. I can see our family, our friends, standing in groups, drinking and laughing. But it's as if I'm not here.

Livia

With everyone still grouped on the lawn from watching Marnie's video, I realize it's a good time to thank everyone for coming. Adam is here, so I'll be able to give him his present before he does another disappearing act. I'm not sure what's going on with him, but something isn't right. Earlier, when I had my arms around him, there was a moment when he slumped against me, as if he suddenly had no strength left. First thing on Monday morning, I'm going to make him an appointment with the doctor.

Despite everything she's done, it was lovely to see Marnie on-screen. I'd been talking to Izzy when Josh set it up, so when I heard *I'm here, Mum!* she sounded so close that I thought she *was* here, that she'd turned up unexpectedly as a surprise. And everything—all the anger I felt toward her—disappeared, and all I wanted was to put my arms around her and hold her close. I would never tell Josh this, but when I realized it was a video and that she wasn't actually here, some of the tears that sprung to my eyes were tears of disappointment. And I think Adam must have thought the same, because when he came bursting through the crowd, I could feel his bewilderment, and I wished I could have warned him and spared him the same disappointment. But I couldn't, because I couldn't take my eyes off Marnie.

When the video came to an end and everyone was clapping and

cheering, my eyes happened to fall on Rob, and the proprietorial look I saw on his face as Marnie waved good-bye from the screen sent another wave of white-hot anger coursing through me. But then I saw Adam and he looked so bleak, so utterly devastated, that I forgot Rob's treachery in an instant.

Kirin and Izzy appear in front of me, their arms laden with gifts.

"Time to open your presents!" Izzy cries.

Before I've had time to work out what's happening, Izzy maneuvers me behind one of the tables, which has been cleared of plates.

Josh cuts the music and I begin opening my presents. Most of my friends have clubbed together to buy me a beautiful gold necklace, and Adam's parents have bought me matching earrings. There are also lovely bath oils and essences, chocolates, a cookbook, a canvas bag for the beach, a leather purse and, from Josh, an intricate silver bangle, which I absolutely love. By the time I've thanked everybody individually, I feel so emotional that I don't know how I'm going to be able to speak, especially as I don't have anything written down. But I manage to say what I want to say, and when I get to the end, I reach for Adam, the bandage on his hand a reminder not to squeeze it too tightly.

"The wonderful thing is that, after tonight, this need for a special day, which came about because I never had the wedding I dreamed of, will finally be out of my system. Thanks to everyone here, I'll have lived my dream. But the person I have to thank most is Adam. He never told me to let go of my dream, or told me that it was unattainable or stupid or selfish or unreasonable, or any of the other things he could have said. He always encouraged me, supported me, championed me." I turn to Adam. "You've given me so much, and now it's my turn to give something to you." I walk over to one of the large plant pots and slide out the large brown envelope I hid under it earlier. "This is for you, with my love."

As Adam takes it, I detect a fleeting panic in his eyes and I feel terrible. I knew he'd hate having to open it in public, but I've gone ahead anyway because I want all our family and friends gathered here tonight to know I'm not completely selfish, that I've thought about Adam too, that this party is also for him. But it's not, I realize. The fact that I want them to believe it is shows I'm only thinking about myself, about how I will look.

"You can open it later, when everyone has gone," I say, trying to rectify the situation. But it's too late; above the clapping and cheering, a cry goes up, urging Adam to open the envelope. There are a few suggestions as to what it might be, including a subscription to *Playboy* magazine from Rob, and a season ticket for Manchester United from Nelson. Adam hides his dismay, smiles good-naturedly and gives me a kiss.

"Thank you," he says.

He takes his time opening the envelope and I'm not sure whether it's because he wants to keep everyone waiting or if it's because he's apprehensive about what it might contain. I'm not worried on that score. I know he's going to love it.

"Is it a parachute jump?" someone asks.

"A drive in a Ferrari, maybe?" Mike says.

I watch Adam's face as he draws out the photo of the Millau Viaduct.

"Well, what is it?" Rob asks impatiently.

Adam clears his throat. "I think my amazing wife is taking me to see something I've always dreamed of seeing," he says, and I breathe a sigh of relief. He holds up the photo. "The Millau Viaduct in the south of France."

The significance is lost on most people, so Nelson starts explaining.

"There's something else in the envelope," I tell Adam, because I want him to know the trip has already been booked, that we're actually going, that it's not one of those promises for a vague time in the future that never will materialize because other things will get in the way. With a questioning look, he takes out the envelope containing the tickets and then he just stands there, staring at it, and my heart sinks, because there's something on his face that tells me he doesn't want to open it, that he's afraid to, in case he sees something that he doesn't want to see.

"Come on, man, when are you going?" Rob calls. "We want to know!"

Realizing that he's not behaving as he should, Adam gives a quick smile.

"I'm trying to prolong the suspense!" he says, but I can see that it cost him a lot to joke about it. And I want to turn around and scream at Rob to leave Adam alone, to tell everyone that the circus is over, because for some reason, this whole present thing has become too hard for Adam to deal with.

He opens the envelope and draws out the tickets. "Tuesday." Only I detect the waver in Adam's voice. "Tuesday," he says again, his voice stronger this time. "We're going on Tuesday!"

"For how long?"

Adam takes his time doing the math. "Four days! We're coming back Saturday." And everyone begins cheering and whooping.

"It is all right, isn't it?" I say to Adam as the music comes back on and people begin to melt away.

He puts his arms around me. "It's wonderful," he says, holding me tight.

"Only I thought you seemed—not disappointed, exactly, but—I don't know."

"It's perfect," he says. "I was just amazed that you remembered how much I wanted to see the Millau Viaduct. I never expected you to give me anything. I was a bit overcome, to tell you the truth."

I move back so that I can see his eyes. "Are you sure?"

"Yes," he insists. "Thank you, I can't wait to go."

"Wasn't it lovely of Josh and Marnie to arrange the video?"

"Yes, it was."

"I thought she was there for a minute—when I heard her say 'I'm here, Mum!' You did too, didn't you?"

"Yes," he says. "I did."

Out of the corner of my eye, I see Rob chatting to a couple of my friends from work. It's hard to put my resentment for him aside, but looking at him objectively—something I've never really done before—I can see why women find him attractive. What I can't understand is how Marnie fell for him when she knows how Adam feels about Rob. She's often teased him that the reason he doesn't really like Rob is because he's better-looking. She adores Adam—yet she's gone headlong into a relationship that she must know will break his heart. What will happen if Adam refuses to accept Rob as Marnie's boyfriend, which he almost certainly will?

Suddenly, I can't bear to be near Adam, knowing what I know. I let go of his hand.

"I'm going to see Jess," I say, although it's not going to be any easier being with Jess than it is with Adam. "I'll catch you later."

I go over to where Jess is sitting, a faraway look in her eyes.

"Jess, are you all right?"

Her eyes come into focus. "Yes, I'm fine. Cleo suddenly seems a bit down, though." She looks around. "Have you seen Rob?"

"Yes, he's over there. Do you want me to take you to him?"

"If you don't mind."

"Of course not."

And taking her arm, I lead her over to where Rob is charming the pants off my work colleagues.

SUNDAY, JUNE 9

---

12 A.M.–1 A.M.

Adam

I can't even begin to describe the horror of the last hour. First the video of Marnie, then Livia giving me my present. When I pulled out the photo of the Millau Viaduct, it was so hard to look happy, because all I could think was that the only place we'd be going was Cairo.

It's dark where I'm standing in the shadow of the tent. The night sky is black, but the garden is a glaring spotlight of color and movement. I've been hiding here since I managed to escape the crowds after Livia's speech. I don't know who to be anymore, or where to go.

I'm holding the blue envelope Liv gave me, but I'm not sure what to do with it. It's identical to the one I got in the travel agent's this morning, and I thought, for one terrifying moment, that I was going to open it and find myself looking at the tickets to Cairo. My fear was so great that my mind began to shut down, so I couldn't do what I was meant to do, react how everyone was expecting me to react, and for once I was grateful to Rob for dragging me back to where I was supposed to be by telling me to get on with it. My relief when I saw the tickets were for Montpellier disappeared when I realized that they were for Tuesday. A sickness rolls through my stomach.

"Mr. Harman?"

I curse silently.

"Amy." I don't know Amy well. Josh has brought her home for the weekend a couple of times, but I haven't seen her since Easter. I know she's at Exeter, studying psychology, I think. Or maybe anthropology. She seems a nice girl and she's obviously very important to Josh. Remembering how off I was with her, I manage a smile.

"I'm sorry if I was rude when you arrived. I was miles away at the time and I wasn't expecting to see you."

"It's my fault, I shouldn't have just turned up. But I wanted to surprise Josh." She hesitates. "I know he's told you about New York and I want you to know that I've tried to persuade him to go because I don't want him to miss out. But he won't listen."

"It's fine, Amy, really."

"You're not disappointed?"

"No, it'll be lovely to have the two of you nearby."

She reaches up and gives me a kiss on the cheek. "Thank you for saying that."

"I'm going to find a glass of something to drink," I say. "Can I get you one too?"

"No, thank you, Josh has one for me."

We walk around from the side of the tent and, with a quick smile, go our separate ways. My head feels as if it's going to explode from the effort of trying to say the right thing, to be who everybody needs me to be, whether it's Livia, Josh, Amy, or anyone else here tonight. The only thing that's keeping me going is that there are only a couple more hours of this party left. The caterers should be bringing out a cake soon; Livia will blow out her forty candles, everyone will sing and gradually—hopefully—people will start to leave. I can't wait for them to go—but I know that once they have, once I'm on my own with Livia and Josh, I'll want to call everyone back so that I don't have to tell them about Marnie, about what I've done.

"Adam!"

This time it's Nelson.

"Sorry, not now." I force a smile and walk past him. I make it safely into the dining room and stand at the window, looking out to the street without seeing. And then, a noise begins to penetrate my brain, a noise so slight that at first I think I'm imagining it.

I listen again. It's coming from somewhere above me, the sound of someone—not talking or moving around, but just being. And I feel a burst of rage, because above me is Marnie's bedroom and nobody, nobody, has the right to be in there.

I run into the hall and charge up the stairs, so angry that when I get to the door, I wrench it open, not caring who's inside.

Cleo's sitting on the bed. She springs up, and the only thing that stops me from howling at her for being in Marnie's bedroom and not being Marnie is the way she's looking at me.

"Adam, where's Marnie?" she asks.

I grab hold of the door frame.

"What do you mean?"

She hesitates, and with a creeping dread, I step into the room and close the door behind me.

"I know I'm not meant to know," she says. "But Marnie told me she was coming to surprise Livia, because she wanted me to pick her up at the airport. She said it would be quicker than getting a taxi, and she wanted to get here as soon as possible. She made me swear not to tell anyone, not even Mum and Dad, and I didn't, I promise." Her hands are moving as she speaks, her fingers unable to be still. "But then I got a text from her this morning saying her flight was delayed and that she'd miss her connection in Cairo. She told me not to worry about picking her up because she had no idea what time she'd actually arrive in London, as it would depend if they could find her a seat on another flight. I was just to come to the party and she'd take a taxi from Heathrow. So I've been waiting all evening for her to turn up, and it's now gone midnight. Have you had any news from her?"

I clear my throat. "No, not yet." I know I should say something more, but the fact that Cleo knows that Marnie was meant to be coming home has thrown me completely.

"The thing is," Cleo goes on, and then stops.

"What?"

"It's just that I heard about that awful plane crash and when I checked, I saw that it was the flight Marnie was meant to be on, and I was so happy that she missed it, I kept thinking how lucky she was that her first flight had been delayed. But now—" She looks up at me, her eyes dark with fear. "There's no way she could have made it, is there? I mean, wouldn't she have contacted us by now to tell us what time she'd be arriving?"

I can't look at her. "Not necessarily. She told me she'd let me know when she arrived in London, and she might have had to go an even longer way around to get here."

She nods slowly. "So you're not worried?"

I don't want to lie to her, but how can I tell her that I'm terrified?

"A little," I say.

"It's just that—no offense—you look awful. Everyone's saying you've got a migraine, but I wondered, you know, if it was something to do with Marnie."

"I definitely have a migraine," I tell her, grimacing.

She takes a shaky breath. "I did think of something."

"What?"

She looks as if she doesn't want to tell me. "There's a number you can call if you think someone you know might have been on the flight. I don't suppose—I mean—would it be a good idea to call it?"

I nod. "I can definitely do that if she hasn't turned up by the time the party is over."

"Oh," she says, deflated.

"Only another hour or so."

She looks earnestly at me. "I suppose if she *had* been on it, they would have let you know. They probably wait for people to call and if they don't, they phone them."

I feel a flicker of hope. Maybe Cleo is right. If Marnie had been on the flight, wouldn't someone have let me know by now? "Yes, I would think so."

"So if they haven't called you, it's probably all right."

I give her a reassuring smile. "Try not to worry, Cleo. Why don't you go back to the party?"

"Would it be all right if I stay here for a bit?"

"Of course."

"If you hear from her, will you let me know?"

"Of course," I say again.

Livia

"You OK?"

I look up. Josh is looking down at me, his eyes almost black in the dark.

"Sorry, I was miles away."

"With Marnie, then," he says.

I laugh. "No, not with Marnie. I was actually thinking about your dad."

"He's all right, isn't he?"

"Yes, but I think he'll be glad when this party is over."

"That was really nice what you did for him, booking a trip to France."

"He deserves it. I would have booked for longer, but I knew he'd be worried about taking time off." I look at him gratefully. "Thank you for the video of Marnie. It was lovely."

"I hope it went some way to make up for her not being here?"

"It did, definitely."

He nods toward the terrace. "So, it seems I have a grandmother?"

I look at him, stricken. "I'm sorry, Josh, I should have told you myself that she turned up."

"Didn't she want to see me?" I can hear the hurt in his voice.

"Yes, she did, but she couldn't stay because someone was waiting for her, which was just as well because we were both a bit overwhelmed. But she's coming back tomorrow afternoon, to see you before you leave."

"Cool." He bends his knees so that he can look me in the eyes. "I'm sorry about your father. Nelson said he died."

"Yes—but I'm kind of OK with it. He wasn't a very nice person. And it's only because he's no longer around that Mum felt she could come tonight. So, you see, every cloud has a silver lining."

A flash of light catches my eye, followed by a collective gasp.

"Beautiful!" Kirin cries, clapping her hands together as two of the caterers carry an enormous cake, lit by what I guess are forty candles. In fact, it's three cakes stacked one on top of the other in order of size.

"Chocolate, vanilla and—your favorite—coffee," Josh explains. He takes my hand. "Come on, Mum, come blow out your candles."

"Where's Dad?" I ask Josh over the noise of everyone cheering as he pulls me toward the table.

"I think he must be inside somewhere. Do you want me to go and find him?"

"No, it's fine, leave him," I say, pushing away my disappointment that he isn't beside me. Hopefully, he'll hear everyone singing "Happy Birthday," because they're making quite a noise, and come out from wherever he is. As I stand there listening, my heart swells with emotion. And then, just in time to make it even more perfect, Adam arrives, pushing his way through the crowd, joining in with the last line of the singing, and then standing next to me while I blow out my candles.

When everyone has finished applauding, because I manage it with one breath, he takes me in his arms.

"I love you," he says softly, to cheers and whistles. "I always have and I always will."

"Thank you." I can't stop the tears from falling. "Thank you for making this the best day ever, for always being by my side, for doing everything in your power to make me happy. I'm so lucky to have you."

"Never stop loving me."

"I'll always love you," I tell him. "Forever."

And behind his eyes, behind his smile, I see terrible doubt, and I want to ask him why he thinks I'll ever stop loving him.

"You need to cut your cake, Mum," Josh says, breaking the moment.

Adam gives me a last kiss. "I'll leave you to it. Nelson looks as if he needs rescuing from Rob."

So does our daughter, I think bitterly.

Josh hands me a knife and, as I cut my cake, I realize that if I *could* rescue Marnie from Rob, I might be able to avoid a complete breakdown of the relationships within our group. If I could make her see sense, and she broke things off with Rob, nobody would ever need to know about their affair and we could carry on exactly as we were before. Well, not exactly as before, because it could never be the same. There would be this horrible secret between me, Marnie, and Rob, and having to be polite to Rob so that no one would guess how much I despise him would be incredibly difficult, if not impossible. But even worse is that I'd never be able to look at Marnie in quite the same way. And that breaks my heart.

Jess catches my eye and gives me a little wave. Rob is standing beside her, his arm around her waist, and I want to run over and beg her not to hate me, which she will when she finds out about him and Marnie. She'll automatically blame Marnie because Rob will spin her a story to make him the innocent, and her the guilty party. He'll carry on lying to her as he's done all along. He'll tell her that Marnie seduced him, that it was a moment of weakness on his part, that when she left for Hong Kong, it was over as far as he was concerned—except that she wouldn't let go and kept begging him to come and see her. And Jess, hoping to preserve her marriage, will choose to believe him. It's why, whatever else she knows, I'll never tell her about the baby. I'll never tell her that Marnie was pregnant and that Rob asked her to have an abortion. That would be too much.

My biggest fear—and one that I can barely voice to myself—is that if Rob does intend to leave Jess, and Marnie is coming home to support him through it, they'll do it openly, not secretly. That instead of being discreet, they'll flaunt their relationship in public. If they do that, it will be the ultimate insult. And how will Adam and I feel about them being a couple? Would we be able to have them around, watch as Rob kisses and hugs our daughter? If it was the only way we could see Marnie, what choice would we have? But it would kill any chance of rescuing my friendship with Jess.

The only way that any of us can escape what is to happen, I think bitterly, is if a massive thunderbolt were to come out of the sky and strike Rob dead. And that's hardly going to happen.

1 A.M.–2 A.M.

Adam

I haven't been back to the party since seeing Cleo. I can't, not yet. I'm in the bedroom, sitting on our bed, my mobile in my hand. There aren't any missed calls. My messages for Marnie still haven't been delivered. The only emails I've received are junk mail. There's nothing on Livia's phone either. When I left Cleo, I went straight to the utility room, leaving the light off as I took Liv's phone out of the laundry basket. She had lots of messages and a few missed calls—but nothing from Marnie, and nothing from an unknown or withheld number.

Mimi is back in our bedroom, keeping her distance. Watching me from the corner of the room. I should call the emergency number; I've typed it into my phone. All I have to do is press Call. But still I can't.

I think about what Cleo said, about being called by the authorities if nobody has contacted them about a passenger on a crashed flight. Do they wait a certain amount of time before contacting the family? Did Marnie even have me down as her next of kin on her passport application form? Had she filled that part in? Maybe it wasn't obligatory, maybe she forgot. Maybe she put Josh down rather than me or Livia, so that we wouldn't be the first to know if anything happened to her.

The sound of people singing "Happy Birthday" reminds me where I'm meant to be.

Taking the stairs two at a time, I race into the garden and reach Livia just in time. It all seems so unreal. But I'm with her, present, and despite the crushing pain of what might have happened to Marnie, I'm able to kiss Liv, tell her that I love her, be who she needs me to be.

"Adam!"

I see Nelson waving and give Liv a last kiss. "I'll leave you to it. Nelson looks as if he needs rescuing from Rob."

"Why are some people obsessed with bad news?" Nelson grumbles, coming toward me, leaving Rob standing on his own. "He keeps going on about that plane crash this morning, the one in Cairo."

I walk over to the wall, where Livia and I sat earlier, the one opposite Marnie's fence. Marnie's fence. It will always be known as that, I realize. Even when the photos have been taken down, it will still be Marnie's fence.

Nelson sits down next to me, stretches his legs out.

"You OK? You don't seem to have drunk much."

"Migraine, that's all."

He turns to me. "Has something happened?"

I try to meet his eye, but I can't. "What do you mean?"

"Just that you only get migraines when you're stressed about something." He pauses. "You know you can tell me, don't you?"

I wish more than anything that I could tell him. I wish I could tell him that Marnie was probably on the plane that crashed. I can't bear it. If it's true, how am I going to tell Livia that her daughter has died? What will she say when she realizes that I let the party go on? She's never going to forgive me.

I lean forward, my elbows on my knees, my head down, trying to hide my distress from Nelson.

"For God's sake, Adam, tell me!" he says.

"I can't." My voice catches. "I need to tell Livia first."

I sense him become still. "Are you ill, is that it? Is that what you need to tell Livia?" There's worry in his voice and I remember that Jess told Nelson she had MS before she told Rob.

"No, no, I'm not ill," I say. "It's something I've done." I need to stop talking, my voice is cracking and I can't cry here, not now, not with everyone so close to leaving.

"It can't be that bad," Nelson says.

"It is. Livia is never going to forgive me."

"Sure she will," he says. "She loves you."

I shake my head.

"If it was anyone else, I'd be really worried you were saying you'd had an affair," Nelson says, and for a moment I wish that was what it was—a horrible mistake and betrayal. "But I know you wouldn't," he goes on. "That's not you, that's not who you are."

Something breaks in me. I start laughing, because the alternative would be to weep.

For a moment, Nelson lets me laugh. And then he lays a heavy hand on my shoulder.

"You must think I'm mad," I say, pressing my eyes with the heel of my hand.

"Whatever it is, you'll get through it," he says. "You all will, we all will. Whatever it is."

Livia

I look over to where Nelson and Adam are sitting together on the wall and another layer of worry adds to the anxiety I'm already feeling about Adam. I watch for a minute, noticing how distressed he looks, and then I catch my name. My heart sinks. This can't be about the present he still hasn't given me, can it?

Just as I'm wondering if I should interrupt, Adam starts laughing. I haven't heard him laugh all day and at first I'm pleased that he's relaxed a bit. But then I realize that there's something almost desperate about his laughter, and Nelson notices it too, because he puts his hand on Adam's shoulder and says something quietly to him. And Adam's laughter stops as quickly as it started.

I'm glad Adam made it out from wherever he was hiding in time for the cake. I thought he might bring the box with him, the one I saw sticking out from under the table earlier, but he didn't. Somehow, I don't think I'm going to be getting my present tonight. I can't help speculating about what it might be. The box is far too large for the handbag I thought I might be getting, but it could be a smoke screen.

It's not only me who's thinking about the box, because suddenly Rob is staggering up the steps with it, not because it's heavy but because of its size.

"Hey, Adam!" he calls over. "Haven't you forgotten something?

This is for Livia, right? The only problem is, I think you might have forgotten to put the present inside."

"Put it down!" Adam's voice rings out, cutting through the music. "Don't touch it!" He leaps to his feet, his face dark with anger. Heads turn toward him. He looks as if he's going to lunge at Rob, and a huge part of me is willing him on.

Nelson places a restraining hand on his arm and for a moment no one moves.

"Sorry, mate," Rob says, dropping the box on the ground. It falls onto its side and the top flaps open, exposing its empty interior. "I didn't mean any harm."

I know how much it is costing Adam to keep hold of his temper.

"It's all right," he says, forcing a quick smile. "It's just that there's been a bit of a problem with my present for Livia and I was hoping nobody would notice that I haven't given her anything yet. Now, everybody has."

"It doesn't matter!" I call over. "I've had the best present ever with this lovely party!"

Everybody begins cheering and clapping and the moment is soon forgotten, especially by Rob, who leaps down the steps onto the terrace and begins dancing along to Village People's "YMCA," while Jess hides her face in mock embarrassment. I turn my back on the scene, unable to look at Rob a moment longer, and bump into Paula.

"I'm going to leave now, Livia," she says.

"Now that you've had the cake?" I tease.

She laughs. "I'm so glad that your mum turned up," she says, because everybody knows now. "It'll be lovely if you can both put the past behind you and move on."

"We're going to have a damn good try," I say, suddenly feeling tearful.

"Make the most of it," she says. "Family is everything. I wish mine weren't so far away. I feel so alone sometimes."

"Oh, Paula," I say, dismayed. "You're not alone. You have friends all around you and look at all the things you've been doing since you retired."

"It's not the same as having family around, though, is it? I look at you and Adam, at his family—Jeannie and Mike are super, aren't they? At Josh, and Marnie, who will be home soon. I envy you, Livia, not in a horrible way, but I envy you."

"I know I'm very lucky," I say, wishing I didn't feel so guilty.

"And me—I'm just an individual, filling in time. Yes, I'm meeting people, but afterward they go back to their families and I go back to an empty house." She shakes her head sadly. "I still can't believe that both my sons chose to live so far away."

"I think maybe life chose for them."

"I know," she says. "I know it wasn't a conscious effort to move as far away from me as they could. And they certainly didn't expect their dad to die so young. What they expected was for me and Tony to live out a long and happy retirement together while they got on with their lives."

"Exactly. If he'd died before they'd gone to live abroad, they might not have gone."

"They keep telling me to come and see them," she goes on. "They say I can stay as long as I like. But it's so expensive."

"Why don't you start saving, like I did for this party? Do you think you could start saving some of your pension?"

"Yes, I'm sure I could."

"Then every couple of years, you'd have enough for a trip to either Australia or Canada. That way, you'd have something to look forward to."

Paula nods. "You're right, I would. That's such a good idea—you never know, this time next year I might be off to Australia!"

"I'd go during the winter months, if I were you. You may as well have some sunshine if you can get it."

"I'll aim for November next year. I'll definitely have saved up enough by then." She gives me a hug. "Thank you, Livia, I feel so much better about everything now." She looks toward the terrace. "Maybe I'll have one last dance before I go."

"You do that," I tell her.

I watch her go, deciding to invite her over more often. Adam won't mind, and he can always disappear to his shed so that Paula and I can have a proper chat together. I'm shocked at how lonely she sounded and also by what she said about being envious of me. I hate that I've made her feel that way, but it must seem to her that I have it all. I know how lucky I am that I have my family, my friends, and my health. At least for now.

2 A.M.–3 A.M.

Adam

I pick up the box from where Rob dumped it on the lawn and move it out of the way. I know I shouldn't have yelled at Rob, but the box was Marnie's idea and I don't want it damaged.

My mind goes to the other things I'll want to keep, things that normally I'd have thrown away, like her old bike. It's leaning against the wall in the garage, waiting for me to take it to the dump. I won't, not now. It was a present for her twelfth birthday. I can see her riding it, the ends of her hair lifting in the wind as she pedaled as fast as she could. And her old desk, which I was going to use for firewood—I'll restore it instead. How can I ever throw away anything that Marnie has touched, that might still have something of her?

And there are all the things that Marnie gave me, things I've never used, or gotten around to wearing. Like the multicolored Red Herring socks she sent me last Christmas, all the way from Hong Kong. They sit in my drawer, still in their box, because brightly colored socks aren't my thing. I wish I'd worn them, just once, and taken a photo to send to her—*See, I'm wearing them!* And the expensive corkscrew that she gave me for my last birthday and which I've never used, because the one in the drawer works perfectly well. I should have used it, I should have at least told her I'd used it.

"So you're off to Millau."

I feel Dad's hand on my shoulder. I turn to face him and just seeing him gives me strength, because I know that he'll be here for me in the next hours, days, weeks, months, like he's always been. He'll understand why I let the party go ahead, he'll understand that I wanted Livia to have these last few hours of happiness before her world fell apart. And if he doesn't—well, he'll say that he does, because that's what parents do, they say what we need them to say, at that moment in time.

"Yes," I say.

"It'll do you good to have a break, even if it's only for four days. Here." He hands me the glass he's holding. "You look as if you could do with a beer."

"Thanks." I take it, but I can't bring myself to drink it. "Dad, if someone did something bad but he had good intentions, would you be able to understand why he did it?"

Dad considers this. "You mean like someone robbing a bank because his family is starving?"

"Yes, something like that."

"Did anyone get hurt while he was robbing the bank?"

"No."

"Then, even though it was morally wrong, I wouldn't have a problem with it. As long as his family really was hungry and it wasn't to buy the children an Xbox."

"But what if his wife was really upset with him when she realized that he'd robbed the bank, even though he'd had their best interests at heart?" I say, adapting myself to his mind-set.

"Once they'd had what they wanted, you mean?"

"Yes."

He moves to the wall and I follow him over. "I think her upset would be more to do with guilt," he says as I sit down beside him. "You know, that she'd enjoyed the food when, if she'd known it had been bought with stolen money, she'd have chosen not to eat it."

"But if he'd told her where the money had come from, and she'd decided not to eat the food, they'd have died of starvation," I point out.

"Which is why he didn't tell her."

"Exactly."

"He just wanted his family to be able to enjoy one last meal."

My throat swells. "Yes."

"I'd be OK with that."

"Even though his family will hate him for it?" I say, my voice tight. "Even though he'll lose them forever?"

"They won't hate him. Maybe at the beginning. But not forever."

"I hope you're right."

He turns and looks at me. "This person—maybe he should have asked his dad for advice before it got to that point."

"Yeah," I say quietly. "Maybe he should have."

"Why can't he tell him now?"

"Because he needs to tell his wife first."

He sits in silence for a while, giving me the chance to change my mind.

"The party will be over soon," he says eventually. "It's been great, exactly what Livia dreamed of."

"What time is it?"

He studies his watch, moving it to catch the light coming from the tent. "Ten past two."

"Can you ask Josh to start winding things down? Get him to play 'Unchained Melody'? It's my song choice, for Livia."

"I hope you told him the Righteous Brothers' version."

"Of course."

It's a couple of minutes before I hear the opening bars play and the memory comes back, of our wedding day, and how we danced to this in the run-down pub and how much I loved her then. How much I love her now.

I walk down to the terrace, to where Livia is waiting for me, and take her in my arms. We don't speak, we just dance, our bodies close together, her head on my shoulder, my hand in her hair. And I wonder if this will be the last time she'll ever let me hold her.

Livia

Adam and I are dancing, and I'm so close to crying I can hardly hold back the tears. I know that anyone watching would take them for tears of happiness. But there's this huge sadness welling up inside me. It's coming from Adam, seeping from his pores into mine, filling me with a sorrow I don't understand. I can feel that he's barely hanging on, that all he wants is for this party to be over and everyone to leave.

He told me he isn't ill, but I no longer believe him. It can't be work; if he's lost an order for a piece of furniture, it wouldn't matter. Unless one of his parents is ill? As we circle slowly, I keep an eye out for Jeannie and Mike and when I see them laughing together, I know it isn't about them either.

Jeannie catches me looking and waves. I smile back. The song comes to an end and I decide to stop worrying. Whatever it is, I'll know soon enough.

I see Jess hovering, trying to catch my eye. I go over to her, put my hand on her arm. "Is everything all right?"

"It's Cleo. She's a bit upset, so we're going to go."

"Oh no! Is it Charlie?"

"I don't know. She just came up and asked if we could go. I could see she'd been crying, but she wouldn't say why."

"Where is she?"

"She's gone to find Adam, to say good-bye. And I need to find Rob."

"It's OK, I'm here," he says, appearing over her left shoulder. He gives me a sad look. "Looks like we're going to have to leave your lovely party, Livvy."

"It's almost over anyway," I say, my teeth on edge. I hate it when he calls me Livvy because it's what Mike calls me and I don't want anyone else using it, least of all Rob.

"I'll go and get the car." He tries to give me a hug, but I turn to Jess quickly.

"Thank you for coming, and for the spa and the swimming costume and for being the best friend in the world," I say, hugging her more tightly than I've ever hugged her before, aware that this might be one of the last times she'll ever speak to me. "I'll always remember today as being one of the best days of my life."

She laughs softly. "You sound as if we're never going to see each other again. Have a lovely holiday in France, and make sure you come over and tell me about it when you get back."

"And you make sure you take care of yourself," I tell her fiercely.

"I will." She looks around. "I don't suppose you can go and find Cleo? Tell her we're waiting in the car?"

"Of course," I say, giving her a last hug. "Bye, Rob." I don't even look at him.

"Bye, Livvy, enjoy your holiday," he says as Jess takes his arm.

But I've already gone, because I've just spotted Cleo and Adam on the other side of the terrace. They're standing close together, and even though they have their backs to me, I know Cleo is in tears. I hurry over to rescue Adam.

"You should tell Livia," I hear Cleo say, her voice wobbling all over the place. "You have to tell her about Marnie, she has to know."

I freeze, a terrible dread spreading though me. Cleo *knows*? I step quickly behind the gray rain barrel, not wanting them to see me, my heart thudding horribly in my chest, questions tumbling through my brain. How does Cleo know? And when did she find out? She was fine earlier on, so it must be recent. Did Marnie tell her? She wouldn't have, not tonight, not during my party. Max, then? But why would he do that, why would he be so cruel? Or did Cleo somehow guess? Maybe Marnie and Rob gave something away while they were in Hong Kong, and she spoke to Max about it, told him what she feared. And Max wouldn't have been able to lie to her. Or maybe she saw an incriminating text on Rob's phone, or overheard a conversation between him and Marnie; maybe Marnie phoned him at the party. But if she managed to get Wi-Fi, wouldn't she have phoned me as well?

"I will tell her, as soon as I know for sure." Adam sounds so desperate, so broken that I hate myself. I should have told him weeks ago; then he wouldn't have had to find out like this.

"Do you still think there's a chance, then, that we're wrong?"

"Yes," he says firmly, and I feel weak with gratitude that they don't actually know, they only suspect.

"So when will you know? When are you going to try to find out?"

"As soon as everyone has gone."

"Will you let me know? Straightaway? Even if it's the middle of the night. Even if it's bad." She chokes on the word.

"Yes," he says, giving her a hug.

"Promise?"

"Promise."

She looks up at him. "You're so brave."

"No, I'm not." His voice is low. "I'm anything but." He turns toward her, puts his hands on her upper arms and moves her back slightly so that he can see straight into her eyes. "Can I ask you to do something for me, Cleo? Will you not say anything to your parents, not just yet. I need to tell Livia first."

She nods. "All right."

His body sags in relief. "Thank you."

He releases her, and realizing that the moment he looks up, he could see me standing in the shadow of the rain barrel, I move out and hurry forward as if I've just arrived.

"Cleo, I'm so sorry, your mum says you're not feeling well," I say, putting an arm around her. "She's gone down to the car with your dad." I stop abruptly. How could I be so insensitive as to mention him when she's just found out that he's been having an affair with Marnie? I wait for her to burst into tears, but thankfully she doesn't. "Shall I take you?"

"No, it's fine, thank you," she mumbles. "Thank you for a lovely party."

She leaves and it's just me and Adam. I'm so tense, I can't look at him.

"Poor Cleo," he says, and I realize that he's not looking at me either. "Is it Charlie, do you think?"

"Probably," I say, playing along. "I think they've been having a few problems."

"Shall we start getting people out the door?"

"Yes, it must be around two-thirty now."

The next thirty minutes pass in a blur of matching phones to owners and saying good-byes and thank-yous.

Sometime during the evening, realizing there was quite a bit of food left over, I invited Jeannie and Mike, Izzy and Ian, and Kirin and Nelson to come for lunch tomorrow, but only because I knew that Jess and Rob wouldn't be able to come, as Jess had already mentioned that they had plans.

"Maybe we should sleep here," I hear Izzy joke.

"Why?" Adam asks.

"Well, we have to be back here in a few hours for lunch."

A frown crosses his face. "What do you mean?"

"Livia invited us to come and eat the leftovers. Mum and Dad too."

"And Nelson and Kirin," I say.

"Right," he says, nodding slowly.

"You can stay if you want," I say to Izzy. "I'll make up Marnie's bed for you."

"No!" We all look at Adam in surprise. "Sorry, Izzy, I love you, but you're not staying here tonight. My migraine wouldn't stand it."

"Why don't you stay at ours?" Jeannie offers.

"Thanks, Mum," Izzy says gratefully.

"You may as well leave your car here and come with us in ours," Mike says.

Ian looks horrified. "Are you telling me that I could have had more than one glass of champagne tonight? That I didn't need to drink fruit juice all evening?"

"I'm sure Izzy will make up for it tomorrow by doing the driving back to Southampton," Mike says, laughing.

"Then I won't be able to drink!" Izzy says.

"Will you all just leave?" Adam says, and I can see he's really struggling now. "Please?"

A couple more minutes and the garden is silent. Josh checks his watch.

"Two forty-five," he says. "How's that for timing?"

"Perfect," I say, collapsing against him. "Thanks, Josh, you did an amazing job, and with the music. And the decorations. Has Max left?"

"Yes, he couldn't get anywhere near you to say good-bye."

I look at Adam and Josh. "That's it, then. Just the three of us."

"And Amy," Josh says.

"Where is she?" I ask.

"In the garden. It is all right if she stays the night, isn't it?"

"No," Adam says abruptly. "Sorry."

Josh frowns. "What?"

"Sorry, Josh, but Amy can't stay the night."

"Why not?"

"How did she get here? Did she drive?"

"No, she doesn't have a car. She came by train."

"Then I'll order her a taxi."

Josh shakes his head. "All the way to Exeter? Why?"

"Wait a minute, Adam," I say, intervening. "Surely Amy can stay the night? I mean, she's already stayed over."

"I know," he says. "But not tonight."

"I don't understand," Josh says. "Why can't she?"

"Because she can't, that's all. Any other night she'd be welcome. But not tonight."

"So you are blaming her for me not taking up the internship in the States!"

"Don't be stupid!"

Josh's mouth drops open at Adam's tone and I can see he's about to erupt. I shoot him a warning look.

"Josh." Adam sounds bone-weary, as if he barely has the strength to speak. "Don't keep arguing. Amy isn't staying the night, all right."

"No. Not all right." Josh folds his arms across his chest. "If Amy goes, I go."

"Sorry, Josh, I need you here," he says firmly.

"What for? We're only going to go to bed. Dad, you're being ridiculous!"

"I just want it to be family. Is that so hard to understand?"

"It's all right, Josh." Amy's voice comes from behind us. "I can stay with my friend Maggie tonight—you know, the one who lives in Guildford. I already told her I might, as I have to be at Grandad's tomorrow for his party and she lives nearby. It makes sense for me to stay at hers."

Adam turns to where she's standing in the doorway and I wonder how much she heard.

"I'd really appreciate that, thank you, Amy," he says, his relief evident.

"It doesn't make sense," Josh growls.

Amy lays a placating hand on his arm. "It's really not a problem. And I'm sure your dad has a good reason."

"Then why the hell won't he tell us what it is?"

"Well, maybe he can't tell you." She gives a little shrug. "It's like that sometimes in families. Things happen." She gives Adam a quick smile.

"I'll call you a taxi," he says. "Where did you say your friend lives?"

"Guildford."

Josh takes out his mobile. "I'll do it."

Thankfully, the taxi arrives quickly, so the agony of us all standing in the kitchen, Josh with his arm around Amy but no one talking, doesn't go on for long.

"We'll see you again, Amy," Adam says. "Thank you for understanding."

I give her a hug and murmur a quick "Sorry." Josh takes her out to where the taxi is waiting, and there's only me and Adam.

"Shall we go to bed?" I ask.

"Yes. But there's something I've got to do first." His face is gray with exhaustion. "Will you wait for me upstairs?"

I feel a rush of alarm. Surely he's not going to try to call Marnie now, ask her if she's been having an affair with Rob.

I put my hand on his arm. "Can't it wait until tomorrow?"

"No." He moves away and my hand drops to my side. "I'll see you in a minute."

3 A.M.–4 A.M.

Adam

I'm on the floor of my shed, teetering on the edge of a void. I don't know how much time has passed since I called the emergency number and heard that my daughter, Marnie Sarah Harman, was a passenger on flight PA206.

Time no longer has any meaning. All hope has gone, there's only darkness. All I want is for it to take me, as it took Marnie. But there's no mercy, just the stark knowledge that she is dead.

I hunch over, my head on my knees, my hands clasped around my legs, a useless attempt to protect myself from what has already happened. I squeeze my eyes shut to block out the images of Marnie's last moments. It doesn't work. All I can hear are her screams.

How will I live, knowing that I wasn't there when she needed me most? If I'd been with her, I'd have buried her face in my shoulder and wrapped my arms tightly around her so that she wouldn't have seen death coming. Even if, weeks or months down the line, we're told that Marnie wouldn't have known a thing, that the plane exploded without warning, there'd still be the possibility that she was alive when she started falling from the sky.

Crushed by an all-consuming, hopeless, terrible grief, I'm barely aware of the sobs that rack my body, the tears that stream from my eyes. What was I thinking, making her take three flights to get home, when she could have taken a direct one? By not wanting to spoil her, I tripled her chances of dying. My body contorts in pain and I feel a flash of hatred for Livia. I would have gotten Marnie the more expensive direct flight, but I knew she'd disapprove, because of Josh and how he'd feel. For a moment, I hate Josh too. But he would be horrified that I'd made his sister take three flights just because I'd made him take two. And didn't the short time she was going to be spending with us—four days—justify a direct flight? The only person I can blame is myself. How could I have been so stupid, so shortsighted—so *illogical*?

Eventually, life intrudes, bringing with it a dull awareness that there are things I have to do. Cleo, I'd promised to tell Cleo.

I find my phone, search for her name, press the Message symbol. What can I even say to her? I can't think, nothing seems right. The only words I find are *Cleo, I'm sorry*. And then I wait for her to message me back, my eyes fixed on the screen, desperate to know that I'm not alone.

Then it comes. *Me too.*

And now it's real. I have to tell Livia. But how? How do I get past the *Livia, I need to tell you?* How can I say the words I can't even say in my head: *Marnie has died*. It's too brutal, too inhumane. I need more words—*Livia, I need to tell you. Marnie and I had arranged a surprise for your birthday—* I stop, because I can already see her face lighting up. Maybe it would be better to go straight to the truth: *Livia, I need to tell you—you know the plane that crashed yesterday on its way to Amsterdam? Well, Marnie was a passenger on it—*and then add something to help ease the pain. *But don't worry, everything's going to be fine, we're going to come through this, you, me, and Josh.* Because grief makes us say the stupidest things.

And I realize that there are no words to tell a mother that her child is dead.

I get to my feet. This is it, this is the moment I tear Livia's world apart.

Mechanically, I leave my shed, walk across the lawn toward the house, down the steps onto the terrace, and into the kitchen. But then I see my bike keys lying on the counter, where I dropped them a lifetime ago, and instead of carrying on upstairs to the bedroom, I grab the keys and walk back through the kitchen and down the side path. I'm running now, no longer thinking about how I'm going to tell Livia, but about the time I picked Marnie up from a party and instead of coming home, we drove all the way down to Southampton and went for a walk along the beach. I reach the garage, take my helmet from the top case, get on my bike, start the engine, and roar off down the road.

I race along deserted streets, scattering a scavenging cat, cutting a corner too tight, shattering the night's deathly silence with the roar of my bike. Ahead of me, the slip road to the M4 looms. I open the throttle and take it fast, screaming onto the motorway, slicing in front of a crawling car. My bike shifts under me as I push faster.

The drag of the wind on my face is intoxicating and I have to fight an overwhelming urge to let go of the handlebars and free-fall to my death. Is it terrible that Livia and Josh aren't enough to make me want to live? Guilt adds itself to the torment of the last fourteen hours and a roar of white-hot anger adds to the roar of the bike as I race down the motorway, bent on destruction.

Then, in the mirror, through the water streaming from my eyes, I see a car hammering down the motorway behind me, its blue light flashing, and my roar of grief becomes one of frustration. I take the bike past one hundred mph, knowing that if it comes to it I can push it faster, because nothing is going to stop me now. But the police car quickly closes the distance between us, moving swiftly into the outside lane, and as it levels with me, my peripheral vision catches an officer gesticulating wildly from the passenger seat.

I add more speed, but the car sweeps past and moves into my lane, blocking my bike. I'm about to open the throttle and overtake him, pushing my bike to its maximum, but something stops me and he slowly reduces his speed, bringing me in. I'm not sure why

I let him. Maybe it's because I don't want Livia to have even more pieces to pick up. Or maybe it was Marnie's voice pleading, "Don't, Dad, don't!" I swear I could feel her arms tightening around my waist for a moment, her head pressing against the back of my neck.

My limbs are trembling as I bring the bike to a stop behind the police car and cut the engine. Two officers get out, one male, one female. The male strides toward me.

"Have you got a death wish or something?" he yells, slamming his cap onto his head.

The second officer—the driver—approaches. "Sir, step away from the bike," she barks. "Sir, did you hear me? Step away from the bike."

I try to unfurl my hands from the handlebars, unstick my legs from the bike. But I seem to be welded to it.

"Sir, if you don't comply, I'm going to have to arrest you."

"We're going to have to arrest him anyway," the first officer says. He takes a step toward me and the sight of handcuffs dangling from his belt shocks me into speech.

I flip up my helmet. "Wait!"

There must be something in my voice, or maybe they read something in my face, because both police officers pause.

"Go on."

"It's about Marnie."

"Marnie?"

"Yes."

"Who's Marnie?"

"My daughter." I swallow painfully. "Marnie's my daughter."

They exchange a glance. "Where is your daughter, sir?"

Livia

I stand at the bedroom window and watch Adam walk across the lawn. He has his head down, as if he can't bear what he's about to do. Is he really going to call Marnie? Or Rob, even? I feel suddenly sick at the thought of Jess's finding out now, in the middle of the night. But then I remember how he asked Cleo not to say anything, because if it was true, he wanted to tell me first.

That's why he didn't want Amy to stay the night, I realize. He doesn't want her here tomorrow morning, when we'll have to tell Josh about Marnie and Rob. We need to face this as a family.

Adam disappears from sight and I imagine him squashing his way through the gap to his shed. Now that everyone has gone, the garden looks strangely abandoned, the tent moored in the middle of the lawn like a huge white ship lost at sea. A few white napkins, missed by the caterers, lie on the ground like discarded flags that might once have SOS'd for help. Burst balloons hang sadly from their strings and the CONGRATULATIONS banner has come unstuck at one end. The scene looks like the aftermath of some kind of disaster and a shiver goes down my spine.

I watch for a while, imagining him on the phone to Marnie, asking her if she's been having an affair with Rob. Is that why he hasn't come out yet, because he's trying to come to terms with it? I should be with him; we should be facing this together. Or, now that he knows the terrible truth, is he waiting until I'm asleep so that he'll only have to tell me when I wake up? It would be like him, to not want to spoil my day, to keep it to himself so that I can have a few hours' sleep before he drops his bombshell. What is he going to say when I tell him that I've known for weeks?

I unzip my dress, slide it off, then kick off my shoes, glad to give my aching feet a rest. I spread my dress out on the bed; apart from a tiny stain near the bottom, it's surprisingly clean, so I slip it inside a plastic cover and hang it on the back of the door. I don't suppose I'll ever wear it again, unless I put it on when Marnie comes back so that she can take a photo of me with her yellow roses. Although, somehow, I can't ever imagine that scene taking place, not now.

Someone—Kirin, I suspect—has brought my presents upstairs to the bedroom and the sight of the oils and essences makes me want to soak in a bath. Much as I'd like to be asleep when Adam comes up, I know I won't be. I'm too wound up and I'm not going to lie there pretending.

In the bathroom, I fill the tub and add a generous amount of one of the oils and some bath foam. Repinning my hair on top of my head, I climb in and sink under the water until it's up around my shoulders. It's absolute bliss.

A film of the evening plays in my head, from the moment everyone arrived until the moment they left. I can't wait to go over it all with Adam. I want to know what he thinks about Kirin expecting twins, about Mum turning up, and how he really feels about Josh not going to New York. But all those things are going to be overshadowed by Marnie and Rob's affair, and I feel a stab of anger that they've spoiled the end of what has been a wonderful evening. Is that what Adam was arguing about with Nelson earlier? Did he tell him about Rob? But he can't have; he didn't know back then. It was after this that Cleo spoke to him, wasn't it? My eyelids feel heavy from trying to work it out.

It's the cooling bathwater that wakes me. Disorientated, I sit up quickly, splashing suds up the sides, wondering how long I've been asleep. I release the plug and the drain gurgles, a too-loud sound in a silent house.

A shiver pricks my skin as I towel myself dry. A memory tugs at my brain. It was a sound that woke me, the roar of a motorbike in the street outside. I pause, the towel stretched over my back. It couldn't have been Adam, could it? He wouldn't have gone off on his bike, not at this time of night.

Wrapping the towel around me, I hurry to the bedroom and look out of the window. The guilty beating of my heart slows when I see, behind the tent, a yellow glow coming from his shed. He's there, he hasn't gone to settle scores. Part of me wants to go down and check that he's all right, but something, a sixth sense perhaps, tells me not to, that he'll come to me when he's ready. For a moment I feel afraid, as if I'm staring into an abyss. But it's just the dark and the deserted garden that're making me feel that way.

Turning from the window, I lie down on the bed. I'll give him another ten minutes and if he's not back by then, I'll go and find him.

4 A.M.–5 A.M.

Adam

The police slowly follow me home. They caution me, but their words are kind. They tell me to get some sleep and I say that I will, as soon as I've told Livia. But I know there'll be no sleep, not once I've told her.

I go into the house, the days ahead weighing heavily upon me: breaking the news to everyone, boarding a plane to Cairo and sitting through the hell of a five-hour journey, thinking of Marnie on her flight, while Livia weeps beside me.

In the hallway, I go to the cupboard, find my leather jacket and take the travel agent's blue envelope from the inside pocket. We don't need these tickets now; the airline has arranged for us to fly to Cairo with Josh on Monday—tomorrow, I realize. I tear the envelope in half and drop it into the kitchen bin. Then I make my way upstairs.

Liv is asleep on the bed, wrapped in a bath towel. Of course she's asleep, I've been gone for ages. I stand looking down at her, taking her in, drinking in the way she looks—her face relaxed in sleep, her hair tumbling around her shoulders, her right arm curved over her head—trying to imprint it on my mind so that I can remember how she looked before I told her.

I sit down on the edge of the bed.

"Livia," I say softly.

But she's in a deep sleep, and suddenly, I can't bear to wake her. Surely it won't do any harm to let her sleep a little longer when she'll never sleep this easy again. The important thing is to tell her before anyone else wakes up, before someone, somewhere, works out what has happened and tells her before I can tell her myself.

I move from the bed, take off my clothes. Reaching past her, I turn off the light. The movement disturbs her, and she stirs in her sleep. My heart starts racing and I hold my breath, willing her not to wake.

She settles and I lie down beside her and stare into the darkness. I feel so alone, so unbearably alone. The need to be held overwhelms me to the point where I reach for Livia and fold her into my body. Her arms come around me in response and for a blessed few seconds I feel comforted. I can tell her like this, I can tell her in the dark, whisper it in her ear, hold her while she breaks. I will be here for her, as I wasn't for Marnie.

"You were a long time in your shed," she murmurs.

"Sorry."

"I didn't mean to fall asleep."

"It doesn't matter. You're tired."

In the dark, her hand finds my face and traces the lines of it.

"You too."

"A little."

"It was a perfect day." Her mouth finds mine. "Thank you, for everything."

I need to tell her. "Livia—"

"Not now." She moves the towel from around her and slides herself closer to me, pressing her body against the length of mine, wanting me, and I shrink away because I can't, we can't. But the softness of her skin and the touch of her fingers draw me in until all I want is to forget, to forget what has happened and be like we've always been, like we'll never be again. So I empty my mind and think only of Livia, of us, one last time.

Livia

Adam's head is heavy on my shoulder, my arms are tight around his back. His exhaustion is so deep that I'm not sure anything would wake him. I feel guilty for falling asleep, for not waiting for him to come back from his shed, and even guiltier for using sex so that I wouldn't have to hear what I know he was going to tell me. Poor Adam. I'd never use the word *fragile* to describe him, but there's a fragility about him that makes me afraid. In the space of a day, something deep within him has changed. I'm not surprised; to find out that your beloved daughter is having an affair with one of your friends, someone you don't particularly like, must be one of the worst things a man can experience. If only he hadn't had to find out at my party.

And that's when I realize—he was already stressed before my party started, so when, exactly, did he find out? I go back over everything. He was fine when we woke yesterday morning, fine over breakfast. Then I went out with Kirin and Jess, leaving him with Josh. At some point he went into town, supposedly to get my present, and came back with a migraine instead. There was the phone call he made to his parents in the afternoon, about seemingly nothing at all. The way he was off with Amy when she arrived and his conversation earlier with Nelson, when he had seemed distressed. There's been too much that's out of character. And what was it he wanted to tell me, when we were together in the garden, before the party started? Was it about Marnie and Rob? If it was, and I can't think of anything else it could be, he must have found out about their affair while he was in town.

Everything points to it, I realize. It's why he was so stressed yesterday afternoon. The effort of pretending he didn't know must have been awful, especially in relation to Rob. It had been hard enough for me, and it would have been harder for Adam, because instinct would have made him want to rip Rob apart. I had secretly cried my eyes out for two days. Adam hadn't had the luxury of coming to terms with it in private before meeting Rob publicly. That's why he looked as if he wanted to kill Rob during the box incident. So his conversation with Nelson must have been about Marnie and Rob after all. Nelson had refused to believe it and had probably said something along the lines of *My little brother wouldn't do something like that,* which would explain Adam's almost hysterical laughter.

The phone call he made to his dad during the afternoon—maybe he'd wanted to talk it through with Mike, and had decided against it at the last minute because he felt he should tell me first. Which means that Cleo must have told Adam about her suspicions during the morning. Maybe they bumped into each other in town, went for a coffee together and it had all come out. It's why Adam didn't have my present, because once she'd told him, all thought of it would have gone from his mind. It also explains his migraine—it was just a made-up excuse to explain his low spirits.

Poor Cleo, poor Adam, I feel terrible for them. I need to wake Adam and tell him that I already know about Marnie and Rob, that I've known since Rob and Cleo went to Hong Kong. But—my heart sinks. He'll be furious that I've let him drink and joke with the man who has betrayed us so horribly. It'll be exactly what I've been afraid of; he'll think I held back for six weeks—six weeks, not just a few hours like he has—because I wanted to make sure I had my party first.

I lie for another while, turning it over in my mind, hating myself for what I'm thinking, which is that I'll let Adam tell me about Marnie and Rob when he wakes up, and pretend I didn't know. I'd have to tell Max, though, so that he won't give me away. A wave of shame washes over me, that I could even think of lying to Adam, and making Max part of that deceit. But it would make everything so much easier. Tensions are going to be running high. Why add to them by telling Adam that I already know what he so desperately wants to tell me?

Moving slowly, I ease my shoulder from under Adam's head and carefully slide my arms from around him, ready to stop if he moves. But he sleeps on, unaware that I'm no longer holding him. I get quietly out of bed, pull a T-shirt over my head, slip on some jeans, push my feet into slippers, and go quietly downstairs. Although the caterers took the crockery, cutlery, and glasses away with them, there are some of my own dishes piled in the sink, and the floor needs a good wash.

My birthday cakes are sitting on the counter, each of them covered in cling wrap. Just seeing them makes me hungry and I realize that I didn't eat very much during the party, or drink. Every time someone handed me a glass, I only took a sip before I seemed to need to put it down. I set to work, loading what I can into the dishwasher and washing the larger dishes by hand. I put everything away, wipe down the counters, then make myself some coffee before washing the kitchen floor.

I carry my coffee out to the garden. It feels as if I'm the only one awake in the world. When Josh and Marnie were small, I'd often get up in the early hours and get the housework out of the way. I'd always have a really good day afterward, no longer stressed about having to get things done. I'm glad that I've been able to get the house back to normal, with everyone coming over later.

It's a while before I realize that nobody will be coming to lunch today, not now that Adam knows about Marnie and Rob.

5 A.M.–6 A.M.

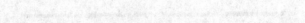

Adam

I jolt awake, my heart pounding. I know something terrible has happened and I struggle to remember what it is. And then I remember. Marnie is dead. I lie still, trying to absorb the pain of loss that racks my body. This is how it will always be, I realize. A first few seconds of unawareness before reality comes flooding in, bringing anguish along with it.

Is it a good thing that Livia is no longer beside me? Yes, because if she was, I'd have to tell her now, this minute. She must be in the bathroom, which means I can wait a bit longer. I try to think of nothing, to close my mind to the horror of Marnie's death, to preserve myself so that I'll be able to tell Livia without breaking. But it's impossible.

It's the not knowing that's going to haunt me. Not knowing if Marnie knew she was about to die. And because I can't know, I'll always torture myself with thoughts that she did, that there were seconds, minutes even, when she knew the horror that awaited her. I'll never get over the fact that Marnie had to face death alone, never.

One of my biggest regrets has always been that I wasn't there at her birth, because I was at the pub with Nelson. By the time Jess tracked me down, it was all over. Is it significant that I wasn't there for her death either? Maybe it's the price I've had to pay for not caring enough about her before she was born. That, and not really wanting her in the first place.

The sound of the back door opening and footsteps on the terrace tell me that Livia is downstairs, not in the bathroom. I wonder how long she's been up. Through the open window I catch the sound of her humming to herself, and feel an aching sadness. Today is the last day she'll have gotten up, excited for the day ahead.

The amount of effort needed to reach for my mobile is huge. I manage only because I need to know the time, I need to know how much longer I can stall before I tell Livia. It's 5:45. The sun will just be rising. It will be beautiful out there in the garden, a little chilly perhaps, but beautiful. Is that the place to tell her, in the garden, sitting on the wall surrounded by memories of yesterday, facing Marnie's fence? Or will the photos of Marnie make everything worse, if it's possible for things to be worse?

Fifteen more minutes and then I'll tell her, before Josh wakes up, before everybody starts phoning to thank us for the wonderful party.

Livia

I love the garden in the early morning, before birdsong is replaced by the sound of voices, the drone of lawn mowers and power tools. I walk across the grass, retrieving the discarded napkins and dropped bottle tops as I go. I catch myself humming "Unchained Melody," the song Adam and I danced to last night, and I can't believe I feel so relaxed when I know what the day ahead holds. I suppose it's because it's going to be Adam telling me about Marnie and Rob, rather than the other way around, which means the worry of telling him has gone. I feel bad that I'm going to pretend I know nothing about the affair to save my own skin. *Maybe I shouldn't,* I think anxiously, *maybe I should just tell the truth.*

I try to take the burst balloons down, but realizing I'll need scissors to cut the string, I go and fetch some from the kitchen, taking the napkins and bottle tops with me. As I go to throw them in the bin, I freeze. Because there, lying on top of remnants of food, is the envelope from the travel agency, the one I gave Adam during my party. Not only that, it's been torn in half.

I reach down and retrieve the two pieces, my heart heavy with dismay. I don't understand. Why has Adam thrown away the tickets I bought him? I thought a trip to see the viaduct would be the perfect present for him. How could I have gotten it so wrong?

I carry the torn pieces over to the table and sit down, feeling stupidly close to tears. It's true that he hadn't seemed excited when I presented him with the tickets yesterday. I thought it was because he was worried about taking time off; now it seems he didn't want to go at all. It's completely out of character for him not to be grateful for a present, even those he secretly doesn't like, like the Christmas sweater his aunt buys him every year. He might never wear it—he has a drawerful of presents that he's never used—but when he opens it, he'll pretend that it's exactly what he wanted. He would never hurt anyone's feelings—but he has hurt mine, not by not wanting to go and see the Millau Viaduct, but by tearing the tickets in half. For him to have done that, he must have been angry, irritated, frustrated.

Frustrated. Maybe Adam has never gotten over his disappointment at not having qualified as a civil engineer. What if it's still there, hidden deep inside him, along with other never-to-be-fulfilled desires? Have I made the most stupid, insensitive mistake? I never thought to run it past Mike or Nelson, ask them what they thought before booking the trip. Maybe they'd have put me right and suggested an alternative. If Adam still has regrets about not having done what he wanted to do, not being what he wanted to be, I'm the last one he'd tell.

Tears escape from my eyes and I dash them away angrily. I'd rather he'd come out and told me, rather than tear up the tickets. What am I meant to do now? Go and have it out with him? I shake my head. Nothing adds up, nothing makes sense. I know Adam, and if he really didn't want to go and see the bridge, not only would he have been honest, he'd also have found a solution. He'd have suggested that we stay somewhere near Montpellier, not Millau itself, and explore the surrounding countryside instead. Maybe he didn't want to tell me last night, so that's another conversation we're going to have this morning. And I'll tell him that it's fine, that we can do as he suggests. What's important is that he has a few days away that he'll enjoy.

I'm not sure the travel agency will refund the tickets, but I can always ask. First, I need to try to stick them back together, because I don't suppose they'll appreciate them being torn in half any more than I do.

I take the tickets from the envelope and piece them together, first Adam's, then mine. And find myself staring, because instead of Montpellier, the destination is down as Cairo. I sit back against the wall, puzzling it out. I don't understand how there could have been a mistake. I remember the girl at the travel agency going through the tickets with me before putting them in the envelope, and she can't have gotten them mixed up with someone else's tickets because our names are on these, in black and white. And then I notice the departure date, and the time—June 9, at 10:30 A.M. Today. In a few hours.

My mind feels as if it's wading through sludge. These aren't the tickets I bought, these are tickets that someone else bought. It must have been Adam. But why would Adam buy tickets for Cairo, leaving today, and not say anything about them to me? Unless he arranged a surprise for me, like I'd arranged a surprise for him. Except that I got there first.

I feel terrible. No wonder he wasn't very enthusiastic when he saw the tickets for Montpellier. He knew we wouldn't be able to go on Tuesday because we'd be in Cairo. It also explains the non-appearance of my present at the party—how could he give it to me when he knew it would spoil the one I'd just given him? But as he's probably booked a resort, it would be more logical to cancel the trip to France than the one to Egypt.

The thought of Adam planning this trip makes me feel quite emotional. We'd seen a travel program a while back about Egypt, and I remember telling him that I'd always wanted to see the pyramids, a throwback to my childhood, when I wanted to be an archaeologist, until my parents told me I'd be a doctor. He must have planned to surprise me with the tickets this morning. Or maybe he wouldn't have given them to me, maybe he'd have told me to pack a case because we were going on a surprise trip, and that I'd find out where we were going only when I got to the airport. It would have been wonderful. And it still can be. From a totally selfish point of view, I'd rather see the pyramids than the Millau Viaduct.

6 A.M.–7 A.M.

Adam

I'm about to get out of bed and go and find Livia, when I hear her footsteps pounding up the stairs, as if she's suddenly discovered something. There's a rush of acid in my stomach. She knows. I spring up in the bed, ready to catch her, but she comes running into the room looking so relieved and happy that I freeze.

"You are just the most perfect man," she says, throwing herself down beside me. She cups my face in her hands and looks deep into my eyes. "I don't know whether to say thank you first, or sorry."

"What do you mean?" I ask warily.

"It's not too late, we can still go." I look at her uncomprehendingly. "To Cairo!" She laughs. "I found the tickets. It doesn't matter that they've been torn in half, I'm sure we can print them ourselves."

I take her hands from my face and hold them in mine. "Livia."

"You should have told me," she says, before I can say anything else. "I understand now why you didn't seem overly pleased about the trip to Millau. You should have told me you'd already booked somewhere. I wouldn't have minded."

Now I'm in another nightmare. "It's not that. We're not going to Cairo. Well, we are, but not this morning."

"Have you managed to get the tickets changed? Oh, that's

perfect! Now we have two trips to look forward to! When are we going?"

"Tomorrow. But listen, Livia—"

"Well, that wasn't very clever, to only change them to tomorrow." Her eyes cloud with confusion. "We still won't be able to go to Montpellier. But I'd rather have a beach holiday anyway."

"Livia!" I say desperately. "Will you listen?" She looks at me in surprise. "We're not going to Cairo for a beach holiday—"

"Don't tell me—I know, it's one of those tour things, where you stay at different places! I know it's not the same as lying on the beach, but it'll still be lovely."

"No. It's not that."

"Well, what is it, then?"

I catch hold of her hands again.

"Livia, I need to tell you something very serious, and I need you to listen."

The laughter finally leaves her and she goes very still. And while I'm trying to get the words out, she utters the most unthinkable words.

"It's all right, Adam, I know."

I go hot, then cold, then hot again. For a blessed moment, the world recedes, and Livia along with it.

"No," I say when my vision clears. "It's not possible. You can't know what I'm going to tell you."

"It's about Marnie, isn't it?"

My mind fragments. I release her hands abruptly. "You—you *know?*"

"Yes, and I'm just as devastated as you are." Her voice breaks and her eyes fill with tears. "What's going to happen to us all?"

I throw the covers off and get out of bed, unable to be next to her, trying to take it in. She's upset, but shouldn't she be distraught? Shouldn't her heart be broken, shouldn't she be weeping? She seemed so happy when she came in—she *was* happy when she came in. How is she still functioning?

"Adam," she pleads, reaching for me.

"When did you find out?" I ask harshly, ignoring her out-stretched arms.

There's a split second of hesitation. "Yesterday."

She's known since *yesterday*? "When, yesterday?"

"At the party."

"What time?" I snap.

"Why are you so angry with me? What does it matter what time I found out?"

"I just want to know if it was after you danced the night away, or before!"

She leaps out of bed and faces me. "What about you? It didn't stop you joking with Rob! Because when did you find out, Adam? Yesterday, before the party had even started! And yet you still let it go ahead!"

"I did it for you, Livia! I wanted you to have one last chance to be happy!"

"Stop being so dramatic! I know it's going to be difficult, but to say that we're never going to be happy again—" She moves closer to me. "Look, I know it's hard for you to accept that Marnie isn't the angel you think she is, but it's not the end of the world."

I stare at her. "Wh—what did you say about Marnie?"

"It's not the end of the world if she isn't the angel you think she is. If you're going to be angry with anyone, be angry with Rob. He's to blame for all of this."

I shake my head. I'm struggling to breathe, to think. "Liv, what has Rob got to do with it?"

Her eyes go wide. "Oh God," she says, her hand halfway to her mouth. "I thought you knew, I thought you knew it was Rob." She searches my face. "Did you think it was Max, is that why you were off with him yesterday?" She puts a hand on my arm. "I'm so sorry, Adam, it's not Max, it's Rob."

"What's Rob?" I ask, my voice thick with confusion.

"It's Rob who's having an affair with Marnie. That's what I'm trying to tell you, Adam. Marnie and Rob are having an affair, not Marnie and Max—although that wouldn't be an affair, because he isn't married, not like that filthy, cheating adulterer!" she finishes angrily.

I thought I'd reached the bottom, I thought that things couldn't possibly get worse. But what Livia has just said—I can't even begin to process it. I sink onto the bed. She has to be mistaken. Marnie would never, ever, have an affair with someone like Rob. She couldn't. She wouldn't. She wouldn't do that to Jess, to us. Livia's made a mistake, she must have.

As if she knows what I'm thinking, she crouches on the floor and leans into me so that our foreheads are touching.

"I know it's hard to believe, but it's true," she says quietly, taking my hands in hers. "They've been having an affair for over a year now. From what Max said, I think it must have started during her first year at Durham. They split up just before she left for Hong Kong. I knew she'd been seeing someone, but I didn't know it was Rob; it wouldn't have occurred to me in a million years that it might be. If it had, I would have—I would have . . ." Her voice trails off. "It's why she was so unhappy for the first few months there. But then he went to see her, last December, when he was meant to be on that business trip to Singapore, and everything must have started up again." She gives a harsh laugh. "Oh, and guess what? He didn't go with Cleo to Hong Kong because Jess didn't want her to go alone; that was just a story. He went so that he could be with Marnie. I saw him on FaceTime, coming out of the bathroom in the hotel, naked. I thought it was a boyfriend, but it was Rob."

I know she's speaking. I can feel her breath on my face as the words tumble out of her. But they barely register because all I can think is that she still doesn't know, she still doesn't know that Marnie is dead.

I move my head back and find her eyes.

"Livia, that's not what I wanted to tell you."

She looks at me in bewilderment. "But you said it was about Marnie."

"Yes, it is."

"What, then?"

I pull her to her feet and make her sit on the bed next to me, keeping her hands in mine.

"Livia," I say, turning to face her.

"Is it about the baby?"

The same feeling comes over me, as if I'm living in some kind of parallel world.

"No, it's not about the baby," I say, my mind unable to keep up, unable to understand why she's started talking about Kirin's pregnancy.

"What, then?" She sounds almost impatient.

I open my mouth but nothing comes out except a shaky sigh.

"You're scaring me, Adam!" Her voice is sharp with fear. "Just tell me."

I would if I could remember how. My thumb rubs the back of her hand.

"Livia, I'm sorry, but there's been an accident."

Blood drains from her face. "Oh God, is it Marnie? What's happened? Is she hurt, is she in the hospital?"

"No, no, she's not hurt. She—she didn't make it, Livia. Marnie's gone."

The world comes to a stop. We don't even breathe.

"Gone?" Livia says, finding her voice. "What do you mean, gone? Gone where?"

"I'm so sorry, Livia." I thought the pain couldn't get any worse. "Marnie—she died. She—she's dead."

She snatches her hands from mine. "Stop it, Adam! How can you say such a thing? Don't! Don't, do you hear me? Don't say such a stupid thing! She's had an affair, that's all!"

I try to pull her toward me, but she twists away.

"Livia, it's true. I wish it wasn't, but it's true. She was coming home as a surprise, she was going to turn up at your party to surprise you, but her plane—well, it crashed. It crashed on takeoff from Cairo."

"Cairo?" She pounces on the word. "Marnie wouldn't have been in Cairo. You've made a mistake. Marnie's in Hong Kong. She went away for the weekend, but not to Cairo. She wouldn't have gone to Cairo, it's too far. Someone mentioned a plane crash at the party, I think they said Cairo. It's all right, Adam, you've gotten mixed up, you've been dreaming and you've gotten mixed up."

"No. That's why we're going there tomorrow, to see where Marnie—"

"No!" She slaps her hands over her ears. "I don't want to hear it! I don't understand what you're saying, I don't understand!"

Of all the ways she could have reacted, I never expected this, that she wouldn't want to understand what I'm telling her. I want to scream at her that she has to understand, because there's no other way to tell her that Marnie is dead. Instead, I remove her hands from her ears and fold her into my arms, holding her tight.

"I'm so sorry, Livia, but Marnie was on the plane that crashed. She was coming home via Cairo and Amsterdam for your party. You know I wouldn't say it if it wasn't true. I'm sorry, I'm so sorry."

A wail starts from somewhere deep inside her, an echo of the one that tore out of her as she pushed Josh from her body, the same that she would have given when she brought Marnie into this world, except that I wasn't there to hear it. I anchor her to me, letting my body take the force of her anguish. The stupid, useless platitudes that I'd been determined not to say stream from my lips.

"It's all right, Livia, it's all right, everything's going to be all right, I promise, everything's going to be all right." But she's beyond hearing, beyond listening, beyond anything but the raw pain of loss.

The bedroom door bursts open and Josh stands there, fear etched on his face. Josh, I'd forgotten about Josh.

"Mum!" He stares at Livia, collapsed against me, and panic

takes hold. "Dad, what's happened? What's happened? Is it Grandad? Gran?"

It wasn't meant to be like this. I was meant to tell Livia, then Josh, separately, one at a time, so that I could be there for both of them. I hold out a hand.

"Josh. Come here."

He stays glued to the spot, paralyzed by fear. "What's happened? Dad, what's happened?"

It's hard to make myself heard over Livia's terrible weeping. "I need you to come here. Please."

He comes over and sits on the bed. "What is it, what's going on?"

I put my hand on his shoulder.

"Josh, it's Marnie." I can't go on because the mention of her name adds to Livia's grief.

"What do you mean, it's Marnie?" Panic spirals in his eyes. "Has she had an accident?"

"There's been a plane crash. I'm sorry, Josh, but Marnie was on it."

"Plane crash? Where? How?"

"In Cairo. Marnie was on her way home; she was going to turn up at the party as a surprise. The plane crashed on takeoff."

Josh stares at me. "You mean—you mean—" He tries another tack. "She's all right, isn't she?"

I shake my head. "No, no, I'm sorry. I'm so sorry." He waits. "She's gone. Marnie died in the crash."

He goes so white I'm afraid for him. I move my hand to the back of his head, draw him toward me and Livia. And hold them while they fall.

Livia

Everything has stopped. I can't breathe; the room is crowding me.

It can't be true. This isn't happening, it can't be true. I don't understand, I don't understand how Marnie was in Cairo. She said she was going away so that she could revise in peace, so what was she doing in Cairo? Cairo is noisy; she wouldn't get any peace there. Adam keeps telling me that she was on her way here, for the party, but that doesn't make sense. Why would she be in Cairo if she was coming here? Adam has explained, over and over again, to me and to Josh, because Josh doesn't understand it any more than I do. He keeps saying that she was on her way to Amsterdam, but that doesn't make sense either. Josh, poor Josh. I'm glad he's quiet now, I couldn't bear it when he was crying, his body shuddering through Adam's to mine. It cut through my pain and made me able to comfort him.

"What are we going to do, Dad?" he mumbles. He sounds so scared that my heart breaks for him. "What are we going to do?"

"We're going to get through it, we're going to be strong for each other," Adam says. "We need to think about the people who love Marnie as much as we do, about how we're going to tell them. We need to be strong for them, for Gran, Grandad—" He breaks off, unable to face the thought of telling his parents.

"No." Josh shakes his head. "I meant—what are we going to do without Marnie?"

"We're going to get through it," Adam says again, and I wonder how he can be so strong. "I don't know how, but we're going to get through it. We have to." His voice breaks slightly. "It's what Marnie would want."

"I still can't believe it. I don't want to believe it."

"I know, Josh," Adam says gently. "I know."

"It can't be true," he says for the hundredth time. "It just can't be. Are you sure, Dad, are you sure?"

"Josh, please—"

Adam sounds as if he's at his breaking point, and that frightens me, because I need him to be strong. So instead of asking him if he's really, really sure that Marnie was on the flight, because, like Josh, I can't believe that she was, I give his hand a little squeeze, telling him wordlessly that I understand how incredibly hard it is for him to have to answer our never-ending questions. But he must be wrong, he has to be. He just needs time to realize it.

So I stay very quiet, giving him time to work it out, and Josh does the same. But the silence drags on and the air in the room becomes heavy with despair. I can feel it on my skin, taste it in my mouth; I can even smell it. And that's when I know.

Tears seep from my eyes. I can't ever imagine them stopping.

"How are we going to tell everyone?" I ask brokenly.

A wave of relief—profound, soundless—spreads through Adam's body, that I've finally accepted the unbearable truth. He clears his throat.

"I thought I'd ask Nelson to let people know. Except Mum and Dad. I need to tell them myself."

"It's good that Izzy is with them," I say, amazed at how calm I must sound.

"Do you see now why I couldn't let Amy stay the night?" Adam says. "I didn't think it was fair on her to be here when—" He falters. "You know, when I told you."

"How did you find out, Dad?" Josh mumbles. "Did you get a phone call or something?"

"No. I knew what flights Marnie was taking; it was our secret. When I heard about the plane crash, I didn't think it was her flight, and when I realized that it was, I didn't think she was on it because she'd messaged to tell me that her flight from Hong Kong was delayed, so she'd miss her connection in Cairo. But then, later, I realized that the flight from Cairo had also been delayed, so there was a chance she might have arrived in time for it. But there was still the chance that she might not have made it."

My head jerks up. "So maybe she didn't," I say, grasping at this new thread of hope. "Adam, what if Marnie didn't make the flight?"

He swallows painfully. "She did. It's been confirmed."

"When? How?"

"I phoned the airline last night, after Amy left. There was a number I could call to find out."

"After Amy left? Is that why you went out to your shed?"

"Yes."

"But—" I draw away from him, running it through my mind. If he knew that Marnie—that Marnie was—when he came back into the house, why didn't he tell me then? And didn't we make love? No, we can't have done, not then, not once Adam knew, we couldn't have. It must have been before. I want to ask him. I need to know. But I can't, not with Josh here.

"Why didn't you tell us, Dad?" Josh says angrily, although I know it's not Adam he's angry with. "You shouldn't have had to go through that on your own. Why didn't you wake us up when you knew?"

"I thought I'd let you sleep. I thought a few hours wouldn't make any difference."

"They would have made a difference to you. It must have been awful for you, having to keep it to yourself." He shakes his head. "You should have woken me up, Dad."

Even in my confusion about when, exactly, we made love, my heart goes out to Adam, for choosing to spare us by shouldering the burden himself. But it comes to a sudden halt, brought to a standstill by another thought, another puzzle.

"So how did it happen?" I ask.

"They don't know. They wouldn't tell me anything. They said there'll be an investigation. We'll know more when we get there, I expect."

"Get where?" Josh asks.

"Cairo. Mum and I are going tomorrow. You too, if you want. They've booked us on a flight. But you don't have to come if you don't want to."

"Of course I'm coming!" he says angrily.

"No," I interrupt. "I meant—how did it happen? How did you find out about Marnie?"

"I told you, there was a number to phone."

"But before then. How did you know you had to call it?"

I sense a slight hesitation. "Because Marnie hadn't phoned me to let me know she was safe. I kept expecting her to, but she didn't."

"Wait a minute." I close my eyes, trying to work it out. "You said the airline has booked us on a flight tomorrow."

"That's right."

"But the tickets for the flights this morning, the ones I found in the bin—you must have bought them, from the travel agency in town. I recognized the envelope."

"Yes."

"When? When did you buy them?"

"Yesterday, as soon as I heard about the crash. I thought Marnie was stranded at the airport in Cairo. I thought, if she'd missed the flight, she'd be there all alone and she'd be frightened because of what had happened—because the plane that crashed was the one she should have been on—and she wouldn't know what to do. So I got tickets for us to go to her, to be with her."

"What? You knew about the crash yesterday?" Josh stares at Adam. "Why didn't you tell us?"

"Because—I told you—I didn't think that Marnie was on the plane. I wasn't going to worry you for nothing."

My heart retracts, coming back to nestle deep inside me.

"That's it, isn't it? That's what was wrong with you, why you were acting so strangely. Wait—was that what you were trying to tell me, before the party?" He doesn't say anything. "It was, wasn't it? You wanted to tell me that Marnie might have been on the plane that crashed."

"Yes," he says again.

"But why didn't you tell me? Why didn't you just come out and tell me?"

He can't meet my eyes. "I tried to," he says, his face gray. "I tried to. But you were so happy. If I'd told you, you would have wanted to cancel the party and I just wanted you to—I knew that once I told you, you'd feel sick with worry, like I did, and I didn't want that for you until I knew definitely."

"But you only phoned at—what?—three in the morning. Why didn't you phone earlier? They give you a number straightaway, don't they, for people to phone if they think someone from their family might be on the plane?"

"Because I didn't want to know," he says, his voice low. "I wanted to hang on to the chance that Marnie hadn't made the flight."

I look at this man, who has suddenly become a stranger to me, and my heart shrivels to almost nothing.

"How did you do it, Adam?" I ask, my voice trembling with rage. "How did you manage to chat and laugh and eat and drink when there was a chance that our daughter was dead? And more to the point"—my voice rises as the realization sets in—"how could you have let me chat and laugh and eat and drink, and dance—*dance!*—when there was even the tiniest of chances that Marnie was dead!"

"Livia, please!" He reaches desperately for me, but I twist away.

"*No!*" I look at him in horror. "What are you, some kind of monster?"

"Mum, don't!"

I round on Josh. "He let me dance! My daughter was dead and he let me *dance*!" Lunging at Adam, I begin hitting him, raining blows on his head, on his chest, anywhere I can reach.

"Mum, stop!"

But I'm too far gone. I carry on hitting Adam with my fists, screaming at him, calling him a coward, and other names, until Josh pulls me away and I collapse onto the floor.

7 A.M.–8 A.M.

Adam

Livia's cries follow me all the way down the stairs and into the garden. I walk blindly up the steps to the lawn, still reeling from the violence of her reaction. I knew it would be like this. I knew she wouldn't forgive me, not once she knew the truth of what I'd done. She might have accepted that I'd kept the news to myself for a couple of hours because she and Josh were sleeping. But to expect her to accept that I knew about the crash long before the party started, and chose to let it go on, was too much. When she asked how I could have let her dance, her words tore through me, and as her hands slammed onto me, I asked myself the same question—how could I have let her dance? Because now, it seems abhorrent.

I need to phone Nelson. I sit down on the stone wall, my back to Marnie's photos. I can hear Livia's sobs from here—or maybe it's just their echo in my brain. I'm glad Josh is with her, doing what Livia wouldn't let me do, comforting her. He hasn't said anything to me. He didn't need to; the look of disbelief he gave as he asked me to leave was enough.

I take out my mobile, sit with it in my hands, reliving the moment when I destroyed Livia's world. It was harder than I ever imagined because she thought I was talking about something else. Something to do with Marnie, but also to do with Rob. I can't think about that now; I have to call Nelson.

His voice is too loud down the line. "Adam! How're you doing?"

"Nelson, can you come over? Just you, not Kirin or the children."

There's a pause. "Is everything all right?"

"No, not really. I'll tell you when you get here. I'm in the garden. Could you come now?"

"I'm on my way."

Five minutes, ten at the most. Just enough time to phone Dad.

"Hi Adam, to what do I owe the pleasure of an early call?"

I close my eyes, press the corners with my finger and thumb.

"Dad." My voice cracks. "Is Mum there?"

There's the sound of movement, then his footsteps on the stairs. "Not anymore. I'm in the kitchen, your mum's in bed."

"Are you sitting down?"

"No. Should I be?"

"Yes."

The scrape of a chair. "Right. Go ahead."

"It's bad news, Dad. It's about Marnie."

I hear him take a steadying breath. "What's happened?"

"She was coming home for Livia's party as a surprise. She had to take three planes. One of them crashed. She's dead, Dad. Marnie's gone."

There's a half-strangled cry that stops as soon as it starts.

"I'm sorry, Dad. I'm sorry." The words won't stop coming out of my mouth. "I'm so sorry."

"When?" His voice is barely a whisper. "When did Marnie—" He can barely speak.

"Yesterday. I knew in the morning, not for sure, because I thought she'd missed the flight; she said she was going to. So I let the party go on because I wanted Livia to have a last few hours of happiness. Can you understand that, Dad? Can you understand why I didn't tell anyone?"

"Yes, I understand," he says, because he knows it's what I need to hear. "I'm so sorry, Adam. I can't imagine—how is Livia, how is Josh? Are they all right?" He gives an angry growl. "Of course they're not, how could they be. I don't know what—I'm coming over. You just stay exactly where you are. I'll be with you soon. Is there anyone with Livia, apart from Josh?"

"No. Nelson is on his way over. I thought, once I've told him, he could tell everyone who needs to know. You don't have to come over; you should stay with Mum. Once you've told her—will you tell Mum? And Izzy? And Ian? Will you tell them about Marnie?"

"We're not leaving you to cope with this on your own," he says fiercely. "It's going to be all right. We'll get you through this, your mum and I. We'll get you through it."

I hang up quickly, before I crumble completely, wondering if I should have told Dad in person. But I don't think I could have. I couldn't bear to see his face, witness his distress. I don't even know how I'm going to tell Nelson.

I lean forward and concentrate only on breathing. I don't have to wait long for Nelson to arrive. He doesn't say anything, he just sits down beside me and I realize he already knows. Josh must have told him, when he let him in.

"I'm so sorry, Adam," he says, his voice barely a whisper.

I clear my throat. "Can you tell Jess? Ask her to come over, for Livia. Not Rob, just Jess."

"Yes, of course. What else can I do? Do you need—I don't know—a cup of tea, or anything?"

I stand up, suddenly needing space. I look around, but there are memories of the party everywhere. I walk blindly to my shed, shoving the tent out of the way with my shoulder. The block of black walnut that I started carving for Marnie is still where I left it, on the floor in front of the bench. I slide down beside it, needing its physical presence, and close my eyes.

Time passes. Dad arrives. He sits down next to me, pulls my head to his shoulder.

"It's all right," he says gently. "It's all right."

Livia

There's a knock at the bedroom door and as it begins to open, I get ready to yell at Adam to go away. Part of me is ashamed of the way I went for him, but if he comes anywhere near me, I know I'll attack him again. I can't believe—I just can't believe—that he let the party go ahead.

It isn't Adam, it's Nelson. As soon as I see his large frame taking up most of the doorway, I start crying again. Josh, his arm around me, pulls me closer.

Nelson comes farther into the room. "Livia, Josh, I'm so sorry, so very sorry."

Josh mumbles something, but I don't say anything, because what is there to say?

"I spoke to Jess," Nelson continues. "She's on her way over. Cleo's bringing her."

Relief washes over me.

"Thank you," I say tearfully, because it's Jess I need at this moment.

I sense him appraising the situation, me and Josh sitting together on the bed, me crying, Josh doing his best to comfort me.

"Josh, can I ask you to do something? Your dad has asked me to let people know about Marnie." I marvel at the way Nelson says her name without any hesitation or embarrassment. It's exactly what we need. "Could you get me a list of names and phone numbers, please?"

Josh gets to his feet. "Sure." His voice is hollow, but there's also a tinge of relief, and I realize that Nelson's purpose in asking him for help is to give Josh something to do.

They stand, their arms clasped around each other, and I'm glad Josh is able to take comfort from Nelson, which he couldn't from me. I wish I'd been able to be strong for him, but the horror of knowing I was laughing and dancing when Marnie was already lost to us was too much. I want to reach out to him, to hug him as Nelson is doing, but more waves of pain and anguish make it impossible.

Josh leaves and I can feel Nelson's sorrow as I sit twisting a sodden tissue in my fingers, trying to get my sobs under control.

"I'm sorry," I say as he settles on the bed beside me. "I wish I could stop crying."

"The worst thing that could possibly happen has happened to you," he says, drawing me to him. "You're allowed to cry as much as you like."

"I can't believe it," I say brokenly. "I can't believe that Marnie's—"

"I know," he says, smoothing my hair. "I know."

I want to tell him that Adam knew about the crash hours before the party started, but something stops me. Whatever I might think of Adam, I don't want Nelson to think less of him.

Jess's voice comes to me, calling from the hall below. I scramble off the bed, but by the time I've opened the door, she's made it up the stairs.

"Livia," she says. And then we're weeping in each other's arms, because she understands my pain, the pain of a mother losing a child.

Nelson squeezes past us, his hands heavy on our shoulders.

"Mike has made tea," Jess says eventually, wiping her eyes. "Come on, let's go downstairs."

"Adam isn't there, is he?"

"No, he's in his shed. Mike came to get some tea and toast for him."

"It doesn't surprise me that Adam is able to eat," I say bitterly, because I don't mind telling Jess. "He knew, Jess, he knew about Marnie and he let the party go on. He carried on as normal, as if nothing was wrong, and even worse, he let me carry on as normal." I shake my head and fresh tears fall from my eyes. "I'll never get over it. I'll never get over the fact that I danced the day my daughter died."

"I don't think he knew for sure about Marnie," she says hesitantly. "From what Cleo said, he didn't actually have confirmation until this morning."

"Cleo? Why has Adam been speaking to Cleo about it?"

"Because she knew that Marnie was coming home."

"Cleo knew?" My mind reels.

"Come on," she says, easing me toward the stairs. "Let's go and have a cup of tea. Cleo is with Josh now. You can talk to her later."

5 P.M.–12 A.M.

Adam

A muffled sob escapes Livia's lips, breaking through the silence as we sit with untouched mugs of tea in the kitchen.

"Sorry," she mumbles.

I long to comfort her, but she doesn't want me, she only wants Jess.

"Don't be silly," Mum says, her eyes bright with unshed tears. "You've nothing to be sorry for."

The day has been punctuated with Nelson disappearing to make calls and coming back to tell us that we're in the thoughts of whoever he's just phoned, and to let them know if they can help in any way at all. It doesn't seem to register with Livia. She doesn't even nod. She's retreated into herself, protecting herself. She didn't even want to see her mum.

We'd forgotten about Patricia until there was the ring of the doorbell in the middle of the afternoon. We left Nelson to answer it, presuming it was a neighbor.

"Livia, it's your mum," he said, coming back into the kitchen. But Livia shook her head and left it to Nelson to explain about Marnie.

I move over to the door and look unseeingly through the glass to the garden. We'd be more comfortable in the sitting room, but nobody has suggested going through. We've been here most of the day: Jess, Mum, Dad, Izzy, Ian, and Cleo sitting around the table; me, Josh, Amy, and Nelson leaning against the countertops, cradling mugs of hot drinks that no one wants. Max was here earlier, and Kirin, but they've left now, taking their quiet grief with them.

Murphy lumbers over to stand beside me. Max brought him back this morning and he's barely left my side since. Mimi has slunk off somewhere, as if she knows her presence is a constant reminder of Marnie. I'm not sure when Amy arrived. Sometime this morning, Josh asked if he could tell her about Marnie and if she could come over. Of course we said yes. He needs her more than he needs us; only she can comfort him as he needs to be comforted. The way that we—Livia and I—need to be comforted. Except that for me and Livia, it's impossible.

Although nobody has mentioned it, they know why she won't speak to me, they know the story of how I let the party go on. Nelson knows why, although I'm not sure the others do. I look at him, the conversation we had this morning a comfort against Livia's hate.

"I can't imagine what it must have been like to go through something like that on your own," he said quietly, coming to stand beside me after I'd gone outside for some space. "Why didn't you tell Livia when you first suspected Marnie was on the flight?" There was no criticism in his voice, just curiosity.

"Because I knew that once she knew, it would change her life forever, just like it had already changed mine." I rubbed my face. "I can't tell you what it's like to live with the knowledge that your child is almost certainly dead. I just wanted to stop what was happening. Let Livia have her party, let her have a last few hours of happiness."

"Jesus, Adam."

"If Marnie was dead . . ." I paused. "If I'm honest, I think I must have known she was, because otherwise she would have called. And I think I thought that Liv knowing then wasn't going to change anything for Marnie. It's not as if we could have rushed over to be with her. Livia called me a coward; she thinks I didn't make the call to the airline until the party was over because I lacked the courage to hear the truth, and the courage to tell her. Maybe she's right. Maybe I was lying to myself all along."

"You should have told me," Nelson said.

"I almost did, when we were sitting on the wall, when you were avoiding Rob. But I knew I had to tell Livia first."

The rehashing of my conversation with Nelson, the mention of Rob, stirs something in my brain. Where is Rob? Shouldn't he be here, sitting in the kitchen with us? He's conspicuous by his absence, and I know Nelson thinks the same, because when Jess left the room earlier, he followed her out and had a quiet conversation with her, but not so quiet that I couldn't hear Rob's name. And ever since, Nelson has been texting on and off. Even Jess is at it, discreetly sending messages under the table.

She looks up suddenly, relief evident on her face.

"Rob sends his apologies, he's on his way over."

I turn from the window in acknowledgment and see everybody nodding in silence, except Nelson, who mutters, "About time too." And Livia, who gets up from the table and walks silently out of the room.

It's the look of hatred on her face that brings the nightmare back, the nightmare of this morning, when I was trying to tell her that Marnie was dead and Livia thought I was trying to tell her something different about Marnie. Something she already knew, something about Marnie being in a relationship with—I close my eyes, trying to remember her exact words—*I'm so sorry, Adam, it's not Max, it's Rob.*

"Are you OK?" Dad is on his feet, moving toward me. "Do you want to sit down a minute?"

"No—no, I'm fine." Realizing that I'm clutching the door frame, I lower my arm and pull the door open. "I just need some air."

"Shall I come with you?"

"I'm fine."

Except that I'm not fine, I'll never be fine again. And I'm going to be even less fine if what Livia said is true.

Marnie and Rob. Marnie and *Rob*? I pace up and down the terrace, trying to work it out, Murphy watching me anxiously from the doorway. It can't be true, it can't be. I mean, how could it possibly be true? Livia said something, about Rob going to see Marnie when he was meant to be in Singapore, but she must be mistaken, she has to be. Marnie wouldn't, she just wouldn't, and neither would Rob; he has Jess. He wouldn't do that to Jess, not when she's ill, not even if she wasn't ill. I need to speak to Livia, ask her why she thinks Marnie and Rob were having an affair. I try to recall everything she told me, but I can't. I can only remember parts of it and I'm not even sure I remember those correctly. But if Livia is right—I try to think what it would mean. But I can't, because my mind can't cope with it.

And then I hear him—Rob—coming up the path. I go to the side gate to wait for him; he opens it and comes through, his head bowed, his sunglasses in place even though the sun is weak today. He takes a breath and as squares his shoulders, he raises his eyes and sees me standing there. A momentary pause, then:

"Mate." He walks toward me, his arms outstretched. "Adam."

But I need to know, so I reach out and take off his sunglasses. And, caught by surprise, he has no time to hide. I look deep into his red-rimmed eyes and as he stares back at me, I see the guilt, and smell the stench of it seeping from his pores. It flushes his skin red, works his mouth wordlessly as he searches frantically to deny what is staring me in the face.

"Adam, I—"

I don't even think about hitting him, I just do it. My fist slams under his chin, lifting him off his feet so that he stumbles sideways, crashing into the wall.

"Get out."

Livia

My heart is pounding as I watch from the bedroom window. From where I'm standing, I see Adam walk toward the gate. I have to crane my neck, press my face against the window to be able to follow him to where he comes to a stop, and although I'm sick to my stomach at the thought of seeing Rob, I need to know if Adam absorbed anything of what I told him about Marnie. I don't think he did. I know now that the private hell he disappeared into while I was telling him was nothing to do with the thought of our daughter having an affair with Rob, but the dread of having to tell me she was dead. Dead. I still can't believe it, even though the fact that everyone sitting around the kitchen table tells me it's true, because why would they be here otherwise?

I hear the click of the side gate, then Rob coming onto the terrace. He sees Adam, takes a step toward him, his arm outstretched and I can't breathe, because if they put their arms around each other, it means that Adam didn't grasp what I was telling him, which means he'll never know about Marnie and Rob, not unless I choose to tell him. And I know that I won't. A part of me rages that I'm going to have to sit down and eat with Rob, laugh at his jokes and accept his embraces so that nobody will guess there's anything wrong. But I can't risk alienating Jess and Nelson by spilling Rob's dirty secret, because without them, Adam and I aren't going to get through this. Not when we no longer have each other.

At first, when I see Adam remove Rob's sunglasses, I think it's because he doesn't want to damage them when they clasp each other, united in their grief for Marnie. But he just stands, staring at Rob, and I know the intensity of his gaze because I've felt it so many times myself; I know he's looking deep into Rob's soul, as he has looked into mine. Just as I'm wondering what he's found there, he hits Rob square on the chin, knocking him against the wall, and as Rob scuttles back down the path, a sob escapes me and I'm crying, crying, crying, not for me, not for Marnie, but for Adam. Because although I'll never forgive him for what he did, what I wanted, more than anything, was for him to be able to remember his version of Marnie, not mine.

Adam

I hear the scrape of the back door opening and Nelson calling me as I head across the lawn to my shed, my eyes averted from the photos of Marnie still tacked to the fence. Because, after what's happened, how could anyone take them down, even if they thought it best to?

"Was that Rob?" he calls.

I turn toward him. "Yes."

"Didn't he want to come in?"

"No. He's pretty cut up. But it was good of him to come by. I'm going to my shed for a while. Can you make sure nobody disturbs me?"

"Of course."

Was it only yesterday that the thing that caused me the most grief was having to squeeze behind the tent to get to my shed? There must have been something bigger, something more serious, more problematic. I rack my brains and come up with nothing. My life really was that good.

Inside the shed, I make it as far as the nearest wall, slide down it to the floor. I lean my head back against the warm wood and close my eyes. The knuckles of my right hand are throbbing, my heartbeat echoing through the pulses of pain. There's a peace to it and I flex my fingers, wanting to feel more pain. The movement opens the gash across my palm and I welcome the sharp twinges of discomfort.

It seems impossible that anything could eclipse Marnie's death. But somehow, her affair with Rob does. I can't stop reliving the moment I looked deep inside him, the moment when everything Livia told me was reflected in his eyes with such clarity, I knew it was true. It spins in my brain on a loop—Marnie and Rob, their affair, his visits to see her in Hong Kong. He didn't accompany Cleo to Hong Kong because Jess didn't want her to go alone; he went so that he could be with Marnie. Livia saw him on FaceTime, coming out of the hotel bathroom, naked. The word makes me feel physically sick.

I hear someone brush against the tent as they make their way to the shed and my rage boils over. I just want to be left alone.

"Go away, just go away," I plead, but whoever it is ignores me and, guessing it's Mum, or maybe Dad, I try to keep a hold on my anger. The door pushes but doesn't open. The familiar sound of claws scraping against wood tells me it's Murphy, so I pull myself up and let him in. He follows me back to where I was sitting and as I slide back to the floor, he leans his body into me.

"How did this happen?" I say out loud. Murphy turns his head toward me and licks my face. I put my arms around him, bury my head in his fur, breathe in the earthy smell of him while I try to come to terms with the devastating truth of Marnie and Rob's affair. All the signs were there, I realize. Marnie's unhappiness in Hong Kong. Livia's pulling back from our group of friends, unable to be near Rob, unable to face Jess. Questions crowd my brain, each of them bringing more confusion than the last. Why didn't Livia tell me? Was she ever going to tell me? Did Marnie know that Livia knew? Or was Livia waiting until Marnie came home to talk to her about it? If that was her plan, how would Livia have felt about Marnie turning up at her party? Maybe it wouldn't have been a wonderful surprise, but a terrible shock. And most devastating of all—who was Marnie really coming home to surprise, Livia or Rob?

I don't know how much time has passed before Mum comes to tell me that she and Dad are leaving, taking Izzy and Ian with them.

"They'll be staying with us for a few days," she adds.

I nod. "That's good."

"We'll be back tomorrow, to see you before you leave for the airport. Nelson is taking you."

"That's good of him."

"You should go in now, Adam."

"I will, in a minute."

"Can I do anything for you?"

"No thanks, Mum. Say good-bye to Dad for me."

"Come here."

I get to my feet and she puts her arms around me.

"It'll be all right," she whispers, holding me tight. "It'll be all right."

I close my eyes. I don't say anything, because I can't. It's a while before she lets me go.

"Good-bye, Adam." Her eyes are bright with tears.

I reach a hand to her cheek. "Bye, Mum."

If Mum and Dad are leaving, it must be later than I think. I look through the window; it's almost dark outside, so it must be around 9 P.M.

I sit back down next to Murphy, worrying that he hasn't been fed. I'm trying to raise the energy to take him inside, when Nelson comes in.

"Adam, I'm going to leave now. Jess and Cleo will be leaving soon and Livia is in bed." He pauses. "Why don't you go in? There's only Josh and Amy, and they'll be going up soon."

"I will, in a minute."

"Do you want me to stay? I can, it's no problem."

"No, it's fine, you should get back to Kirin. Can I ask you to do something? Can you give Murphy something to eat?"

"Of course."

He has to take Murphy by the collar to get him away from me.

"Go on, Murphy," I encourage. "I'll see you later."

"Try and get some sleep," Nelson says from the door. "I'll see you tomorrow."

What would he say if I told him about Rob, told him that his thirty-eight-year-old brother was cheating on Jess with my nineteen-year-old daughter? It would destroy him, it would destroy his relationship with Rob, it might even destroy ours. And even if it didn't, things would never be the same.

More time passes. A discreet knock and Josh comes in.

"Dad?" I sense him peering in the darkness. "Where are you?"

"Over here."

"Do you want the light on?"

"No thanks."

"Are you going in?"

"Not just yet."

He waits until his eyes adjust to the dark, then comes over and sits down beside me, adopting the same position, his back against the wall, his knees drawn up, his forearms resting on his knees.

"Wouldn't you be more comfortable in a chair?" he asks after we've sat in silence for a few minutes.

"Probably. But I like it here on the floor."

"Mum's gone to bed."

"Yes, Nelson said."

"You don't mind if Amy stays over, do you?"

"No, of course not."

We sit in silence for a while longer.

"We will get through this, won't we?" he asks.

"Yes, of course we will."

"I mean, you and Mum—"

"We'll be fine."

"I get why you did it, Dad. I get why you didn't tell her until the party was over. I didn't at first, but I do now. Anyway, it's what Marnie would have wanted." He pauses. "I've been thinking—I might try and get my motorcycle license. It would be great to have a bike for getting around London, and when I come down on weekends, we could go for a ride together."

My eyes blur, because I know what he's doing, I know that my son, who has never shown the slightest interest in riding a bike, is already looking for a way to fill the void he knows Marnie will leave in my life.

"That would be great," I say. "But get settled in London first."

"I don't have to live in London, I could stay here for a while. I can travel in easily from Windsor."

"No, you do have to live in London, with Amy. Nobody is going to change their plans. It's already enough that you're not going to New York."

"I'm glad I decided not to go," he says.

"Me too. You should go in, Josh, I'll be along in a minute."

"It's fine, I'll wait."

Knowing that he's not going to leave without me, I get to my feet. I'm so stiff that he has to help me up.

"Thanks. I must be getting old."

He pulls me into a hug. "Never," he says fiercely.

We squeeze behind the tent, walk across the garden.

"I think I'll go for a shower," I say when we get to the house. "Good night, Josh, I'll see you tomorrow."

"Night, Dad. Try to get some sleep, won't you?"

I follow him slowly up the stairs and when I get to the landing, I stop, because our bedroom door is shut tight, a warning not to go in. I have my shower in the family bathroom, but I need clean clothes, and anyway, I'm desperate to talk to Livia.

Our bedroom is in darkness apart from the moonlight coming in through the window. Livia is lying under the quilt, only the top of her head visible. I know she's awake, I can sense it. I dress as silently as I can, then sit down on the edge of the bed.

"Liv," I say.

I don't know which is worse, her angry silence or the desperate tears of before. I ache for the touch of her hand, needing her like I've never needed her before, because she's the only one who knows Marnie like I know Marnie. But it's as if I don't exist.

Livia

I lie in bed, not knowing how I managed to get through the day. After I'd seen Adam punch Rob, I went downstairs to tell everyone I was going to have a rest and found an envelope lying on the mat by the front door. I hadn't realized I was tearing it into pieces until Nelson's fingers prised it from me.

"It's all right, Livia. I'll take that."

"I don't want it, I don't want to see it," I told him, choking back an angry sob, hating that someone had already pushed a condolence card through the letterbox.

"I know," he said, taking my arm. "Why don't you try to get some sleep, at least rest for a while?"

"I want to say good-bye to everyone first."

"Would you like me to stay?" Jess asked once Adam's family had left and we were in the bedroom. Cleo was in Josh's bedroom with him and Amy, and Nelson had gone to see Adam, who was still hiding in his shed.

"No, it's fine," I told her. "You go home, I'll be fine."

"It's just that I don't understand why Rob didn't come in, why he left. And now he's not answering his phone. I'm worried about him."

I turned away, praying that Rob wouldn't tell her about him and Marnie, not tonight. Not ever, I realized, because what did it matter now?

She left to get Cleo, and Nelson came in. "Will you go and see Adam?" he asked. "He needs you."

"No. I can't, I just can't." More angry tears filled my eyes. "How could he do it, Nelson, how could he let the party go on when he was almost a hundred percent sure that Marnie was on that plane? How could he have laughed and joked with everyone?"

"To be fair, I don't think he was laughing and joking with everyone."

"Even Cleo knew before me." I couldn't keep the anguish from my voice. "Did you know too? I saw you talking to Adam at the party; he seemed distressed about something. Is that when he told you?"

"No, I didn't know anything. I knew something was going on with Adam and when I asked him, he said he'd done something terrible and that you'd never forgive him."

"He was right about that! I thought all the fuss—you know, his migraine, the way he kept disappearing into the house—was to do with my present. I didn't realize it was because he was too much of a coward to tell me about Marnie."

"Adam isn't a coward, Livia. He's the strongest person I know. Can you imagine what he must have gone through, from when he first suspected Marnie was on the plane until he actually found out? What he had to go through alone?"

All my resentment burst out of me. "If he'd told me, he wouldn't have had to go through it by himself," I hissed. "I would have shared it with him. *Stop* defending him, Nelson. He was wrong and you know it."

"But—"

"No." I slammed my hand down on the bed. "I don't want to hear it! This isn't about Adam; this is about Marnie!"

He didn't say anything, just gave me a kiss.

"Get some rest, Livia," he said gently. "I'm going now, but I'll be back in the morning."

That was five minutes ago and I wish I could have asked him

not to go. I don't want to be left alone with Adam. I don't want to think about Marnie either, so I concentrate instead on the sounds around me: Nelson saying good-bye to Josh and Amy, then he and Cleo going downstairs, followed slowly by Jess. The sound of two cars pulling away from the house, Nelson's, then Cleo's. Then silence, which quickly becomes too loud, and I feel a mounting panic until Josh's bedroom door opens and he goes downstairs, giving me other sounds to focus on. The back door opening and closing, his footsteps as he crosses the terrace. I strain my ears; I can't hear him pushing back the tent as he squashes his way to Adam's shed, I can only imagine it. But it's not enough, so I force my ears to pick up other sounds: Amy moving about in Josh's room, the neighbors respectfully quiet in their gardens as they tidy up for the evening. And later—I don't know how much later—a sound that makes my heart start racing, of Josh and Adam coming back to the house, and as they come up the stairs, I hold my breath until my lungs hurt, because I don't want Adam here, I don't want to see him. He heads in the other direction, to the other bathroom, and I breathe a little easier while he takes a shower. But then he's here, outside the door, and I huddle under the covers and shut my eyes tight.

He moves quietly as he dresses. *Please let him go away again,* I pray.

I feel him sit down on the bed.

"Liv," he says and I flinch at the need in his voice. It makes me angry, because why should I feel guilty for not being able to give him what he wants? All this is his fault anyway, I realize with mounting fury.

"Why did you have to let Marnie come home for my party?" I say, my anger muffled by the covers. "When she was already coming back at the end of the month?"

"Because she wanted to surprise you," he says.

"And you couldn't resist indulging her."

He gives a harsh laugh. "If I'd indulged her, I'd have insisted on her taking a direct flight."

"Then why didn't you?"

"Because I hadn't let Josh take a direct flight to the States."

"Right, so it's Josh's fault."

He gives a tired sigh. "Don't, Livia."

Enraged, I throw the covers off. "Don't tell me what I can and can't say!" I cry. "Don't sit there and preach at me when you're the one who let Marnie take that flight! If you hadn't been so stupid, she wouldn't be dead! And to not tell anyone." I shake my head, spilling tears from my eyes. "I'll never understand how you could act as if nothing had happened, never! When did you become so hard? You haven't shed a single tear for Marnie. What's happened to you, Adam? When did you become so damned unfeeling?"

He gets slowly to his feet.

"How long have you known about Marnie and Rob?" he asks softly.

In the dark, I can't see his face.

"What has that got to do with it?" I say, suddenly afraid.

"Everything."

"What do you mean?"

"You've known about their affair since he and Cleo went to Hong Kong for Cleo's birthday in April."

"So?"

"That was six weeks ago. Marnie told me she wanted to come back for your party three weeks ago. If you'd told me about their affair when you first found out, do you think I'd have let her come home?" He pauses. "Why didn't you tell me, Livia? Why didn't you tell me about Marnie and Rob?"

"Because I wanted to protect you! Because I wanted to preserve what we had!"

"So when were you going to tell me? Never? Or once you'd had your party?"

I reach behind me and grab one of my pillows. "GET OUT!" I yell, hurling it at him. "GET OUT AND DON'T COME BACK! I HATE YOU, DO YOU HEAR? I HATE YOU!"

Adam

I stand outside the bedroom door, listening to Livia's heart-breaking sobs. I don't know where it came from, what I said to her. I hadn't worked out that if I'd known about the affair, I wouldn't have let Marnie come home, so why did I say it? Why have I made Livia think it's her fault that Marnie is dead when it's mine? How could I be so cruel?

I run a hand through my hair, wondering what to do next, where to go. Before, I might have gone to Marnie's room, tried to find some comfort there, but I can't. I don't know who she is anymore. I thought I knew her, but I didn't. I thought she would never lie to me, but she did. I thought she would never do anything that she knew I'd disapprove of, and yet she did the worst thing she could possibly do, the one thing that would hurt me more than anything in the world, because of who Rob is, because of what he stands for. She knew how I felt about him, yet that didn't deter her from having an affair with him. I can't understand it; I can't understand how she could do it.

I go downstairs, feeling more alone than I've ever felt in my life. I can feel the pull of my bike, but after what happened—when was it—yesterday?—when Marnie was still the person I thought she was, I'm scared of what might happen now that she isn't. The only place I know I'll feel safe is my shed, so I go outside and pick my way across the lawn, using the moon to guide me. As I go in, I reach automatically for the light switch; light floods the room, dazzling me. I'm about to turn it off again, when my eyes fall on the block of black walnut. A dark rage consumes me and, grabbing an ax from the shelf, I begin smashing it to pieces.

Livia

The sound stops my sobs of guilt in their tracks—because deep down, no matter how much I try to dress them up as tears of hurt and indignation, that's what they are, tears of guilt. Everything Adam said was true; no matter how much I try to blame him for what happened to Marnie, the fact is that if I'd been up front with him, she wouldn't have been on that plane. I told Adam that I hated him, but it's me that I hate, for not wanting Marnie to come home. Is that why she died, because I didn't want her here, because I wanted to be able to carry on living the life I was living?

The sound comes again, the thud of splintering wood, followed by a cry of such pain and anguish that I leap from the bed and run out of the bedroom toward the stairs. Josh's door opens.

"Mum!" he says, looking scared.

"It's all right, I'm going," I tell him.

"Shall I come?"

But I'm already gone.

Adam

"Stop, Daddy, stop!"

I hear Marnie's voice, but I don't take any notice, I just keep swinging the ax.

"Please, Daddy, stop!"

I give a roar of frustration. "Don't! Don't you dare ask me to stop when you've been having an affair with Rob!" I bring the ax down on the largest remaining piece, scattering fragments everywhere. "My best friend's brother—" I raise the ax again. "Jess's husband—" Another swing of the ax. "Your best friend's FATHER—"

"Daddy, STOP!"

Turning the ax in my hand, I use the head as a club and send the mass of broken wood flying around the shed. "Don't tell me what to do!" I yell as pieces smash off the walls. "You don't have the right! How could you do it, Marnie? How could you leave us?"

"ADAM!"

Livia

He stops in mid-swing and whips around, and for a terrible moment I think he's going to bring the axe down on me. Then confusion replaces the fury in his eyes and he looks at me in bewilderment, as if he can't believe that it's me standing there and not Marnie.

I reach out a hand. "It's all right," I say gently. "It's all right."

He lowers his arm and the ax thuds to the ground. His face turns ashen. And then he sinks onto his knees, covers his face with his hands and begins to sob uncontrollably.

I kneel on the floor among the shards of black walnut, trying to take him in my arms. But he won't let me in. Ashamed of his tears, he won't let me move his hands from his face. With him trapped in his own private hell, all I can do is hold him, tell him that I love him, that I'm sorry, that everything is going to be all right, that we're going to get through it. All the things he said to me, all the things I couldn't say to him, until now.

At some point I look up and see Josh standing in the doorway, his arms by his side, his face streaked with tears. When he starts to move toward us, I shake my head and give him a quick smile, letting him know that Adam wouldn't want him to see him like this: broken, crushed, defeated. And understanding, he moves quietly away.

Eventually exhaustion overtakes him and I'm able to pull him to me, smooth his hair, kiss the tears from his eyes.

"It's going to be all right, I promise," I say softly. "It's going to be all right."

He doesn't answer, because he can't. But the sigh, from deep within him, is enough.

A YEAR LATER

JUNE 8, 2020

Adam

We're having a party today, for Livia and Marnie. Josh has organized it. Everyone who was at Liv's party last year is coming, plus Marnie's friends from school and university. All the people who've become an important part of our lives during these last twelve months.

In the aftermath of Marnie's death, and at her memorial service, the one thing people wanted to know was what they could do to help. We thought about it and decided that what we wanted, what would help the most, was for them to keep Marnie alive in our minds by keeping her alive in theirs, and talking to us about her. And it has helped, hearing stories about her that we never knew. It isn't always easy, but it's better than never mentioning Marnie at all.

That was one of my first mistakes, not mentioning Marnie to save people embarrassment. It's normal for clients, while we're talking about the piece I'm going to make for them, to show me photos of their house so I can suggest the best type of wood to use to harmonize with the rest of their furniture. Inevitably, talking about "home" leads to talking about family, and if I was asked about my children, I would only mention Josh. But each time, it felt like a terrible betrayal of Marnie. So now this is what I say:

My son, Josh, lives in London with his girlfriend, Amy. I did have a lovely daughter, Marnie, but she died some months back in a plane crash— the Pyramid Air one, perhaps you heard about it?

And when they look shocked and mumble that they're sorry, I say:

It was terrible at the time, and it still is most days, but we try to remember how lucky we were to have her.

It's usually enough.

For the first few weeks after Marnie's death, Liv was definitely stronger than me. I was a physical and emotional mess. Crushed not just by guilt and grief but also by Marnie's affair with Rob. I couldn't reconcile the Marnie I knew with the Marnie she had become. I couldn't eat, I couldn't sleep, and quickly lost about fourteen pounds. Whenever I thought about her last moments, I imagined her calling, not for Livia, or me, but for Rob.

We never made it to Cairo. The night Livia came to find me in my shed, when everything finally became too much, the thought of boarding a plane a few hours later filled me with such dread that I knew I wasn't going to be able to do it.

"I can't go to Cairo," I murmured shakily as the sun began to rise in the sky. "I don't want to see."

"Then we won't go," she told me gently. "I don't want to see either."

In the aftermath of the accident, it was Nelson who dealt with the official side of things and kept us up-to-date with the investigation into the crash. Trapped in a deep, dark tunnel with seemingly no light at the end of it, I was incapable of doing anything.

The turning point came about six weeks after Marnie's death, when I wandered down to the kitchen one morning and found a note from Livia, saying she'd gone out. Josh didn't seem to be around either and I vaguely remembered that he and Amy had gone away for a few days' break. It was the first time I'd been on my own since Marnie had died, and although I'd retreated so far into myself that I barely spoke, their absence began to weigh on me, until I couldn't stand it any longer. I tried phoning Livia, but each time, my call went through to voice mail.

I phoned Nelson.

"I can't get hold of Livia," I told him, feeling near to tears. "I don't know where she is. What if she's had an accident?"

"She hasn't."

"How do you know?"

"She's gone to the park," he said, referring to Windsor Great Park. "Have you just gotten up?"

"Yes," I admitted, because it was nearly midday.

"Then have a shower and a shave and go and join her."

"No," I said, shrinking back inside myself. I hadn't left the house for weeks, not since Marnie's memorial service, and I didn't want to go a place that held so many memories of her.

"You have to."

"Why?"

"What date are we at?"

"I don't know."

"It's the twenty-fourth of July."

I knew that date. Marnie's birthday. "It can't be," I stuttered, unable to believe that most of July had gone past without my noticing.

"You need to get a grip, Adam," Nelson said firmly. "You can't go on like this."

I felt a surge of anger. "In case you've forgotten, my daughter died," I said, my voice cold.

"And so did Livia's. Go and find her. She needs you, Adam. She can't go on carrying you anymore."

I hated him then. But when I went to the bathroom, my hate turned toward the shell of a man staring at me from the mirror. I barely recognized myself and that frightened me. How could I have let myself become such a mess? It wasn't Nelson's voice I could hear telling me to get a grip, but Marnie's. She'd have been appalled to see me in such a state.

While I shaved for the first time in weeks, I thought about what Nelson had said about Livia carrying me, and felt a growing shame. I couldn't remember the last time I'd looked at her properly, or had had a conversation with her. Consumed with guilt, I'd let Marnie's death become all about me.

I guessed that Livia would have walked into Windsor and used the Cambridge Gate entrance to get into the park. I kept my head down as I walked through the town, imagining that everyone recognized me as the man who had lost his daughter in the plane crash. When I reached the gate, I found myself faltering. We had always started the Long Walk with Marnie here, and I wasn't sure I could do it without her. And then the strangest thing happened. As I stood hesitating, with memories of Marnie crowding my thoughts, I felt myself being propelled forward. I was so sure someone was pushing me that I turned my head to see who was there. But there was no one. And yet there was, because I could feel this presence walking along beside me.

"Hello, Marnie," I murmured. "Happy birthday." A gentle breeze stirred the air around me and for the first time since Livia's party, I found myself smiling.

I wasn't worried that I wouldn't find Livia. I knew that if I kept walking, I'd eventually meet her as she made her way back to the gate. It was a while before I saw her coming toward me. I was shocked at how thin and tired she looked, and wondered how I could have been so selfish.

She didn't see me as she trudged along with her head down. As she went to move around me, I caught her arm.

"Livia."

It took her a moment to realize it was me. And when she did, she slumped against me and burst into tears of relief and exhaustion.

From the kitchen, I hear Josh and Amy moving around upstairs as they get dressed. I left Livia sleeping, but I heard the shower running, so she'll be down soon. I open the back door and Murphy stirs in his basket. He comes to stand beside me and we go out to the garden to wait for Livia.

I miss Marnie every minute of every day. There's an aching void inside me that will never be filled—how can it be when I've lost a part of me? But Livia and I have come a long way in a year, thanks to the love and support of our family and friends. She has Jess, Kirin, and her mum, and I have Izzy, Ian, and my parents, especially my dad. His sixth sense knows when I'm drowning and he'll miraculously appear to throw me a lifeline, usually in the form of a drink in town, or a walk along the river with Murphy, whichever he feels I need most.

I also have Nelson, who came and stood in the doorway of my shed one day, and I knew from the look on his face that he'd found out about Marnie and Rob. He was heartbroken over their affair, furious that Rob was willing to risk everything he had, everything we had, for something that could never be.

"What was he thinking?" he kept repeating, the same question Livia and I had asked ourselves over and over again in relation to Marnie. "I'm so sorry, Adam, I'm so sorry."

I tried to comfort him, telling him it took two to have an affair. I was glad he didn't know about the baby Marnie had lost. I almost wished I didn't, but Livia hadn't wanted there to be any secrets between us. Sometimes, I try to imagine what it would have been like if Marnie hadn't lost the baby and if she hadn't died. It's heartbreaking to think how it could have been. But I also know it would have been extremely difficult to adapt to such a situation.

Nelson asked what Livia and I wanted to do, saying he'd understand if we never wanted to see Rob again. Under any other circumstances, that's what we'd have chosen, to never see him again. But we had Jess to think of. If we cut Rob out of our lives, she would want to know why. I also had Livia to think of. To lose her best friend, which she inevitably would, on top of losing her daughter, would be too much. And there was Cleo and Josh to consider. We didn't want either of them to know about the affair.

In the end, it was Liv's decision. She said she wanted us to carry on as before, as if nothing had happened, as if we didn't know. So that's what we do. It's incredibly hard, and despite our best efforts, things aren't quite the same when we meet up. If Jess, or Kirin— because Nelson preferred not to tell her—notice that Rob is more subdued around us, they probably put it down to the strain of Marnie's death. Normally, Kirin might have dug deeper, but she has her hands full with the latest additions to their family, Rose and Bertie, who are now six months old.

I think Livia finds it easier than me. There are days when the weight of the lie becomes almost too heavy; when I don't know how I'm going to bear being in the same room as Rob, or breathe the same air as him. But I do it for Livia, for all that she's been through, for the way she has coped with losing Marnie, for the way she carried me during those first weeks, putting her grief aside to get me through mine. And because I love her more now than ever.

Livia

I close the card I was reading and put it back in my drawer, hidden beneath the roses I saved from Marnie's bouquet. The card arrived on the Tuesday after she died, the day after we were meant to fly to Cairo. It was the birthday card she had promised to send me, and tucked inside, I'd found a hastily scribbled handwritten note.

There's something I need to tell you, Mum. I think you know I've been keeping something from you but I'm hoping you don't know what it is because I want to explain it face to face so that you can at least try to understand. I'm not sure you'll be able to, and Dad even less. You're going to be disappointed, and ashamed of me, but I need you to know that I never intended it to get to this, it just happened. And now that it has—well, all I can hope is that you'll find it in your hearts to forgive me.

As I read it, I was glad that I knew what Marnie was alluding to. If I hadn't known about her affair with Rob, I'd have tormented myself forever, wondering what she could possibly have done to need my forgiveness. But there are other things to torment me. I guessed that Marnie had written the note straight after our phone call, when I'd tried to tell her not to come back. I've never stopped wishing that I'd managed to persuade her, just as I've never stopped wishing that it hadn't been our last conversation. I can't remember if I told her that I loved her, as I usually did at the end of a call, and I torment myself that I didn't.

I have a shower and get dressed. I'm not sure how I feel about this party today, although I'd never tell Josh that. I wouldn't mind if we never celebrated my birthday again. I know it's stupid, but sometimes I wonder if Marnie dying was payback for me being so over the top about my party last year. It seems almost abhorrent to have put so much store on something so materialistic.

It might seem strange, but I feel lucky to be where I am today, to have what I have. First and foremost, Adam. For a few terrible weeks after Marnie's death, I thought I was going to lose him too. There were times when I couldn't see him ever clawing his way out of the grief and guilt that consumed him. If it hadn't been for Josh and Amy, I don't know how I would have coped.

I finally hit the bottom on Marnie's birthday, as I walked the Long Walk in Windsor Great Park. I'd been hoping that Adam would come with me, but as the date approached, I could see that he'd forgotten it was her birthday and I was too scared to mention it in case it pushed him over the edge. As I walked along, the exhaustion I felt frightened me, because I knew I wasn't going to be able to carry on much longer.

"Please, Marnie," I prayed, close to tears. "Please bring your dad back to me. I can't get through this without him." And then I looked up and he was there, and as he held me while I wept tears of relief, all I could think was that somehow Marnie had heard me. I talk to her every evening now, in the quiet of my bedroom, while Adam is downstairs, or walking Murphy. I lie on the bed, Mimi curled against me, and tell her about my day. And I know that she's listening.

I'm also grateful to have Mum, who turned out to be my rock when it came to deciding what to do about Rob. I finally contacted her about three weeks after Marnie died, to invite her to the memorial service, and from then on, we began to meet once a week for coffee in town. Maybe if Marnie hadn't died, we wouldn't have bonded so quickly, but I desperately needed someone who hadn't been close to Marnie, because it was too much to have to cope with everyone else's grief as well as my own. Mum was sad about Marnie, and no doubt cried her own tears of regret. But she hadn't known her, which somehow made it easier.

Because Adam was in no state to talk about anything, Marnie and Rob's affair remained a festering sore until the day Nelson went to see him, a couple of weeks after Marnie's birthday. Rob had finally admitted to him why he'd been avoiding us, and Nelson was understandably furious. It meant that Adam and I were finally able to discuss what had happened. But we couldn't work out what to do. We didn't want Rob to get away with it, but we couldn't decide whether or not to tell Jess.

One day, when Adam had gone to see a prospective client, Nelson came by to speak to me about Rob, to appeal to me on his behalf. He said that Rob was full of remorse for what he'd done, that his affair with Marnie had started unintentionally when he'd been struggling with depression after Jess's diagnosis. He had tried to end it several times and his biggest regret was the pain it was going to cause Jess when the truth came out. He hoped that Jess would forgive him, because he truly loved her, and he asked only that we let him be the one to tell her.

I despised the way Rob was trying to slip from what he he'd done. The words he didn't dare say—*Marnie started it*—were behind every calculated word he said. I wanted to tell Nelson that his brother was a liar and a coward and a vile, vile man. I tried to imagine the scene where Rob broke Jess's heart, but I couldn't.

I asked Nelson to tell Rob not to say anything to Jess until I'd thought things through. The next day, I met Mum for coffee and as we sat together in the Castle Hotel, I found myself telling her about the affair and asking her advice. And Mum pointed out what neither Adam nor I had thought of, which was that even if we told Jess, she might choose to stay with Rob anyway, either because she loved him enough to forgive him or because she preferred to be with him than be on her own. And because we were the messengers, it would put an intolerable strain on our friendship. Not only that; if we told her, Jess might feel that she should leave Rob because that was what we were expecting her to do. And if she didn't meet anyone else, she would have a difficult future in front of her. On the other hand, Mum said, if we didn't tell Jess, Rob would no doubt be a devoted husband to make up for the affair and because—as he'd told Nelson—he truly loved her.

I talked it over with Adam, and then with Nelson. And in the end, we decided to keep Rob's affair with Marnie to ourselves. On balance, in view of Jess's illness, I think we made the right decision. Rob is certainly devoted to her, and although it's horribly difficult to have to see him, we do it for Jess.

I look out of the bedroom window and see Adam walking around the garden, Murphy by his side, and feel a rush of something I haven't felt for a long time, something I don't dare pronounce, because it doesn't seem right. I hurry downstairs and when Adam sees me crossing the lawn, he holds out his hands to me.

"Happy birthday," he says, kissing me.

"Thank you," I say, putting my arms around him. "You're up early."

"Well, it is an important day."

Hand in hand, we walk over to the wall and sit facing Marnie's fence. There's a burst of laughter from inside the house and I smile at the sound of Josh and Amy teasing each other.

I turn to Adam and see that he's smiling too.

"Happy?" I ask without thinking. And then feel dreadful, because how can we be happy? I glance worriedly at Adam, but he pulls me toward him.

"Yes," he murmurs, kissing the top of my head. "You?"

"Yes," I say softly.

It's not the happy of before—how could it be? But it's our kind of happy, and it's enough.

Acknowledgments

After four books, I've come to the conclusion that the Acknowledgments section is far harder to write than the novel itself. The list of people to thank becomes ever longer and "thank you" never seems quite enough. This time, as well as the most dedicated and supportive agent I could wish for—Camilla Bolton—and my editors in the UK and the United States—Kate Mills, Jennifer Weis, and Catherine Richards—I would like to thank my publishers abroad: Aleksandra Saluga (Poland), Bertrand Pirel (France), Fernando Paz Clemente (Spain), Haris Nikolakakis (Greece), Jennifer Boomkamp (the Netherlands), Siren Marøy Myklebust (Norway), Sigrún Katrín and Egill Arnarsson (Denmark and Sweden), Barbara Trianni (Italy), Jana Drápalíková and Kateřina Hájková (Czech Republic), Hülya Balci (Turkey). Thank you for inviting me to your beautiful countries, for giving me the opportunity to meet my wonderful readers, and for making me feel so welcome. I would also like to thank my other publishers worldwide for their continued support and enthusiasm, especially Ásmundur Helgason in Iceland, and all who translate my books, with a special mention for Ireen Niessen in the Netherlands and her amazing eye for detail.

All the teams who work tirelessly behind closed doors, sometimes—no doubt—to the point of breakdown, to bring me back for each new book until I disappear once more to contemplate the dilemma of what to write next. The bloggers, who use their precious time to read and review. The readers, for continuing to buy books and for giving us, the authors, an audience. My fellow writers, for your support and encouragement. Thank you.

Special thanks to my family and friends, especially my husband and daughters, who listen patiently and offer advice when I bore them with new plot lines, who are my first readers, my first copy editors, my first champions. Thank you for being truly amazing. And extra thanks to Calum, for the endless car journeys where I never speak because I'm writing in my head, and for never asking me to step away from my computer, unless it's to eat. I'd starve without you.

Turn the page for a sneak peek at
B. A. Paris's new novel

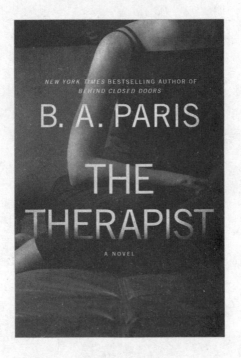

Available Summer 2021

Past

My office is small, perfect and minimalist. It's decorated in calming shades of gray, with just two chairs; a cocoon-style gray one for my clients and a pale leather one for me. There's a small table placed to the right of my chair for my notepad, and on the wall, a line of hooks to hang coats, and that's it. My relaxation treatment room is through a door on the left. The walls there are the palest of pinks and there are no windows, just two ornate lamps that cast a golden glow over the massage table.

Through the slatted blind shading the window of my office, I can see anyone who comes to the door. I'm waiting for my new client to arrive, hoping she'll be punctual. If she's late—well, that will be a black mark against her.

She arrives two minutes late, which I can forgive. She runs up the steps, looking around her anxiously as she rings on the bell, her shoulders hunched up around her ears, worried that someone might recognize her. Which is unnecessary, because there is no plaque on the wall advertising my services.

I let her in, tell her to make herself comfortable. She sits down in the chair, places her handbag at her feet. She's dressed in a navy skirt and white blouse, her hair tied back in a neat ponytail, as if she's come for a job interview. She's right to treat it as such. I don't take just anyone. The fit has to be right.

I ask her if she's warm enough. I like to have the window open but spring hasn't quite shifted into summer yet and I've had to put the heating on. I gaze out of the window, giving her time to settle, my attention caught by an airplane trailing through the sky. There's a polite cough, and I turn my attention back to my client.

I angle my body toward her and, in full therapist mode, ask the standard questions. The first meeting, in some ways, is the most boring.

"This doesn't feel right," she says, when I'm only halfway through.

I look up from my pad, where I've been taking notes.

"I want you to know, and remember, that anything you say in this room is confidential," I tell her.

She nods. "It's just I feel incredibly guilty. What could I have to feel unhappy about? I have everything I want."

I jot the words "happiness" and "guilt" on my pad, then lean forward and stare directly into her eyes.

"Do you know what Henry David Thoreau believed? 'Happiness is like a butterfly; the more you chase it, the more it will elude you. But if you turn your attention to other things, it will come and sit softly on your shoulder.'"

She smiles, relaxes. I knew she'd like that one.

One

The sound of excited voices draws me away from the box of books I'm unpacking. It has been so quiet all day that it's hard to believe I'm actually in London. Back in Harlestone, there would have been familiar external noises; birds, the occasional car or tractor, sometimes a horse going past. Here, in The Circle, everything is silent. Even with the windows open there's been only the occasional sound. It isn't what I was expecting, which I guess is a good thing.

From the upstairs window in Leo's study, I look down to the road outside. A woman with a white-blond pixie cut, wearing shorts and a vest top, is hugging another woman, tall, slim, with coppery red hair. I know the smaller woman is our neighbor; I saw her late last night outside number 5, pulling suitcases from the back of a car with a man. The other woman I haven't seen before. But she looks as if she belongs here, with her perfectly fitting navy jeans and crisp white T-shirt hugging the contours of her toned upper body. I should move away, because if they look up at the house, they might see me standing here. But my need for company is too strong, so I stay where I am.

"I was going to call in on the way back from my run, I promise!" the small woman is saying.

The tall woman shakes her head, but there's a smile in her voice. "Not good enough, Eve. I was expecting you yesterday."

Eve—so that's her name—laughs. "It was ten in the evening by the time we arrived, way too late to disturb you. When did you get back?"

"Saturday, in time for the children going back to school today."

A sudden wind rustles the leaves of the sycamore trees, which line the square opposite the house, and snatches away the rest of her reply. It's very pretty here, like a movie set depicting an enviable life in the capital city. I didn't really believe places like this existed until Leo showed me the photos and even then, it had felt too good to be true.

My attention is caught by a delivery van coming through the black gates at the entrance to The Circle, directly opposite our house. It turns down the left side of the horseshoe-shaped road and drives slowly round. Leo has been filling our new home with things I'm not sure we need, so it could be for us. Yesterday, a beautiful but unnecessarily large glass vase arrived, and he spent ages wandering around the sitting room with it in his arms, trying to find a place for it, before finally depositing it by the French windows that open onto the terrace. But the van continues past and comes to a stop at the house on the other side of us, and I move nearer to the window, eager to catch a glimpse of our neighbors at number 7. I'm surprised when an elderly man appears on the driveway. I don't know why—maybe because The Circle is a newish development in the middle of London—but I'd never considered older people living here.

A few moments later, the van drives off and I look back to where Eve and the other woman are standing. I wish I felt confident enough to go and introduce myself. Since we moved in ten days ago, I've only met one person, Maria, who lives at number 9. She'd been loading three little boys with the same thick dark hair as their mother, plus two beautiful golden Labradors, into a red people carrier. She'd called "hello" to me over her shoulder, and we'd had a quick chat. It was Maria who explained that most people were still away on holiday, and would only be back at the end of the month, in time for school starting again in September.

"Have you met them yet?" Eve's voice pulls my attention back, and from the way her head has turned toward the house, I realize she's talking about me and Leo.

"No."

"Shall we do it now?"

"No!" The force of the other woman's reply has me stepping back, away from the window. "Why would I ever want to meet them?"

"Don't be silly, Tamsin," Eve soothes. "You're not going to be able to ignore them, not somewhere like this."

I don't wait to hear the rest of what Tamsin says. Instead, my heart pounding, I escape into the shadows of the house. I wish Leo was here; he left for Birmingham this morning and won't be back until Thursday. I feel bad, because a part of me was relieved to see him go. The last two weeks have been a bit intense, maybe because we haven't got used to being with each other yet. Since we met, just over eighteen months ago, we've had a long-distance relationship, only seeing each other at weekends. It was only on our first morning here, when he drank straight from the orange juice carton and put it back in the fridge, that I realized I don't know all his quirks and habits. I know that he loves good champagne, that he sleeps on the left side of the bed, that he loves to rest his chin on the top of my head, that he travels around the United Kingdom so much that he hates going anywhere and doesn't even have a passport. But there's still so much to discover about him and now, as I sit at the top of the stairs in our new home, the soft gray carpet warm under my bare feet, I already miss him.

I shouldn't have been eavesdropping on Eve's conversation, I know, but it doesn't take the sting out of Tamsin's words. What if we never make friends here? It was exactly what I was worried about when Leo first asked me to move to London with him. He promised me it would be fine—except that when I suggested having a housewarming for everyone on the street so that we could meet them, he wasn't keen.

"Let's get to know everyone before we start inviting people over," he'd said.

But what if we don't get to know them? What if we're meant to make the first move?

I take my phone from my pocket and open the WhatsApp icon. During our chat, Maria had offered to add me and Leo to a group for The Circle, so I'd given her both our numbers. We haven't messaged anyone yet and Leo had wanted to delete himself when notifications kept coming in about missed parcels and the upkeep of the small play area in the square.

"Leo, you can't!" I said, mortified that people would think he was rude. So he'd agreed to mute the group instead.

I glance at the screen. Today, there are already twelve new notifications and when I read them, my heart sinks a little more. They are full of messages from the other residents welcoming each other back from holiday, saying they can't wait to catch up, see each other, start yoga, cycling, tennis again.

I think for a moment, then start typing.

Hi everyone, we're your new neighbors at number 6. We'd love to meet you for drinks on Saturday, from 7 p.m. Please let us know if you can come. Alice and Leo.

And before I can change my mind, I press send.

Philippe Matsas

B. A. PARIS is the internationally bestselling author of *Behind Closed Doors, The Breakdown,* and *Bring Me Back.* She grew up in England but has spent most of her adult life in France. She has worked both in finance and as a teacher and has five daughters. *The Dilemma* is her fourth novel.